Destruction

SHARON BAYLISS

Published October 2019 by Animus Ferrum Publishing
Mishawaka, Indiana
http://www.animusferrum.com/

ANIMUS FERRUM
PUBLISHING

978-1-948661-55-3 - ebook
978-1-948661-56-0 – paperback

Format design graphics by Curiosity Quills Press

For my mother.
When I was a little girl and couldn't sleep, my mother told me to make up stories in my head. Best advice I've ever gotten.
I love you, Mom.

"Though my soul may set in darkness it will rise in perfect light. I have loved the stars too fondly to be fearful of the night." – Sarah Williams

CHAPTER ONE

David had waited for an important call for eleven years, and even after all this time, his heart raced every time he heard the phone ring. Even in church, or while making love to his wife, his fingers itched to pick up on the first ring. Any call could be *the* call.

The call finally came when David lay in bed with Amanda watching television. She slept with her head on his arm. His fingers tingled from the weight of her head cutting off his circulation, but he didn't push her away. She never seemed to slow down until she lay in bed next to him. Only then could he see the blonde tips of her eyelashes and the freckles between her breasts. No one else noticed these things, perhaps not even Amanda herself. These details belonged to him alone.

When David's phone rang on the nightstand, Amanda opened her eyes. An unfamiliar 432 area code lit up the display.

"It's almost midnight," Amanda said.

"I'm sorry."

"All your kids are at home, babe, so it's nothing important. Business can wait until morning."

"Hello," David said into the receiver.

"May I speak with David Vandergraff?" The woman on

1

the end of the line had a thick West Texas accent and she stretched out the vowels in his last name.

"This is he," David said.

Amanda shook her head and rolled over in bed. She had given up on trying to fix his phone answering habit a long time ago.

"My name is Josie Barstow. I work for the Odessa Police Department. I'm calling about the missing persons report you filed for your children in 2002."

David stopped breathing. He slipped into their master bathroom and closed the door. He had waited a long time for this, but he could never have prepared himself for the rush of hope and terror that came with the prospect of finally knowing. Her words swam around in his head, and he couldn't seem to hold on to any of them, until he heard the one word he really wanted to hear.

"Alive."

He expelled a breath he had held for years.

"Where are they?" David asked.

"A children's shelter here in Odessa."

A brief moment passed where the gravity in the small room seemed to increase. He could feel the weight of his next words, feel them hovering in the air like a wrecking ball about to come down. Without thinking about it, he picked up Amanda's night cream, unscrewed the top, then sniffed it. It smelled like flowers, and something summery, like citrus. That's how she smelled when she crawled in bed next to him every night.

"I'm coming to get them."

"There are legal arrangements that will need to be made."

"That's fine. But I'm bringing my children home with me."

David tried to slip out of the bathroom quietly, but Amanda had not gone back to sleep. She sat up in bed.

"What's wrong?"

"Nothing."

"Don't bullshit me. You're all pale, like you haven't breathed in the last five minutes."

"It was Liza, you know, my VP of human resources," he said. "Her mother died and she wanted to let me know she wouldn't be coming in for a while."

Amanda nodded solemnly.

"Sorry to hear that," she said, and slid under the covers again.

He couldn't tell her yet. He needed another night with her. He needed another ten thousand nights.

CHAPTER TWO

David spent the better part of Thursday afternoon figuring out the best way to tell Amanda what he had done…and what he had to do next. He wrote down phrases like, "It was a long time ago. I've been faithful ever since," and "I love you more than anything. I'll do anything to make our marriage work." No matter how true the words were, they fell flat on the page. He knew they wouldn't be good enough.

He folded his talking points into a stiff little square and taped it to the underside of his desk. He doubted Amanda ever looked in his office, let alone ran her hands under his desk to search for work-in-progress confessions. This reminded him of writing his vows. And, just like when writing his vows, he couldn't get advice from the only person who would know what to say…Amanda.

Amanda's car appeared at the top of the driveway, and he went downstairs to meet her. David could sense her elevated blood pressure from the long Houston commute without needing a cuff. Her face looked a little shiny. Eyes glassy. Hair frizzy. She kissed him with the same passion she had for taking off her heels and hanging up her coat…in fact, she took her heels off with more passion, complete with a sigh of pleasure. He wanted to grab her and press her against the wall, hold her head in his hands and give her a movie kiss. He hadn't kissed her that way in a long time, and if he didn't do it now, he might miss his chance.

"How was your day?" David asked.

"Ugh," she said.

He should wait to tell her on a good day. But, he had said that every day since he'd gotten the call from Odessa a week ago. He would leave tomorrow, so he had run out of chances. His marriage would end tomorrow, whether he gave her a heads-up or not. He owed her so much more than an explanation; he had to at least give her that.

She didn't elaborate on her "ugh" and went straight to the wine rack. She chose a thirty-dollar Pinot Noir. So, she had a bad day that called only for moderately priced wine, not vodka and cranberry, or even Cherry Garcia. Maybe he should remove all the vodka and Cherry Garcia before he told her, or stock up on it; he didn't know which would be kinder.

"How was your day?" she asked.

"Oh, fine."

"You didn't have to go into the office?" she asked.

"Not today. Conferenced in."

"Bastard," she said. "Maybe when I'm the big boss man like you, I can work in my PJs. Soon enough."

"Hell, yes."

He waited for the update on whatever department did whatever stupid thing that day. As always, he had prepared phrases like, *that sounds frustrating,* and *they should have listened to you,* and plenty of *you're right*s for her. But, she switched topics.

"Oh, I keep forgetting to tell you. Ashlynn's Baptism is on Sunday. So, we're going to Carson and Jess's church this week. They're having a family thing on Saturday, too. You don't have to work, do you?"

Work, no. Drive to Odessa, yes.

"Did you hear my question?"

"Yeah. That should be fine. I can't believe she's already twelve."

"I know. Soon enough, she'll be another little Emmy. God help Carson. He never even liked it when I dated guys in high school. If he was that protective of his little sister, I can't imagine what he will do with his daughters."

David's stomach lurched. He hadn't even considered how Amanda's brother Carson would react to the news. Carson had threatened David on many occasions in the first years they knew each other. David heard a lot of, "If you ever hurt her, I swear I'll…" followed by a variety of creative threats, most of which involved Carson's extensive gun collection. However, in the over twenty years that had passed, Carson and his wife Jess had become David's best friends. He realized now that he'd probably lose them too. David would also have to tell his own younger brother, James. James had always looked up to him, wanted to be like him. He could already imagine hearing the disappointment in his brother's voice.

"Oh…also, Emmy's friend Samantha will be staying with us for a few days next week. Her parents are going to Europe."

"What? Now is not really a good time."

"Why not?"

"I mean, shouldn't they have given us more notice?"

"You know how her parents are. We have the room. Besides, she spends most of her time here anyway. I thought you'd barely notice the difference."

David reached over and removed the clip from Amanda's hair and let it fall around her shoulders. The light color concealed the few strands of gray, a secret only he got close enough to see. He combed his fingers through her hair to smooth it down. Her hair smelled like their bed. Like her pillow.

"Was my hair messed up?" she asked.

"No. It just looks nice like this."

She ran her fingers through her hair self-consciously.

"I doubt that. It's all creased from my clip and unwashed." She gave him a hard look. "Is something wrong with you? You're acting drunk." She leaned in and sniffed his lips. "I didn't think you'd be drunk on a random Thursday, but who knows what you do when you work from home."

Talk to lawyers. Plan confessions. Pack bags. He took her face in his hands and kissed her. He tasted the wine on her lips and knew it would never taste that sweet right out of the bottle. He relished the flavor and inhaled deeply while he kissed her to take in the rest. He smelled her shampoo, her face cream, and a touch of sweat from her commute. He had to store every detail, just in case.

After he released her, she smiled like she had in their wedding photos. Perfect. Just the kiss he had intended.

"Dear God," she said. "What was that for?"

He shrugged. "You look nice today."

"That's a bold-faced lie. I didn't even get a chance to do my eyes this morning."

"Let's go upstairs." Having sex with her right before he admitted his affair seemed creepy, but he didn't care. He hadn't even left yet and he feared he might forget her. He had forgotten how her nipples felt against his tongue, how it felt to be inside her.

She gave him her half-smile, which always meant *yes*.

"I don't know what you've been drinking, but keep drinking it," she said.

The fear set in after. He wrapped his arms around her and pressed his body into her back. He held her so tightly, he knew she couldn't get up until he decided she could. She would notice it soon. She would hear his heart beating too fast. Speeding up instead of slowing down, as it ought to after a good release. She would notice him holding his breath to keep himself together.

She squirmed in his arms. "Honey, if we don't go downstairs soon, the kids are going to come looking for us. You know how they get when they're hungry. Thank God I have frozen pizzas. So much for the healthy dinner I didn't really want to make anyway. Oh well."

"Amanda," he said.

She turned and squinted at his face, thankfully obscured by darkness. This didn't feel right. He couldn't tell her with them both naked. He definitely needed clothes for this. Maybe even a suit of armor.

"I think we'll have to order something," he said. "I saw the boys break into the pizza yesterday."

"Those vultures," she said.

CHAPTER THREE

David blinked, and his alarm was going off the next morning. Friday had finally come and he had chickened out again. If he had any doubt before, now he knew for sure…he was a coward. He had been too afraid to tell Amanda the truth for twelve years, and now he had run out of time.

He called Amanda before he even brushed his teeth. He had to get it done. Voice mail. He shouldn't have felt so relieved.

"Hey honey, I'm afraid I have to drive out to a job site this weekend. I would have given you more notice if I could. There were some serious problems with the construction of a subdivision in Conroe. Dangerous stuff, faulty wiring. I have to take care of it right away. I'm so sorry, honey. I'll call you from the road. I love you."

Liar, liar pants on fire. Amanda would have been pissed even if that story had been true. She didn't like being stuck as the single parent for their three teenage children for a whole weekend. He grabbed the bag he had pre-packed in case Amanda had kicked him out last night, and headed for the garage.

Of course, Amanda just happened to need the Expedition on today of all days. She must need to take Emmy or Patrick somewhere after school. Jude had taken his truck. He had no choice but to take the brand new Mercedes with its pristine silver paint. He needed the Expedition. He needed the room.

He needed the room.

His heart rate spiked and he couldn't breathe. Heart attack, maybe? Only a very dedicated coward could actually manufacture a heart attack to avoid what he feared. He had no chest pains, so, unfortunately, he must be fine. Just panic. Wishing he had the car with more cup holders and a built-in Blu-ray player had made it real. He would return with two more children.

Texas seemed massive when driving three hyper kids to Schlitterbahn, but this time, it sped past him like Connecticut. The smaller the trees got, the more he panicked. After San Antonio, he felt like he'd entered a different planet. He had visited West Texas, of course. He'd driven the kids out to Big Bend several years back, but this time it felt more alien—full of red rock and skeleton-like plants. The dry air chapped his lips and the dust made his eyes itch. The road passed through nothing after nothing after nothing. In Houston, his family lived in the middle of a vast terrain of everything.

He had arranged to pick up his children at 10:00 a.m. the next morning, which meant that he had a whole night to kill in Odessa. He wished he had just left in the middle of the night so he would arrive exactly at ten, and wouldn't have to wait. He'd spent a good amount of his evening at Walmart, deciding whether or not to buy his children gifts, his stomach so knotted that his Dairy Queen dinner threatened to make a reappearance. Buying gifts and snacks for the drive did nothing but remind him that he didn't know anything about his children except their names and ages. He didn't even know his daughter's birthday.

Crystal disappeared when she was pregnant with Evangeline, and Xavier had been just a toddler. He searched for them long after their disappearance became a cold case. He hired private investigators, and even hackers. Based on what he found, Crystal never again paid taxes, had a job, or paid bills of any kind. She didn't give birth to Evangeline in a hospital, her children never went to school, and they had no medical records that could be found. And, if they had all died, he found no record of that either. They just didn't exist anymore, as if his "other" family had been nothing but a figment of his imagination. The only thing that proved they ever existed at all was his grief, and even that had to be kept hidden.

CHAPTER FOUR

David arrived at the children's shelter right on time the next morning. A ballerina-like young woman opened the door and David couldn't tell right away if she lived in the shelter or worked there. She managed to have the inviting quality of a grandmother, while barely out of college. She wiped her fingers on a dishtowel she had tucked into her pants pocket and held her hand out to shake.

"Mr. Vandergraff?"

"Yes, ma'am."

"I'm Shawna, associate shelter director. I'll need to see some ID before I let you in. Standard procedure."

David showed her his driver's license and she inspected it carefully.

"Come on in."

The house smelled of bacon, and someone had turned the heater on too high. Halloween decorations filled the house and children's artwork lined the hallway. He felt bad taking them away. He'd known Shawna for about one minute, but this barely-out-of-college stranger already seemed more qualified to raise his kids.

She took him into an office with a fat orange cat sleeping

on the desk. The room had an overpowering pumpkin pie-scented candle smell.

"We'll have to work around Pablo. He never moves unless he wants to."

She pulled out a thick stack of paperwork and asked for a second form of ID. He gave her his passport. She went over what the forms meant and pointed out the places he should sign. This reminded him of signing a mortgage.

"I'll be sad to see them go," she said. "They're good kids. Haven't caused any trouble."

"What are they like?"

"Quiet. Sweet."

"Can you give me any more to go on?"

She smiled. "Evangeline is a little more expressive. She has a lot of imagination and she will talk to me a little bit. She doesn't talk much to the other kids, but she does like to watch them play and talk to each other. She likes to draw and paint. But, she doesn't like to show me her artwork. She also draws elaborate designs on her skin with a ballpoint pen. Some of the other workers want her to stop, but I don't see the harm. Xavier hasn't said more than two or three words to me or the other children. Mostly, 'yes,' 'no,' 'okay'. I see him talking to his sister sometimes. But, he mostly keeps to himself. He watches movies a lot, but, it doesn't seem like he cares about them too much. My guess is that he just likes the excuse to sit quietly and not be disturbed."

"The officer told me that their mother died." Hearing those words out of his own mouth was like hearing a balloon pop right next to his ear. He had chosen not to think about it much. "How did she die?"

Shawna suddenly showed her age, like the confidence from all her schooling and training melted away, and only the young woman remained, unsure and naïve.

"I'm sorry for your loss," she said, and her eyes brimmed

with more sympathy than David could ever have mustered for a stranger, but then she averted her eyes. She pulled out some more papers, one of which was a thin pamphlet that read, *A Guide for The Foster or Adoptive Parents of Sexually Abused Children.*

The span of missing years suddenly felt as vast, dark, and cold, as deep space. So happy they were alive, he hadn't spared much thought for what that life had been like. He had just assumed they had lived with their mother, off the grid, but okay. Happy. Safe. He should have put the pieces together based on what he had been told so far. Surely, this hadn't been the first clue, but his brain had refused to see it. The information had to seep in painfully slowly, like the drip…drip…drip of water slowing carving a gash into rock.

"In your packet, there is the card for the caseworker you've been assigned in Houston," Shawna said. "She'll help you arrange care for your children. And she can answer all your questions."

David stared at her, aware that his glare probably looked threatening. Part of him wanted to shake her until she gave away all the information she feared giving him. And another part just wanted to pocket the pamphlet and the business card, and nod politely, maintaining his ignorance as long as he could.

"What happened to my children?" he said. He had to work hard to speak each word, and his voice sounded breathy and hoarse.

She took a deep breath and looked at her papers as if she had her script written there. "Crystal re-married, a man named Whitman Colter."

"We were never married."

"Right. Well, she was married. She and the kids lived with him, Colter, completely separate from society. We didn't even know they existed. I've never seen anything like it. If you told me they had been invisible up until the day we found them, I might believe it. I'm not sure how they managed it, really."

David felt impatient with her explanation, but she seemed to warm up as she spoke, re-gaining her confidence.

"The police found the kids on the side of the road in the middle of nowhere. It took them a long time to find where they had come from. When they finally found the house, the police swear they had already looked at those coordinates several times, as if the house suddenly popped into existence. Even after they had found it once, they had trouble finding it again.

"Anyway, when they found the house, they found Crystal's body. Her husband had killed her. The ground is hard here…so it's tricky to bury someone. He…he burned her body atop a pile of sticks. And, the kids saw everything."

White spots appeared in David's vision. He could see her body, with dark hair that always smelled of sandalwood, lying on a pile of sticks. He could see her toes, probably painted green or purple, and the tattoo of angel wings on her back, blistering as the fire covered her.

David's thoughts must have shown through his eyelids, because Shawna's eyes became watery. She picked up the papers on her desk and straightened them, even though they already seemed straight.

David couldn't find the words to ask his next question aloud, so he picked up the pamphlet, *A Guide for The Foster or Adoptive Parents of Sexually Abused Children*, and pushed it across the desk toward her.

She nodded solemnly, and continued, once again regaining some of the strength in her voice. "When they were examined, the doctor found a series of small cuts about a half inch long in a neat row on their backs, starting with old scars and gradually progressing to cuts that were still healing. They are like tick marks. Colter added a tick mark every time he completed his "ritual", as Evangeline calls it…when he raped them."

"Both of them?"

"It's not about sexuality…it's about domination. Evangeline has fifty-two tick marks. Xavier has seventy-seven."

David didn't say anything. He couldn't imagine what he should say. That the most horrible thing he had ever heard of happening to anyone, had happened to his own children? And since he chose Amanda instead of Crystal, it was his fault? He made note of the nearest trashcan, just in case he threw up.

"What should I do?" His voice now sounded like a croak.

"The caseworker will help you. For now, just be cautious. Respect their personal space and privacy. Don't ask too many questions. Keep things calm. And be very careful about touching them; even a pat on the back might be inappropriate."

The advice sounded reasonable, but a hard way to live. How long would this mandate stay in effect? Could he shake Xavier's hand when he graduated high school? Dance with Evangeline on her wedding day?

"And make sure your family knows, too. They also need to keep things calm and respect their privacy."

The image of his kids flashed into his mind. Emmy—the loud, touchy-feely quizmaster who entered every room like she twirled a flaming baton. Jude—who thought punching people was the supreme form of affection. Patrick—whose sense of humor bordered between hilarious and verbal abuse. Amanda—control-freak who had to be involved in everything and always had an opinion. His family felt like an atomic bomb.

"I read in your file that your children with your wife are similar ages," she said hesitantly.

"Yes. Jude is seventeen, Patrick is fifteen, Emmy is thirteen, almost fourteen. And I know Xavier is fifteen and Evangeline is twelve."

Shawna crinkled her nose slightly, and David assumed she had done the math and came to the obvious conclusion.

"So, you know what you're doing then," she concluded. She must have majored in looking on the bright side. "Kids who have been abused are still just kids. Just be kind to them and show them you're safe. It will all come together eventually. They are actually very well developed, considering their situation. I've seen much worse. They're resilient."

"That's good advice," David said. "Thank you."

She looked like she might cry again, perhaps with relief that she had said the right thing. "One other important thing," she continued. "Evangeline has created a magical narrative to help her cope. She needs to believe it for now. One day, it will fall apart and she'll have to face what has happened to her, but you shouldn't rush her."

"A magical narrative?"

"She thinks her stepfather was a wizard. I know, it's strange. But, in my opinion, good imagination is one thing that keeps kids resilient. Just go with it, for now."

"What about Xavier?"

"He has more of a grasp on reality. He understands they have been abused. At least, he must understand, because he chose to run. Shortly after his mother's death, he took his sister in the middle of the night and they walked ten miles to the road, then three miles along it, before they were found and someone called the police."

He couldn't help but feel…pride. Xavier saved his sister. He ran. They walked thirteen miles and never gave up.

"I've been keeping something for them," Shawna said. "I wasn't sure if it would be a good idea to give it to them. I didn't know if they'd be ready. But, it's theirs. It should go with them."

She opened a drawer, pulled out a wooden box and placed it on the desk next to Pablo. David reached to open the box, but Shawna put her hand on top of his.

"It's their mother's remains."

His breath caught in his throat. He had his hand on *her*. Shawna must have noticed the look on his face because she squeezed his hand before she let go.

"Will you take them?"

"Yes, of course."

"There is this, too."

She handed him a Ziploc bag containing a platinum ring set with an opal, accented by small diamonds. David's eyes burned with tears he didn't want to shed in front of Shawna. Seeing the ring made it completely real. It really had been Crystal's body that burned atop a pile of sticks. *His* Crystal. Many years ago, he had given Crystal this ring. She had said it looked like an engagement ring and wouldn't take it at first, but he convinced her he just thought she would like the ring, he didn't mean anything by it. In truth, he did mean it as a wedding ring. He wanted a symbol. Something to mean that even though he wasn't married to her, he loved her…she was his. He thought she had tossed it over a bridge when they broke up.

"It was with her body."

"This was the only piece of jewelry she was wearing?"

Shawna shrugged. "I suppose."

Perhaps everything else melted in the heat. She always wore lots of jewelry, but mostly cheap bangles. He held up the bag and stared at the ring for a long time.

"Are you all right?" she asked.

He couldn't be further from "all right," but he nodded and put the ring in the inside pocket of his jacket. He tucked the wooden box in, too. The box, unnervingly small to contain a person, fit into the large pocket inside his jacket. Crystal lay against his chest where she could hear his heartbeat. He never wanted to take her out again.

"Are you ready to meet them?" she asked.

"Right now?"

"They're ready. And we're all settled here." She pushed a folder toward him. "Here is your copy of all the paperwork."

"Okay."

She smiled and patted him on the shoulder as she got up. "Wait here. I'll go get them."

He liked Crystal waiting with him, his little secret tucked into his pocket. But, it didn't stop him from feeling like he might pass out. He held his breath. He always did that when he felt nervous. He could hear the words, "Breathe, David," in a voice which could have been Crystal's or Amanda's. They both said it in the same gentle but exasperated tone, as if they couldn't believe they had to remind him to complete the basic functions of life, but also satisfied they needed to. They liked knowing if they didn't remind him to breathe, he might stop.

Then his children appeared.

A beautiful boy and girl looked at him with the same indiscernible expressions their mother had mastered. He thought, *these are my kids*. They looked so much like his children, they could have lived with him the whole time, and now he was picking them up from a friend's house. In some ways, they looked even more like his children than the ones he had raised. Jude looked like Amanda's brother, tall and broad with blue eyes and blond hair. Patrick looked like David's brother, lanky and dark-haired. Emmy looked like a carbon copy of Amanda.

But, Evangeline looked like her mother. She had Crystal's thick brown hair and pouty lips, but had green eyes exactly like David's mother's. A little ghost of the women he had loved and lost. Evangeline had drawn an elaborate tree on her arm with roots drawn on her five fingers. David thought Evangeline meant to mimic her mother's tattoos, and he appreciated that the shelter workers didn't make her stop. And, Xavier...Xavier was David. He had the same no-color gray eyes and brown hair, only slightly darker than David's. But, the eyebrows showed the most similarity. They both had striking, slanted eyebrows that Amanda said made David look like a movie villain. And, there the eyebrows appeared again, on a ghost of David himself. A David with tick marks carved onto his back.

They looked like normal kids. He had expected…well, he didn't know what he had expected. Only their silence seemed unusual. No, "Hello, nice to meet you," or even a distant teenage, "Hey," or the probably most appropriate, "I hate you, abandoner. Go to hell." Nothing.

He already didn't know what to do. Should he stand up? Or, would that be aggressive? Was staying seated too rude? How should he introduce himself? *Hello, I am your father, the married man your mother had an affair with for seven years?*

He stood up. Slowly. "Hello," he said. "I'm David. It's really nice to meet you."

They didn't say anything right away, but Evangeline finally filled the expanse of silence with a quiet, but confident, "Hello."

And that was it. Several trees' worth of paperwork, a discussion that lasted all of two minutes, and a five-page pamphlet for the foster or adopted parents of sexually abused children. They were his. He felt like he did the first time the nurses left Jude alone with him in the hospital. *That's it? You are just going to hand me a little bundle of life and hope for the best? What's wrong with you?*

David carried their bags to the car. His kids at home carried bags this big to soccer practice. These bags included everything they owned. Xavier ran a finger along the hood of David's Mercedes with his eyebrows slightly raised in apparent amazement, which pleased David. David asked them if they needed anything from their bags before he put them in the trunk. Xavier shook his head. Evangeline said she wanted to keep her bag. David opened the back door for them and they climbed in. Before he closed the door, he noticed Xavier held his breath. Evangeline whispered something in his ear and he took a breath.

CHAPTER FIVE

Shawna had suggested he give them the basics of what to expect, even if they didn't ask.

"The drive is about eight hours long, but we'll stop for lunch. I was going to stop every hour and a half or so for a bathroom break, and you can get a drink or snacks. Let me know if you need me to stop before that. It's no problem. I was thinking pizza for lunch. I saw a pizza place along the way. Do you like pizza?"

"Sure," Evangeline said.

Everyone liked pizza. Good.

"I could put on music. What kind of music do you like?"

"No, thank you," she said.

They seemed most comfortable with silence. He would try to be, too. He let the miles pass under them and considered his plan of action. He hesitated to tell them about their new home. He couldn't be sure where it would be. If David didn't keep them in his own home, as he had said, would the state take the kids back? One of the many pages he signed said something about following through with the plan they had agreed upon, which implied David's wife would welcome them into their two extra rooms without issue.

The meal felt like a first date from hell. David had never met anyone who could stay quiet like that. He kept glancing at them to make sure they hadn't disappeared into thin air, just spirits he had imagined.

After pizza, back in the car, he figured they had enjoyed several hours of their preferred state of silence, and he would try again.

"Is there anything you want to know about me? Anything at all." He glanced in the rearview mirror. They didn't shake their heads right away this time, which seemed like progress. Evangeline looked as if she wanted to say something. He could tell because she looked the same way Emmy looked all the time; words jumping inside her like firecrackers, just waiting for a moment to release them. Evangeline glanced at Xavier, as if wanting his approval. David couldn't tell if Xavier had given any sign either way, but he needed a microscope to read his body language when he looked right at him. He had no hope of reading him while driving eighty miles per hour down the highway.

"Go ahead. Ask me anything, really," David said.

"Are you a wizard?" Evangeline asked.

He had expected an easy question such as, "Do you have a pool?" or, "When do we have to start school?" This question stumped him. Not that he didn't know if he was a wizard or not, but how should he answer without crushing her magical narrative?

"What do you think?" David asked.

"I don't know," Evangeline said.

"Do you hope that I am a wizard, or would you prefer it if I wasn't?"

She opened her mouth and then closed it again. "Never mind."

He completely deflected the only question she dared to ask.

"Are you a wizard…or, a witch?" he asked her.

He watched Xavier for hints, at least, the best he could without drifting into oncoming traffic. Her older brother would understand her narrative and know how to respond. Xavier had moved ever so slightly closer to his sister and looked at her. But, that didn't tell David much. Only that he cared more about this conversation than the endless empty hills out the window.

Evangeline paused and examined David with his mother's green eyes.

"Yes, I am a witch," she said.

He needed to respond without sounding patronizing or sarcastic. She was twelve. This wasn't like playing princess games with Emmy when she was six. To her, this was real. He pretended she had told him something normal, like she knew how to play the piano, and responded accordingly.

"That's very cool."

"I shouldn't tell you more if you're not a wizard. I shouldn't have even told you that."

"That's understandable. But, if you want to tell me more, you can. I won't tell anyone."

"Magic runs in families," she said.

Then maybe she *did* expect him to be a wizard? He didn't have a problem with that as long as she didn't ask him to prove it. He thought about Crystal pressed against his chest. He hadn't taken off his jacket since he had put it on. *What am I supposed to say?*

"As far as I know," David said. "I am not a wizard. But I've never tried to do magic."

He glanced in the mirror and saw her nod. She cast her eyes down.

"So if magic runs in families and I'm not a wizard, then that must mean your mother was a witch?" David regretted it as soon as he said it. Dangerous territory. For some reason, he regretted the word 'was' most of all. He wished he could see their reactions, because they didn't say anything right away.

"Yes," Evangeline said. "We all are. Our mother and stepfather are very powerful dark wizards."

Discuss their dead mother and their abuser during your first casual family conversation didn't appear in the pamphlet. Of course, the pamphlet didn't say anything about how to handle witchcraft-related questions either, so screw it.

"When I knew your mother, she was a *good* witch," David said.

The phrase came out of his mouth fairly easily—the perfect description of her.

Silence. David's stomach turned. He had finally crossed a line.

"Something bad happened to her while she was pregnant with me," Evangeline said. "She was cursed."

David's back tensed. Something bad did happen during her pregnancy. The man she loved left her.

As they approached Houston, civilization broke out around them like a rash. The exits and stores became increasingly familiar.

Then, *his* exit.

He had officially reached the point where he could no longer stall, and turned into the parking lot of a Pappadeaux restaurant. David parked by the dumpster and stared at the brick building.

"What are we doing?" Evangeline asked.

"I just need to do something before we get home. I'm sorry."

He pressed speed dial one. He couldn't think about it. Just

jump in, as if diving into a cold lake.

"Hey, babe," Amanda said. "You almost here?"

"Yes."

"Finally."

"I know this might seem a little odd to you, but can you come meet me in the Pappadeaux parking lot?"

"That does seem odd. Is something wrong with the car? Oh, I think I know what it is. Hang on, we're driving right by."

She hung up. *We? No. No. No.* He redialed. Too late. The Expedition drove into the parking lot. They must have been on the way back from Jess and Carson's family gathering. *Fuck. Fuck. Fuck.*

"Would you please stay in the car?" he asked his newest kids. "Please."

He got out of the car and so did Amanda. A cold front had come in and her hair whipped around her. She hugged her bare arms.

"Are there people in the car?" Amanda asked. "Who is with you?"

Patrick got out of the Expedition first, and then Jude and Emmy.

"Stay in the car," David commanded.

He could tell they sensed the darkness in his voice because they stopped in their tracks. But they still didn't get back in.

"Where is it?" Patrick asked.

"What are you talking about?" David asked.

"We thought you were going to surprise Patrick with his new car," Amanda said.

Evangeline and Xavier got out of the car, bringing the number of his children who ignored his command to stay in the car to a full one hundred percent.

"Who's the guy? He's cute," Emmy said.

"Shut up, Emmy," David said. "For once in your life, just shut up."

For all she talked, David had never told her to shut up like that. All the Vandergraffs glared at him, even Patrick, who told Emmy to shut up several times a day.

"David, what is the matter with you? I can't believe I'm asking you this, but did you kidnap these children?" she said with a weak laugh.

David saw something in her eyes now, a trace of panic bubbling up under the cool blue. She knew. She didn't know what she knew, but she could feel the wrongness coming. She kept looking at Xavier. The eyebrows. Some part of her already had figured it out.

"I really need everyone except Mom to get back in the car." He tried to say it in his most deadly serious tone. He looked back at Evangeline and Xavier so they knew the command included them. They climbed back into the car.

His other kids looked unwilling to budge, but Amanda said, "Go on," and they obeyed her. Before Patrick got in behind his siblings, he gave David a look that could sour milk. He had always been the brightest one. He had caught on to something, too.

Amanda shivered and rubbed her arms. She seemed different in silence. Vulnerable. Talking was her super power and she stood in a vat of Kryptonite. She waited for him to explain.

"I don't know how to say this," David said. "So, I'll just say it. The people in the car are my children. Xavier and Evangeline. Their mother is dead. I am taking custody."

Amanda laughed, but her eyes made it clear she didn't think it was a joke, perhaps only hoped so. "What?"

"I had an affair when we were first married. It ended twelve years ago. These are my kids."

"I don't think so," Amanda said.

"I'm sorry."

"Your kids?" she asked absently.

He had expected fury. This was worse. She looked frightened and confused, a child lost in a strange place.

"Their mother is dead. She was murdered by her husband, their stepfather. I'm taking custody."

"Custody," she repeated as if she learned a new word.

"I'm sorry." He hated the way it sounded. So far from good enough. "I don't want to lose you."

"Two children. Years apart," she said. "Years apart," she repeated. "Who was she?"

"Do you remember Crystal Carr?"

Her whole body tensed, but her eyes came to life, as if flares lit them from behind. Amanda took a few quick steps forward, and hit him in the face. Not a slap. A punch. His cheek vibrated with the sting. His eyes rattled in their sockets. Then she sat down on the curb, put her face in her hands, and whispered, "Crystal."

David couldn't take his eyes off her and didn't notice when his Vandergraff kids came back out of the car. Emmy put her arm around her mother.

"What did you do?" Patrick asked him.

Jude didn't look as if he needed to hear a reason before he planted a punch on David's other cheek. But, he didn't get the chance. Amanda got up and herded them all back in the car like she had the stretchy arms of the woman from *The Incredibles*. And they drove away. Gone. Just like that.

David got back in the car and turned to Xavier and Evangeline with a bright pink cheek.

"I—"

"You didn't tell them we were coming?" asked Xavier. At least he had finally said something.

CHAPTER SIX

David took the kids to Golden Corral for dinner. The concept of a buffet baffled his newest children. *I can eat whatever I want? I just go up there and take it? Are you sure?* They made odd meal choices. Evangeline got a big pile of fruit, a hard-boiled egg, pizza, and a pile of shredded cheese from the salad bar, and then ice cream with sprinkles at David's suggestion. Xavier got cottage cheese, macaroni and cheese, sweet potato casserole, and an egg roll, and then ice cream as well.

"We're going to stay in a hotel tonight," David explained while they took tiny bites of their soft serve. They looked overstuffed. No one eats ice cream that slowly. Feeding them too much too fast and risking vomiting seemed like the least of his mistakes. "You'll like the hotel. It has an indoor pool."

"I don't know how to swim," Evangeline said.

"Oh. Okay, well, you'll still like it, I think."

"Shawna said we were going to stay at your house," Evangeline said.

"I'm afraid I'm not sure if we will or not. My wife is upset with me."

"Because you had sex with our mom and had us,"

Evangeline said. "And didn't tell her about it until just now when you were about to bring us home?"

"Yes."

"That was stupid," Evangeline said.

"Yes it was."

She wrinkled her nose. Disgust. Or judgment. Either way, he had disappointed her. Her father turned out to be a non-magical adulterer with no house.

"It was a mistake…. Not having you, that wasn't a mistake. Not telling my wife until now was a mistake. But I was afraid to tell her."

"Because she will want a divorce," Evangeline said.

"Yes."

"You don't think having us was a mistake?" Evangeline asked.

"No. Of course, not."

"Why not?" Evangeline asked.

"Because then you wouldn't exist," he said.

She looked thoughtful, considering the concept as she would a new food.

"And because I loved your mom," he continued. "If I had to do it over again, I would."

"That's stupid," Evangeline said.

David smiled. He couldn't help himself. She had called him stupid twice. A man she barely knew. A father. She didn't act like a scared, abused girl. She acted spirited and fiery, like her mother.

"What?" she asked.

"Nothing," he said.

They didn't ask the questions he knew they must have. *So…if you loved her, why didn't you stay? Why didn't you marry her? Raise us? Why didn't you save us?* They must have wondered.

Xavier had the same look he had during the wizard conversation. Hardly readable…but listening. He watched

Evangeline while she talked, and then turned to David when he talked. It wouldn't seem like much to someone else, but David knew better. Unlike most conversations that went on around him, Xavier cared enough to listen.

"It probably is stupid. But, I'd do it again because I still haven't come up with any other alternative. I love your mom and I love my wife too."

Present tense. He didn't even mean to say it, but he hoped they caught that.

They looked at him as if they would have been less shocked if he transfigured the plates into mice.

The phone rang. Amanda. Fear shot from the pit of his stomach to his heart. He stopped breathing.

He answered the phone and said, "Amanda."

"Bring them here."

"What?"

"What are you going to do, take them to a hotel? Bring them here. Now."

She hung up and he breathed.

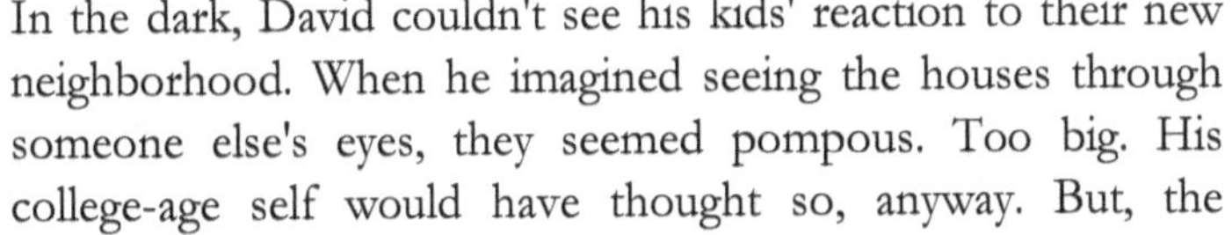

In the dark, David couldn't see his kids' reaction to their new neighborhood. When he imagined seeing the houses through someone else's eyes, they seemed pompous. Too big. His college-age self would have thought so, anyway. But, the houses would have impressed the kid David. The kid David had wanted to be rich more than anything, but had parents who considered poverty a badge of honor.

He parked the car and unloaded the trunk and the kids, while Amanda watched from the doorway, her dark silhouette looming ominously. David's attraction to fiery women had a dangerous side effect; if he pissed one off, anything could happen. He couldn't rule out the possibility Amanda had taken a gun out of the lock box and tucked it under her sweater.

When they reached the front door, she spoke to the kids as if she couldn't see David.

"Come in," she said. "Have you eaten?"

"They have," David said.

Amanda put her hand on Evangeline's shoulder as she led her through the doorway. *No touching.* But, neither of them burst into flames upon contact. After Xavier and Evangeline had passed, Amanda blocked the doorway.

"Just them. Not you," she said.

"What?"

"They need a place to stay and haven't done anything wrong. But, we're done. You're out of the house. You can come by and get your stuff while I'm at work."

"I can't leave them here with you. I am their legal guardian. You're no one… I mean, you're no one legally…to them."

"If you think I'll let you in, then you don't know me."

"Can we discuss it privately?" Evangeline and Xavier stood right behind Amanda.

She shut the door in his face. He had no inclination to turn and leave. Everything that mattered to him slept in that house. And, he legally owned that house. So he would live here unless the police dragged him away.

CHAPTER SEVEN

avid woke to the sound of breaking glass. Cube-like shards littered the floor of the Expedition. The back window, the one closest to where he had slept, had shattered. He sat up fast, but didn't see anyone outside. He shook pieces of glass off his jacket and inspected himself for cuts.

He climbed out of the car and saw Emmy and Amanda run through the doorway into the garage.

"What the hell?" Amanda demanded.

"I—"

"Did you break the window?" Amanda asked.

"Of course not. I was sleeping. I don't know how it broke."

"That's it. We're not going to church." Amanda threw her hands in the air.

"How did it break?" Emmy whispered. Someone had turned her volume down.

"I don't know, honey," David said. "Stay back. You don't have shoes on."

"Give me your keys," Amanda said.

"I'll take the car and get it fixed today. I don't want you to have to worry about that on top of everything else."

"How considerate," she said acidly. "Give me the keys."

He removed the house key from the ring and handed only that one over. "Let me keep the car keys. I can sleep there."

"Go to a hotel, David."

"No."

"You can stop sleeping outside, there's no point. You can't pull off the romantic guy thing anymore. Romantics don't cheat on their wives."

He disagreed. Too much romance caused his downfall, not too little.

"Emmy, can you go inside, please?" David asked.

"It's not like she doesn't know what's going on," Amanda said. "She's smart. She's an Honors student." But, she nodded Emmy back inside.

"How dare you?" Amanda said, as soon as the garage door closed behind Emmy. "How could you not at least tell me about this before showing up at our door?"

"I meant to, but I chickened out. I wanted my last day with you to be good. I couldn't give any of it up."

"Just get out. I think I've done a damn good job managing a surprise adoption, and I'll continue to do it well. Everything you touch turns to crap."

"I've touched you and you're not crap."

"Shut up."

"Can I talk to Evangeline and Xavier? I want to make sure they're okay…I mean…I know they're okay with you. I just think I should check in. And may I come in and brush my teeth and take a shower?"

"No. Shower at a hotel. Or, even better, go ahead and rent your own place. You can come in and get some stuff and talk to the kids. You have half an hour. Oh, and don't forget you have five children you've screwed up, not just two."

"I haven't forgotten."

Xavier and Evangeline entered the kitchen around the same time David did. Evangeline wore a LHS volleyball T-shirt and Victoria Secret PINK pajama pants, both a size too big which made her look even thinner. Emmy's clothes. They didn't look right on her. Patrick's clothes fit Xavier well, but they didn't look right on him either, unless he had in fact attended soccer camp in Fort Collins last summer. The pair looked like they'd woken up in someone else's lives. Which, of course, they had.

David wanted to make them chocolate chip pancakes with whipped cream and a cherry. But, he knew Amanda wouldn't give him the time. He made them frozen waffles and helped himself to the coffee pot. Amanda had made enough coffee for two, out of habit.

"Did you sleep okay?" he asked them.

"When you bought the house, did you know Xavier and I would live here some day?" Evangeline asked.

"What do you mean?"

"Why do you have two empty bedrooms in your house?"

"They're guest rooms," David said.

"Do you have guests a lot?"

"No. Sometimes my wife's parents."

She paused and considered him, as if checking for holes in a weak story.

"I brought in your bags," David said. "I'm sorry I didn't bring them in last night."

"It's okay. I don't need stuff. I'm okay as long as I have this." Evangeline opened her palm to display a black rock. He didn't know how it appeared there. He had seen both her hands a moment ago, and he didn't see any pockets.

"It's my magical object." She handed the rock to David.

She watched him carefully while he held the rock in his

palm. *Would it glow or dance around if I was magic?* It lay in his hand as a rock always does.

"What is a magical object?" he asked.

"It's something a wizard keeps with them when they do magic, sometimes called a talisman. They leave a little bit of their magic in it with each spell. In time, the object collects power. Keeping it with you when you do magic makes you more powerful because all the other magic you've ever done is with you, too. And, talismans can be anything. Objects. Animals. People."

"People?"

"Sure. They're the best ones. Except for their unpredictability."

She glanced at Xavier. *Was he one of her talismans? Certainly, he must be.*

Xavier didn't listen as closely to this conversation. He looked at Evangeline periodically, but mostly enjoyed conversation with his waffles and syrup. David wanted to engage him, but had no idea how.

Evangeline seemed to read David's mind and helped him out.

"Show him yours," Evangeline said to Xavier.

In a look, Xavier's eyebrows said twice as much as he'd ever said out loud. One eyebrow rose, saying *are you kidding?* and the other slanted, saying *how dare you?* David hadn't considered asking Xavier about a talisman. Evangeline had the magical narrative, not Xavier. Did Xavier play along for her?

"No," Xavier said.

She rolled her eyes at him. "It's not a big deal. He's not going to try and take it or anything. He doesn't even believe."

"If it's not a big deal, why do you want me to so badly?" he asked her. He squinted at her as if reading the fine print on the tip of her nose.

"Just do it."

While glaring at his sister, he tugged a chain out from under his shirt and pulled it over his head. A heavy silver object clattered onto the counter. A Christian cross.

David didn't know if this meant Xavier was secretly a wizard or secretly a Christian, or which one of those things seemed more unbelievable.

"Are you a Christian?" David asked him.

"No," Xavier said neutrally. He grabbed the cross again, put it back around his neck, and tucked it into his shirt.

"Thank you for showing me," David said to Xavier, who ignored him.

"Our mom gave it to him to use as his object. It's more powerful as an object than my stone, but I wanted something of my own to build from scratch. The cross comes with built-in magic. Millions of people across the world and across time have used it as their talisman. People sing to it. Speak to it. Put it over the bodies of their dead. It all adds up. But you still have to make it your own, put your own magic in it, or it's still just an object." She swished a piece of waffle around her plate with her fork. "You have these in your house," she said, still looking at her plate.

"Yes," he said. "We're Christian." He didn't know if she expected any more explanation.

"I thought you might understand then, if you saw his," she added.

"I do," he said, even though he wasn't entirely sure.

"You have another talisman, too." She put one finger on his hand, on his wedding ring.

He smiled. "I guess I do."

CHAPTER EIGHT

Patrick stood at the edge of the family room and watched his "brother" peruse their bookshelf. This strange boy had hijacked the family room. Patrick lingered in the hallway, a good ten feet away, as if Xavier emitted radioactive waves he wanted to avoid. But, Emmy blew past Patrick like a stiff wind of cherry vanilla body lotion. She came from behind Xavier and grabbed his arm. He jumped and pulled away, but this didn't discourage Emmy. She grabbed his arm again and pulled him away from the bookshelf. Patrick wanted to tell her to lay off…because she should…but he didn't, because he wanted Xavier to know he stood firmly on Emmy's side.

"When is your birthday?" she asked him.

Emmy generally got her questions answered, but Patrick didn't know if she would this time. Xavier looked at her as if her voice just sounded like an annoying buzz.

"October 17," he said finally.

"That was just a week ago," Emmy said.

He stared at her without response.

"Happy Birthday, I guess," Emmy said.

"Thanks," he said. He looked at the bookshelf, then back at Emmy and Patrick in turn, to see if the exhausting one-question interrogation had ended. He didn't know Emmy.

"Patrick's birthday is June 25." She stated the fact with a hint of malice, as if this should upset Xavier.

Patrick didn't know why Xavier should care. Xavier already knew he lived with the *other* family, already knew his father had cheated and lied. Instead, Patrick had the truth poured down his throat with a funnel, over one night.

"Patrick is only four months older than you," Emmy said. She stared Xavier down.

"It's not his fault when he was born, Emmy," Patrick said.

"Did our dad come visit you? How often did you see him? Did you know he had other kids? How long was he with your mom? Did she know he was married? Did you? Did he love her?" Emmy asked.

"I don't know," Xavier said.

"What do you mean, 'you don't know'? Which question are you answering? You have to at least know if he visited you. You know whether or not you *know* my dad and when you saw him last. It's a simple question."

"He's *your* father," Xavier said. "Ask him your questions."

"You're evading my questions on purpose."

"It's none of your business."

"It is my business, *brother.*"

Then Emmy got quiet so suddenly Patrick thought Mom had entered the room. No one except for Mom could shut Emmy up like that. But, he couldn't have been more wrong this time. Patrick saw the other half of the weirdo twins, Evangeline. Her wet hair from the shower explained why brother and sister had parted for longer than a few seconds. Evangeline looked at Emmy the way the cat looks at frogs she plans to impale with her claw. Patrick moved between them without realizing he had done it. Xavier did the same thing.

Emmy didn't seem bothered by the obstruction or Evangeline's threatening stare.

"Why aren't you wearing the clothes I gave you?" she asked Evangeline. "You'd rather wear the ratty clothes the shelter gave you? You think I *want* you to wear my clothes? I'm trying to help you."

Evangeline didn't answer. She approached Emmy, and Patrick and Xavier hovered nearby. Evangeline touched Emmy's arm, as if she poked a mountain lion.

Emmy gasped and tears streamed down her face as if they had already amassed inside her, waiting to fall.

Emmy turned to Patrick, rubbing her arm. "She hurt me."

Her arm appeared undamaged. "Jesus, Emmy, she's not even five feet tall. Grow a pair."

"No. She *hurt* me."

"What do you mean?"

"Forget it. Where's Jude?"

Okay, so that's how it would be. Only Jude could possibly understand the pain of, and defend her from, twelve-year-old girls who lightly touched her arm.

Patrick followed Emmy to Jude's room and saw Emmy's friend, Samantha, alone in the room with Jude. What a crappy time to be dumped here so her parents could roam around Europe. Samantha looked as if she was made of spun glass and had no business around a horny bull like Jude. Jude lay on his bed staring at the ceiling, and Samantha applied a Band-Aid to his finger, for some reason. She did it way too slowly, as if she wanted the excuse to hold his hand. The sight of her manicured baby-pink nails made him think about how it would feel to have her nails graze his back or run through his hair. It didn't take much for her to get him excited. And, he had to live in the same house with her for a week. Eventually, she'd notice he stared at her like she was an IMAX movie screen. *Apply the fucking Band-Aid already.*

Emmy held out her arm to Jude. "She hurt me."

At least this caused Samantha to drop Jude's hand and

place hers on Emmy's arm.

"The girl?" Jude asked.

"Yes."

"What did she do?"

"She touched my arm, and it hurt me."

"How?" Samantha asked.

"It wasn't physical pain. It's like she hurt my feelings."

Silence.

"She made me feel like I was insignificant," Emmy continued. "Like, no one cared about me. And, I really believed it. I hated myself. I wanted to hurt myself. It was the freakiest thing I have ever felt."

Still nothing.

The accusation sounded completely insane. But, Jude looked at her seriously.

"I'm so sorry," Samantha said. "What a bitch."

Always Emmy's puppy, Samantha would blindly console her even when she said something completely crazy. Did Samantha actually hear what Emmy had said?

Emmy started jabbering to them about the injustice of it all. When things went wrong, Patrick thought his siblings secretly loved it. They loved any reason to brood and conspire and stare at the ceiling and have Band-Aids applied for them. As Emmy talked, her cheeks flushed as if nothing in the world exhilarated her more than misery. Patrick figured she really just loved change, good or bad. She wanted things to happen. She loved all kinds of change. New school years. Change in seasons. Change in the weather. Big news events. Bad news.

Jude and Emmy once made him late for school when they decided to follow a tower of smoke to see what burned. They watched hurricane coverage with the same rapt attention most people gave the Super Bowl. They liked personal disasters, too. Gossip. Scandals. Especially Emmy. Occasionally, Patrick saw Emmy around school with an unlikely new friend. And, he could always guess the reason. Something bad had happened to this person. Someone died. Or, her father lost his job. Or, his brother was arrested. Emmy could sniff out scandal like a shark sniffs out blood.

He had seen Jude do this, too. When Patrick's friend Tyler got injured in a car accident, for some reason, Jude wanted to go to the hospital and visit him, along with Patrick. Jude had once thrown Tyler against a locker for looking at him funny, but once Tyler was attached to an IV, Jude collected money at school for a balloon bouquet.

Emmy and Jude managed to toe the line between creepy people who like to burn ants for fun and Mother Theresa. Whenever Mom and Dad would let them, they'd volunteer to help disaster victims. Emmy actually started a volunteer chapter of the Red Cross for kids. They would do things such as bring old toys to wildfire victims. Emmy even got on the news once for her good deeds. Patrick suspected Jude and Emmy didn't want to help people as much as they liked getting a chance to go see the aftermath of disasters. But, the end result remained the same. Someone got helped. A lonely person got a friend. A homeless child got a toy. Did it matter why?

"She's evil," Emmy said, bringing her tirade to conclusion. "Evil. There is something wrong with her. Do you think that's what *she* looked like? That girl looks nothing like us. Maybe she's not even his."

"She looks like Nana," Patrick said. "You know, like from pictures when she was young."

"No," Jude said. "That's not okay."

'No' she doesn't look like her or 'no' it's not okay she does? Before now, only one other really bad thing had happened to the family—their grandmother committed suicide. Patrick could still remember what Dad's face looked like when he found out. That's when he saw him cry for the first time.

Thankfully, Samantha sat on the floor now with her legs tucked under her, not touching Jude. She looked as if she wanted to disappear. Patrick didn't blame her. It really sucked that her parents dumped her here this week of all weeks. He would have been afraid that she wouldn't come back, if she hadn't been stuck to Jude and Emmy like a magnet.

David spent most of Sunday at his office. He always had emails to answer and plans to review. After he had killed as much time as possible, he drove home. He thought Amanda might wear down if he could prove himself an asset to the family. She didn't want to raise five teenagers by herself. She didn't like it when he left her with three for a weekend. Maybe he'd start with offering to pick up dinner so she didn't have to cook. But, she didn't answer his calls.

He didn't let the unanswered call stop him. He picked up some pizzas anyway and headed home.

David rang the doorbell, which felt strange. Amanda opened the door. She looked at him as if she had gotten a phone call from a solicitor at 6:00 a.m. She left the door open and walked back into the house without a word.

An unspoken invitation? David's stomach lifted.

He entered the house and closed the door behind him quietly. He feared she might change her mind and kick him out any minute.

She waited for him by the stairs as if he had arrived late for a pre-existing appointment.

"I brought pizza," he said.

"Put it in the dining room and follow me," she said, and walked up the stairs.

He did as she said, and followed her up the stairs and into

his office. She closed the door behind them.

"We need to discuss some practical details," she said in the same tone she probably used to read off agenda items during a budget allocation meeting. David half expected her to hand him an agenda and suggest he take careful notes. But, he had the feeling he would remember what she would say.

"I've started shopping around for a divorce attorney," she said. "You should do the same. I really want it to be as quick and painless as possible so it's easier on the kids. You know how I operate. I don't care to quibble over stupid details. To the point, and done."

David had expected it. But, that didn't help at all. To him, it seemed like being told he had only a five percent chance of surviving a disease. That five percent could stretch to hold every second of every day of the forty more years he'd hoped to live. Or, in this case, years he hoped to be married.

"No. Let's shop around for a marriage counselor. You can't just divorce me. We haven't even talked. We haven't attempted to save our marriage. You never just give up like that."

Amanda chewed on the inside of her cheek unconsciously.

"Stop doing that. You'll rip up the insides of your mouth," David said. "It will hurt when you drink coffee."

"Tell me this, David. What kind of woman would I be if I didn't divorce you? If I hesitate…if we spend months or years in therapy, maybe I'll…I am not the kind of woman who stays married to a man who cheats on me."

"You're saying you don't want to try counseling because you're afraid it might work?"

"We're getting divorced. There is no other option that makes me feel okay with myself."

"Do you want to get divorced or are you just doing it because that's what you think you ought to do?"

"Get a divorce attorney, David."

David didn't remember ever changing Amanda's mind about anything, unless he counted convincing her to try sushi. But, he could find plenty of space to live in that five percent chance.

"Before we move on to the next topic," Amanda said. "I need you to understand our marriage is over. Nothing I am about to say should give you any hope about us. It's all about the kids. Period. Do you understand that?"

David couldn't bring himself to say yes, or nod. "I hear you."

Amanda squinted at him. He expected her to call him on his word play, as she usually did, and force him to say yes. But, she let it go.

"I don't you want you here," Amanda said. "Just the sight of your shoes in the closet makes me want to cry. Or tear the house down. I hate the thought of having to see you every day. Talk to you. It's the worst thing I can think of."

She paused. *Dear God, let there be a 'but.'*

"You need to move back in," Amanda said. "Since the guest rooms are full, I figured you could sleep in your office. I need you to co-parent with me and it looks better to the case manager if our family looks solid. And Evangeline asked me if you could live here." Amanda stared at the palm of her hand for a long time before she spoke again, as if she had written her lines there in invisible ink. "I couldn't refuse her."

"Thank you."

"You're my roommate. Not my husband. You understand?"

"If that's what you want."

"I don't want any of this."

She hadn't looked him in the eye since they had started talking. She ran her finger along the blue vein lines on her forearm as if noticing them for the first time.

"I talked to the case manager in Odessa," she said.

"What did you tell her?"

"I didn't tell her the truth, if that's what you mean." Amanda flashed him her blues for a half second, as if she wanted to slap him in the face with her eyelashes. "She told me about what happened to them…and to Crystal. About the tick marks on their backs."

She picked up a glass orb paperweight from his desk and balanced it on her palm. The long-ago Father's Day gift had never looked more like a deadly weapon.

"I think she's lying," Amanda said.

David weighed her words as Amanda did with the paperweight. "What do you mean?"

"Or perhaps, she is mistaken," she amended.

"How could she be mistaken?"

"Crystal Carr," Amanda said. Her name sounded so odd on Amanda's lips. Especially…like that. She slung her name at him as a decisive point that could end any argument.

"What about her?"

"Crystal was a feminist. She didn't seem like the type to take a man's last name, let alone let him abuse her and her children for years. And Odessa? She wanted to move overseas. I'm sure she would have moved at least out of Texas. Really though, she wouldn't have moved anywhere. She didn't even like to eat at the same restaurant twice. She would have travelled. She was always looking for something."

A tingling sensation shot from David's fingertips to his earlobes. He felt as if he had fallen asleep halfway through a movie and then woken up and couldn't follow the story. What the hell had he missed?

She snapped her fingers in his face. "What's the matter with you? Breathe."

"You knew her?"

She clenched her hand into a claw shape and looked as if she might use it.

"I *introduced* you, you asshole…or, did you forget?"

"But, it wasn't like that. I remember. It was in the laundry room at your apartment building. It was a Friday night. We went in there to get your clothes out of the dryer before we went downtown. She was in there guarding her clothes while they dried, reading a book. She was drinking something that looked really weird and I asked her what it was. She said it was bubble tea. You told me her name and told her mine. We both said hi. I asked her if she was going to spend her whole Friday night reading. She laughed at me and didn't answer. And that was it. You never mentioned her again."

Her eyes had narrowed with each word he spoke and he didn't realize why until a second before she said it out loud.

"Oh my God." She sucked on her tongue as if she wanted to remove a bad taste. "The detail…you remember what she was drinking the first time you saw her?"

"It's not a big deal. You're a big picture person, but I'm more into details. I remember stuff like that. About everything…not just her." Sort of true, but he hoped she wouldn't test him. "I remember the details about when I met you, too." That test, he would pass.

"Did it start then?" She asked it quietly, as if she hoped he wouldn't hear and wouldn't answer.

"No. Not right away. It was…"

"Never mind, I don't want to know."

"You were friends with her?" he asked.

"Sort of."

"Sort of? You said she never wanted to eat at the same restaurant twice. That must mean you ate at restaurants with her. Which ones? When?"

"For God's sake, David, that's hardly relevant."

To David, it seemed critical. Which restaurant they ate at, what they ordered, and what they talked about. He couldn't imagine any information more interesting—evidence that truly fascinating things happened in the world he knew nothing about. *What else happened when I wasn't paying attention?*

"I'm just saying I knew enough about her to know there is a hole in the story somewhere. She would never let that happen."

She probably didn't realize this comforted him. She might as well have stroked his hair and whispered, *It's okay…none of it is real. She wouldn't have done that to you.*

"Those are my kids," David said. "And hers. I know they are."

"I know."

"I agree with you. Of course, I do. The woman I knew wouldn't have let that happen…but she did."

"What happened to the *man*? Did he go to prison?"

"No, he wouldn't go quietly, so they ended up gunning him down. He died before he was cuffed."

"Good."

CHAPTER NINE

David had fallen in love with Crystal shortly after he had fallen in love with Amanda. He had never intended to fall in love with her, of course. He should have known better than to even spend time with her. To him, she stood out among all the rest at the crowded University of Texas campus. As if she wore red when everyone else wore black. He had thought they could be friends. But, he didn't tell Amanda about his "friend." He should have recognized that as a dangerous sign and gotten away from her as fast as he could.

It didn't take long for their friendship to turn into more. The second time they studied together at a coffee shop, she kissed him. They sat side by side on a couch sipping double espressos. David had been talking about something…he couldn't remember what…something boring, something unsexy. And, out of nowhere, she leaned over and kissed him. A quick, innocent kiss, like a twelve-year-old trying it for the first time. After her peck, she leaned back and waited, biting her lip.

If David had said what he should have said in that moment, such as, "I'm in love with my girlfriend," or "Thanks, but no thanks, I don't cheat," everything would have changed from that point forward. But, he didn't. He didn't say a thing. He smiled. Then after a moment or two of silence, which probably drove Crystal mad, he leaned in and kissed her, a lot less like a twelve-year-old. It had felt right.

Four months later, they went away together, but not on purpose. On a random Wednesday, when Amanda had class, Crystal suggested they go for a drive.

"Where?" David asked.

"Let's just see what we can find," she said.

They took the highway out of town and turned down the first road that looked interesting. They drove purely on gut, and always agreed on which way to go, based on absolutely nothing. Without planning it, they drove almost directly to Enchanted Rock, a huge natural dome of pink granite outside Fredericksburg, Texas.

They hiked to the top of the dome and arrived at sunset.

"Is this what you were looking for?" he asked. No planned trip could have ended better, and he expected a wistful 'yes', but got a different answer.

She wrapped her arms around herself and looked across the orange-streaked sky. He remembered that moment clearly. She had on a thin white sweater that she hugged to herself as if it had protective powers, and her dark hair twirled and twisted madly in the wind.

"No," she said. "I want more."

His tongue got dry and his heart hammered in his chest. But, he couldn't remember why he had felt so agitated.

She turned and stepped toward him. Her brown eyes pleaded with him. "Is there more, David?"

"I don't know what you mean," he said, but the blood rushed through his head as loudly as the wind. He remembered he had been lying to her. But, that made no sense. This memory, like a lot of his memories, felt a little off. Maybe he had drunk enough in college to burn holes in his brain.

She kissed him. Her lips tasted salty from the hike.

"Why do they call this place enchanted?" she whispered in his ear.

He could barely hear her over the wind. "The sign at the bottom says the rock moans at night. When it gets cool, the rock contracts, and that makes the sound. The Indians thought it was ghosts."

"I see," she said. "Maybe we can spend the night and check for ourselves."

"I didn't pack," he said. "I don't have a toothbrush or anything."

She kissed him again.

"Okay, we can stay."

"I know you have the answers," she said. "You have to tell me."

"Crystal...I don't understand what you're talking about."

"I know there's more. I want the *more*."

"Who says more is better? What's wrong with what you can see with your eyes?" He had shouted it. Why had he been so pissed? Probably because he had thought the day was perfect and she hadn't. The amazing view wasn't enough for her. *He* wasn't enough. But, he hadn't felt angry, exactly. He had felt scared.

Amanda announced they would have dinner together. Jude, Patrick, and Emmy responded as if she had asked them to rip out a tooth and hand it over. But, it didn't matter. They would do it. Amanda wore a quiet simmering rage like vest of TNT. So, everyone would sit and the table and eat the lasagna she made. Even her stepchildren lacked immunity to her force of command.

Never had the task of eating lasagna felt so dangerous. His family members hovered around the dining room, choosing seats an impossibly difficult task. David tried to help Amanda in the kitchen, but she created a force field in the doorway with a firm and biting, "I do not want your help."

So he sat at the head of the table and waited patiently. Samantha placed the silverware and napkins on the table with a ballerina's grace and a paid-by-the-hour inefficiency. She took one piece of silverware out of the kitchen at a time, seeming grateful to have something to do. Poor girl. Wrong place, wrong time.

"Isn't anyone going to help her?" David asked the room at large.

"I don't mind," Samantha said. "I'm pretty much finished anyway."

"Thank you, Samantha," David said. "Everybody sit down."

The kids acted as if snakes hid under the napkins. Evangeline sat on his left. Maybe he had one child who didn't hate him. Better than zero.

"Thank you," he said.

Then Xavier had no choice but to sit down on the other side of his sister. Samantha headed toward the other side of the table, but had a sudden change of heart and filled the spot next to Xavier, leaving three seats on the other side for the Vandergraff siblings. David thought she did this on purpose; she knew the two halves of David's kids should not risk touching elbows.

When Amanda came in with the lasagna, Emmy, Jude, and Patrick sat down. Patrick sat on David's right. David didn't know if that meant anything. Patrick had the coolest head of his kids…at least, of the three he knew well. Patrick usually wanted everyone to "shut up and stop the drama." He yelled something to that effect at his siblings several times a week. As the least likely to stab a fork through his hand, Patrick may have sat next to David just to avoid drama.

The lasagna looked huge. Everything needed two more servings now. Aside from plates scraping and a few quiet "pass-me-the's", the diners remained silent. The longer no one talked, the heavier the silence got, and the harder it felt to break. Emmy talked more than this when she had the flu. She talked more than this when she had tonsillitis. She may have never gone this long without speaking in her life.

"Samantha, I talked to your mom today. They arrived in Switzerland safely," Amanda said.

Samantha nodded. "What did she say?"

"They checked in. Said the place is nice. They're sure it will do them some good."

David's daughters distracted him. They had both engaged in that specific type of sibling *looking* that inspired many children to say, "she's *looking* at me." He knew he shouldn't, but he smiled slightly. They acted like sisters.

"Emmy, Patrick, it was nice of you to share your clothes. Thank you for doing that," David said.

Patrick shrugged. Emmy appeared to have about three million words held in with a cork.

"As soon I get the chance, I can take you to buy some clothes of your own," he said to Xavier and Evangeline.

Patches of flush had broken out on Emmy's neck. She would boil over any minute.

"Emmy, is there something you want to say?" David asked.

Patrick winced and shook his head, which David took to mean, *you should not have asked that, you stupid, stupid man.*

"She's a witch," Emmy said. She pointed her fork at Evangeline in accusation. She would have made the Puritans proud.

"Emmy!" Amanda scolded.

"That's not an insult," Evangeline said, calmly. "You are something much worse. You are a Mundane."

"What does that mean?" Emmy spat.

"It means you are *nothing*. Ordinary. I would rather die than be a Mundane."

"Jesus, you're completely crazy, aren't you?" Jude said. "You really think you are a witch. Psycho."

"Jude!" David shouted.

A slender crack branched up the side of the water glass Jude held. Then the glass shattered.

"Fucking shit," Jude said. Drops of blood dribbled down his fingers onto his placemat.

"She did that," Emmy said. She stood up and pointed at Evangeline again and said, "Witch," in classic *Crucible* fashion.

Amanda examined Jude's hand. "You're fine. It's not that deep. Go clean yourself up." Then she turned to her daughter. "Emmy, we don't point at people and shout 'witch.' That's completely unacceptable. Sit down right now."

"She's right, Emmy," David said. "Apologize to…Evangeline." He had gotten very close to saying "your sister."

"It's okay. She doesn't have to apologize," Evangeline said. "It's not a mean thing to say. I am a witch."

An expected amount of silence followed this pronouncement. But, for some reason, Amanda was the only person upset by this statement. Her eyebrows rose and then furrowed as if she had to massage the words into her brain. Her hands shook.

"Emmy," she said. "Go get the broom and dust pan and clean up the glass."

"She should have to do it," Emmy said. "She broke it."

"Emmy, if you don't go get the broom, I swear to God…"

She didn't have to finish her swear because Emmy left to get the broom.

And that completed their first family dinner.

Amanda went to go check on Jude and David stayed with the rest of them. He told them to take their plates and finish eating in their rooms.

"Why am I being grounded?" Patrick asked. "I didn't even say anything."

"You're not being grounded. I just want everyone to chill out."

"You know what," Patrick said. "That's fine. I vote that we all stay in our own rooms all the time from now on."

"Fine with me," Emmy said.

Evangeline and Xavier picked up their plates and got up to leave, too, glowering at Emmy the whole time. He had to admit, when they glowered, they *glowered*. He thought maybe he *should* actually scold them for looking at her.

"Emmy, I need to talk to you," David said.

"No."

"It's not optional."

He waited until the other kids had left the room and sat down in the chair next to her. She started crying before he even started.

"I'm not speaking to you," she said with wet cheeks. "You're an adulterer."

"It's okay for you to be mad at me. You should be."

She used her napkin to wipe away her tears as soon as they left her eyes, as if somehow he might not notice them if she grabbed them fast.

"But it's not okay for you to be mean to Evangeline or

Xavier. They didn't do anything to you. And they're going through a lot. You have to be nicer."

Emmy's lip quivered. He could sense she had a lot of responses to this. But, David figured Emmy knew as soon as she opened her mouth she would start to sob.

"Do you know what happened to them?" he asked her. "Did Mom explain?"

She didn't answer. He had hoped she'd nod. He didn't want to say it again.

"Their mom was murdered," he said.

"Your girlfriend," she clarified.

"Not since a long time ago."

"How long?"

"Twelve years."

"I'm thirteen," she said.

"Yes."

Emmy stared down at the broom and dustpan she held. Apparently, Amanda's punishment of holding the broom and dustpan hadn't ended, even though she had already cleaned up the glass.

"They were there when she was murdered. They saw it. And…it was more than that. Their stepfather abused them." He couldn't explain to his baby girl that their stepfather had raped them repeatedly. He didn't want her to know something like happened in the world.

"Does it make you sad?"

"Of course, I'm sad my children were abused."

"No, are you sad she's dead?"

"Yes. Emmy, she was a human being. What happened to her is sad."

"I didn't mean it like that. I just…never mind."

"What?"

"Did you love her, or was it just for sex?"

A question you don't want from your daughter.

"I loved her."

"As much as Mom?"

He hesitated. Honestly, he couldn't answer that question. He had chosen Amanda. But, he had never really known why. The decision had come from his gut, not his head, or even his heart.

"No, not as much as Mom."

"You hesitated before you answered. Are you lying?"

"No."

"Was she a witch, too?"

"You mean, Crystal?"

"Her name was Crystal? That's a stripper name."

He had to chuckle. "Well, she wasn't a stripper."

"Was she a witch?"

"Emmy, none of them are really witches. Witches aren't real."

"Mom said they think their stepfather was a dark wizard. And, that's why he abused them. They say he wasn't always a bad guy. The dark magic broke him, messed up his brain."

"They believe that because it's harder to believe the truth."

"Which is?"

He shifted in his seat uncomfortably. He didn't know at which point she began lecturing him, but the conversation had gotten off track.

"That they were abused by their regular human stepfather, who was a very bad guy."

"That's what you believe?"

"Of course."

"Then you're an idiot."

"Are you saying you really believe they are dark wizards?"

"I know they are."

"You're thirteen. You're too old for that kind of thing."

She narrowed her eyes at him. Emmy had been pissed at him before, almost every day, in fact. But, not like this. He could feel her hate making his throat burn.

"They're cursed, too," she said. "Just like their stepfather."

"That's a terrible thing to say."

"It's not their fault, but they are. It's sticking to them. The evil is getting on my clothes."

Reason had left the conversation before it had even started. Since when did Emmy believe in witches? Maybe he should have listened to her more carefully when she talked.

"I'll take her shopping tomorrow. You don't have to share your clothes anymore if you don't want to." As if this would fix everything. Emmy would no longer get curses on her clothes.

Amanda knocked on the door to his office—a small but unsettling change, since she usually just walked in. He opened the door and she handed him sheets and a comforter. She wore the gray pajama pants he found oddly sexy. He guessed the pants themselves didn't do much for him, but she wore them with a tank top that showed her midriff when she moved at certain angles. Most importantly, she wore these pants to bed and he had pulled them off her many times. He also happened to know she wore her sleeping clothes without a bra or panties. Useless and tortuous information now, like how he still had the salad dressing choices memorized from the restaurant he waited at in college.

No small talk. She went straight to business.

"I made their first therapy for appointment for Thursday. They're scheduled with different counselors, but it's at the same time. I can drop them off on the way to work. Do you think you can pick them up? Also, do you think you can work from home as much as possible until they start school? I know they're old enough to be on their own, but it doesn't feel right."

"Yeah. I—"

"I emailed you some links to private schools. I was thinking that might be better. I just can't imagine sending them to public school right now. The high school has almost 4000 students. I think it would crush them. I thought maybe somewhere with small classes, where they could give them more attention, get them caught up with their peers. It would be less overwhelming, don't you think?"

"I like that idea. Can we afford it?"

"We'll manage. It would have to be temporary. Maybe for just this school year. Patrick may have to wait on getting a car."

David groaned.

"I know," Amanda said. "It's not very fair to him. But, he's a sensible kid. I think he'll get over it. We'll make Jude share his truck."

"What do you think the counselors will make them do in therapy?"

"Talk…I'm assuming."

"They hate that."

"Evangeline likes to talk."

"Only about witchcraft."

Amanda chuckled, the closest she had gotten to a smile since she'd met her stepchildren.

"Maybe we should postpone therapy," he said. "They're not going to want to talk."

"David, they watched their mother murdered, and then proceeded to watch her corpse burn just weeks ago. They're going to therapy. That's not negotiable."

"I know…" *Please don't say things like that out loud.*

"Honestly, I don't think they've dealt with any of it. They just float around the house like ghosts. They're in shock. Completely numb. Xavier doesn't even talk, for Christ's sake.

I'm afraid of what's going to happen when the shock wears off and they have to feel it. Trust me, you want them in therapy."

"That's what scares me. The therapist will make them talk about it. Make them say it all out loud. I don't like thinking about what that's going to be like for them."

"They'll be okay," she said. This felt less comforting coming from the same woman who explained why they were not okay less than ten seconds ago.

"I'll see you in the morning," she said. "Good night."

They had kissed each other before bed every night they had slept under the same roof for the past twenty years. He could tell she felt the absence. She suddenly looked too tired to stand.

"I love you," he said.

Her eyes got red and wet, but her mouth contorted as if she might spit on him. She looked like she might come back with an angry retort, but he knew her well enough to know if she opened her mouth, she would cry. Just like Emmy. She left without saying anything.

It seemed wrong not to follow her. She didn't like him to see her cry, but he always at least made an attempt to comfort her before she pushed him out the door with an, "I'm okay. Leave me alone." But, things had changed.

He let go of the breath he held and sat down at the computer. He Googled "Helping Teenagers Deal with Grief." The authors of the articles seemed to have written them about other people's kids. The only thing that seemed true was teens worked very hard to hide their feelings, especially boys. He found a Mad Libs-type fill in the blank, *About Me Storyboard*, to give a teen to help them share their feelings.

The person I lost was_______________.
When found out about the death I was_______________.
Now I feel_______________because_______________.

DESTRUCTION

I get mad sometimes when______________.
The thing that makes me saddest is____________.
One thing I miss about the person is______________.
I wish I could tell them________________.
His kids lived in those blank lines. He couldn't imagine them
having to live with words in them.

CHAPTER TEN

A few days later, the three Vandergraff siblings plus Samantha wore jackets to school for the first time in the season. When the cool air blasted Emmy on her way out, she giggled, the only happy sound she'd made since "the others" had arrived. She stood in the driveway with her arms out and her face to the sky as if she expected snowflakes to land on her tongue, which in Houston was only slightly more likely than a plague of locusts. She took a deep breath.

"Winter," she said. "The trees are going to get all gray and spindly. And of course, there are the Pumpkin Lattes."

Samantha shivered in her open-toed sandals. She could have borrowed some of Emmy's shoes easily enough, but for some reason she didn't. She wore gold sandals with ribbons wrapped around her ankles, like a Greek Goddess who would deem it summer as long as she liked.

While Patrick stared at Samantha's feet, he got hit in the chest with Jude's keys. They fell to the ground with a jingle.

"Good catch," Jude said.

"Why are you throwing shit at me?" Patrick asked. Had Jude caught him looking at her? *Who cares?* Jude could kiss his ass.

"Why don't you drive?" Jude asked.

He waited for the punch line. Jude didn't let other people touch his truck. Jude did *not* let other people drive his truck. He didn't like it when Dad borrowed it to go to Home Depot. And, Dad had bought the truck and had been driving since before Jude was born.

"Why?" Patrick asked.

"You have your learner license, don't you?" Jude asked.

"Yeah."

"Then learn."

Everyone responded differently to a family crisis and Jude must have gone with good old-fashioned crazy. But, as long as the crazy benefitted Patrick, he could live with it.

Patrick picked up the keys and climbed into the driver's seat before Jude could change his mind. Jude got in the passenger's seat and the girls climbed into the half-cab.

"Buckle up," Jude said. "The seat belts in back don't work right. If you crash, Emmy and Samantha will probably go careening out the windshield headfirst. No pressure."

"Shut up," Emmy said. "I know the seat belts are fine."

"We'll see," Jude said.

Patrick had driven before, but not with an audience of two overbearing siblings and one painfully hot girl, plus a truck with displays and knobs he had never seen before. *How do you turn on the wipers? No clue. The headlights? No idea.* If it started to rain, he would probably turn on the emergency blinkers, honk the horn, and crash into a tree.

"Anytime," Jude said. "You're not turning the key to launch a nuke."

Patrick started the truck and proceeded to back out. The truck felt colossal and it took him forever to pull out of the garage because he stopped every time he made it within six feet of any possible obstruction.

"I do have a Spanish test fifth period," Samantha said. "If

we could at least get to school by then, that'd be great."

Patrick laughed, but his cheeks burned. *Was she flirting or making fun of him?* He could never tell the difference.

Learning to drive in Houston resembled learning to surf in a tsunami. As they approached the Expressway, Jude shouted instructions.

"When you get on the ramp, your instinct will tell you to slow down, but you have to speed up. Don't listen to your instinct. Your instinct will be fear. Do the opposite of whatever your instinct tells you."

"Always great advice," Patrick said.

"The cars will be coming from all directions," Jude continued. "You can try to see them with your eyes, but your eyes will always miss something. Humans are unpredictable, so your eyes won't be enough to anticipate the other drivers. You have to *feel* where the other cars are."

"Yes, Obi-Wan."

"Quit fucking with him," Emmy said.

"Please use your eyes to see the cars," Samantha added.

Patrick didn't appreciate Emmy screaming, "You're going to crash," when he pulled on to the highway. Or, when Jude yelled, "Exit now! That's the middle school," three lanes over from the rapidly approaching exit. But, they survived.

Patrick pulled around the side of the massive red brick middle school.

"When do you think they'll have to start school?" Emmy asked quietly.

"Soon, I guess," Patrick said. "They can't just not go."

"They haven't so far," Jude said.

"Do you think they'll be smart enough for classes?" Emmy asked. "Do they know science and math and stuff? Can they read?"

"They're so weird," Jude said.

"They're going to be ripped to shreds," Patrick said.

Patrick didn't think Jude and Emmy would understand this. They didn't get bullied much…they appeared more on the other side of the equation. Patrick saw high school as a minefield of potential humiliation and random acts of violence. And, although he may not be the most normal guy every, Patrick certainly fit in better than Xavier and Evangeline would. Patrick couldn't do much to help, except perhaps if he stood next to Xavier, it would cause the bullies to have to split focus.

"Yeah, they are," Emmy said.

"So, are you just going to let that happen, or what?" Patrick asked. He meant the question for both Jude and Emmy, who each had considerable power at their respective schools. If Jude watched out for Xavier, and Emmy watched out for Evangeline, they wouldn't have anything to worry about.

"What do you mean?" Emmy asked.

"Whether you like it or not, everyone will know they're your brother and sister. Are you just going to let people mess with them?"

Emmy made a sort of grumbling noise in the back seat that Patrick couldn't sort into words.

"Oh, fuck me," Jude said. "I guess I'll have to be his bodyguard, too. Patrick, you're going to have to dial down the freak if I'm going to be able to manage both of you. I'm only one man."

Jude didn't offer to let Patrick drive the next morning, and Patrick didn't complain. His brother's temporary psychosis must have passed. The air had become colder today—but still not uncomfortably cold—that refreshing first cold after the way-too-long Texas summer, that meant football and time off for holidays. Just right.

Samantha dressed more warmly today, but made up for it by parting her lips and exhaling slowly so she could see the steam rising from her lips. No one else in the family had dressed up for Halloween. Patrick couldn't figure out Samantha's costume, but she wore glittery green eye shadow and had a sprinkling of yellow glitter on her cheeks and in her hair, which she had swept off her neck in an elaborate twist held with a green butterfly clip. She looked like Tinker Bell. The glitter from her hair sprinkled all over her—her jacket, her neck, and her chest. He wondered how far down the glitter went.

Mom had let them trick-or-treat as kids, but other than that, they never got into Halloween. No decorations. No costumes. Mom usually bought one small package of the cheapest candy, gave huge handfuls to the first few kids that came by, and then turned off all the lights and locked the door.

She would say, "Who do they think they are, coming to our house at dinnertime and demanding candy and making threats?" And not in a joking way. Trick-or-treaters genuinely pissed Mom off.

"Hey, Emmy," Jude asked. "Are you okay?"

Until then, Patrick hadn't noticed Emmy's unusual quietness, but Jude did, and he had the emotional IQ of a troll.

"Yeah, I'm okay," she said.

Jude smiled at her reflection in the rearview mirror. "I have something that will cheer you up."

He had a devilish grin on his face that made Patrick want to jump out of the car at the next light. Something insane always followed that look, such as *let's put fireworks on Patrick's skateboard and roll it down the stairs* or *let's see if Patrick can fly*. And Emmy always enthusiastically agreed with whatever idea he had.

"I'm going to give Patrick an advanced driving lesson."

Yep. He would jump out at the next light. He did not want to find out what that meant.

"What I said about *feeling* the cars on the highway," Jude said. "It wasn't a joke. I can."

"What do you mean?" Emmy asked.

"Emmy, when I pull on to the interstate, cover my eyes."

Patrick could hear his heartbeat in his ears. He and Samantha argued this point with various statements of reason, such as, "No, we might die," and "No, we'll definitely die." Patrick didn't know if Samantha knew them well enough to realize they might not be joking.

"Jude," Patrick said. "You better be joking. I swear I'll…"

"You'll what?"

"I could tell Mom. She'll take away your car."

"Patrick, don't be such a momma's boy," Emmy said.

"I am not a momma's boy. I just want to live to be sixteen."

"Is he seriously going to do this?" Samantha leaned toward Patrick from where she sat in the half-cab behind him. She smelled of spearmint gum and glitter spray.

"Probably," Patrick said. "Don't worry. I'll do something. I'll grab the wheel."

"Don't, Patrick," Jude said. "You'll mess me up. You wouldn't want to put us in any danger, would you?"

"Do you really know how to do that?" Samantha asked. The question worried Patrick. *No one* knew how to do that.

"Do you trust me?"

"No," Patrick and Samantha said. But, it didn't matter. He meant the question for Emmy.

"Do you think I would do something that would put you in danger?" he asked Emmy, watching her in the rearview mirror.

"No. You wouldn't," Emmy said.

Jude smiled. "Then let's do it."

Morning commuters clogged the interstate, making it extremely dangerous with *both* eyes open. Cars darted from lane to lane unpredictably as their drivers became impatient. Unexpected pockets of traffic caused brake lights to go on and off in chaotic patterns. *Please be joking. Please be joking.*

They weren't.

Emmy placed one small hand over each of Jude's eyes. Patrick considered his options. He had to do something. He didn't want himself and his siblings to die in the stupidest way possible. That should have been his only real concern, but he also thought about Samantha. He wanted to show her he had some power over Jude, that he could do *something* to stop a terrible thing from happening. But, what?

Patrick put his hand on the wheel, between Jude's. The brake pedal concerned him more, but without climbing on top of Jude, he couldn't reach it. If it he had to, he would jump on his brother's lap and take over. He unbuckled his seat belt.

"Patrick," Jude said. "Buckle your damn seatbelt. Are you suicidal or something?"

Well, he did have good hearing, anyway.

"Are *you*?"

"Don't yell at me. I'm trying to concentrate."

Only about twenty seconds had passed, but it felt like twenty years. Either way, Jude had stayed within the lane lines. A freaking miracle.

"Okay. We're all really impressed. Emmy, take your hands off." Patrick said. "There is a car braking in front of you! Open your fucking eyes."

Jude applied the brakes lightly and didn't hit the car.

"Patrick, get your hand off the wheel," Jude said. "You're in my way."

Patrick thought everyone in the car could hear his heart pounding behind his ribs.

"Okay. Amazing. Now open your eyes….no don't change lanes! What are you doing?"

Jude put on his blinker and moved into the lane to his right to pass the car that had slowed down in front of him. Samantha grabbed Patrick's shoulder and dug her fingernails into him. This made his heart start beating wildly for a completely different reason.

"Okay, Emmy," Jude said.

She took her hands off his eyes. Jude sighed happily and grinned at Patrick.

"Pretty cool, huh? You want me to teach you that?"

"I'm never getting in a car with you again," Patrick said.

CHAPTER ELEVEN

David picked his kids up from therapy. They waited in the lobby patiently while he introduced himself to their respective therapists. They had an impressive spread of qualifications and strong handshakes. He asked them what he should do. They both wrote down book recommendations. Evangeline's therapist, a composed and inviting African-American woman with perfect skin, suggested a memorial service for their mother. He felt like an asshole for not thinking of it himself. David asked Xavier's therapist, a librarian-type older white woman with a Bible on her desk, if Xavier had talked at all. She said he had, but didn't expand. "Teenage boys are always tough nuts to crack," she said. "Try talking to him about the things he likes. Easy things."

David wanted to ask for examples, but didn't want to make it obvious he knew almost nothing about his son. If they thought his kids were hopelessly broken, they didn't say so.

He asked the kids if they wanted to go shopping on the way home, but they said no. He let them stay silent on the drive. He asked only one question.

"Was therapy okay?"

They both nodded in the rearview mirror.

"Okay," he said.

His phone rang. He answered with his Bluetooth.

"This is David."

"Hey…David. How are you?" asked Liza, his Vice President of Human Resources. He could already tell she *knew*. She didn't talk usually talk to the CEO with that sad little *How you doing, Champ* voice.

"Fine. How are you?"

"Good. Are you coming in today? If you aren't…I understand. There's just a thing."

"A thing?"

"A crisis sort of thing. We can handle it if you need us to. But I know you want to be looped in to the big stuff."

"What happened?"

"Maybe you should come in."

He glanced at his kids in the rearview mirror. "All right, hang on."

He took them with him to his office. At least, he would make the gossip hounds happy for a few months.

"Do you want to see where I work?" he asked them when he pulled into his office space.

Xavier's eyebrows said, *no, don't care* and *I hate you.*

"It's okay," Evangeline said. "I know you have to go in."

"It won't take long. You can hang out in my office. You can get on my computer."

Everyone in the office greeted him by his first name. He liked to keep it familiar. He had always thought "Mr. Vandergraff" sounded intimidating. The whole office stopped and watched as he passed with his kids. Their appearance would cause a ripple effect of work stoppage for a while. Liza greeted him outside his office.

Her concerned expression didn't mesh with her odd choice of clothing for the day. Liza had her thick legs stuffed in fishnet stockings and wore long, black, press-on nails. Fake blood covered Mark, the VP of Finance. At least Andy, the site foreman, looked normal.

Either they, or David, had lost their minds.

"Why are you dressed like that?" David asked.

"It's Halloween," Liza said.

"Today?"

"Yes."

Now it made more sense why the accountant had worn a cape and the receptionist had pink glitter on her face.

"My costume does look a little funny without the hat. I'm a witch," Liza said.

Naturally.

"I'm sorry," she said.

"You don't have to apologize for it being Halloween."

Apologizing for the calendar date didn't bode well. She acted guilty. Something about the three of them standing there reminded him of aged, bloated versions of his kids. They had done something wrong and waited for him to scold them. Liza gasped dramatically at the sight of Evangeline and Xavier hovering behind him.

"Is this them?" she said.

No. I found these two random children on the street.

"They are so precious. He looks just like you."

She started to approach them and David stood in her path. He remembered that she liked to do things such as tousle boys' hair and tug on little girls' ponytails.

"Don't touch them," he said.

She shrank back, her cheeks bright red. "I wasn't going to. I'm sorry."

"It's okay."

"Do they want anything to eat? There are tons of Halloween goodies in the break room."

David showed them the break room, turned on the computer in his office, and met with his team in the conference room.

When he came in, he heard them speaking in whispers.

"Let's go," he said. "Give me the worst."

None of them said anything.

"David." Liza started.

"Yes?" he prompted.

"There was a problem in Tangled Forest," Andy said.

Their largest project—a forty-acre subdivision near Magnolia.

"Fucking Tangled Forest," David said. "It's always something. I was out there last week. All that's left is landscaping. What could possibly go wrong now? The landscape architect put in red oaks instead of black?"

"It burned down," Mark said.

Tears formed in Liza's eyes. She wiped copious amounts of black eyeliner onto a tissue.

"What do you mean?" David asked. "How much of it?"

"All of it," Mark said.

"That's not possible," David said.

"There was a wildfire," Andy said. "It took out two hundred acres of forest outside of Magnolia, including all of Tangled Forest."

"Imagine, if it had happened two months from now, hundreds of people would have lived in those houses," Liza said. "I guess it's a blessing, in a way."

"No, Liza. They would have all been evacuated," Mark said acidly. "And their insurance would have paid for it. The property is still ours."

"No one was hurt," Andy said. "But we had sixteen vehicles on site. They're gone. We had to stop work in Cherry Woods because that equipment had been scheduled to be moved over there. I sent the workers home without pay."

"Our insurance will cover the vehicles, and will help cover part of the loss from Tangled Forest," Mark said. "But we're covered only for up to twenty million."

The words 'disaster recovery' floated to the top of David's mind. He hadn't spent much time thinking about it, and the mistake would cost him.

"Twenty million," he repeated

It had seemed like an excessive amount of coverage. He had wanted to buy less. How could they lose that much in a disaster? They would have to lose a hundred homes at once. It would take a meteor hitting the Earth for that to happen. A hurricane wouldn't do much this far inland. Tornadoes didn't usually take out that much at once.

"Get the claim going as fast as possible," he said.

"Already done," Mark said.

"Andy, start placing orders for new equipment so we can purchase as soon we get the money. We need to get Cherry Wood back up. We're on a deadline."

"David?" Liza asked.

"Yes?"

"Do you think it's worth it to start work again on Cherry Wood?" She looked at Mark and Andy for support. "Or should we start the process of bankruptcy?"

David stared at her blankly.

"We've lost money before," he said.

"I've done the calculations," Mark said. "We can't come back this time."

"You called me in here to tell me that we're bankrupt?" David asked. "Just like that?

"I'll email you the projections," Liza said, tears still spilling down her face.

Mark spun his wedding ring around his finger.

David's ears rang. He couldn't hear anything anyone said to him as he left with his kids following behind him.

"Are you okay?" Evangeline asked when they climbed back into the Mercedes.

"Let's go shopping," he said. "You need clothes. I'm going to take you to the mall and you're going to buy clothes. End of discussion."

He wished he had handled it differently, but he didn't know how much longer he could afford to buy them clothes and wanted to do it now. He took his silent, baffled children into The Galleria, the largest and loudest structure they'd ever visited, took them to Hollister, and ordered them to pick out clothes. Evangeline walked around the store with her nose wrinkled, but eventually gave in and began pulling things off the rack. She went for bright colors and picked out outfits that defied all sense of matching or reason. David's ears didn't stop ringing until he noticed Xavier. He had his arms wrapped around his chest, and stared at a rack of cargo shorts, holding his breath. He looked as if he was trying not to cry.

David snapped out of it.

"I'm sorry. I shouldn't have brought you here if you didn't want to come. Try to relax. You're fine." As an afterthought, he added, "Breathe."

Xavier looked at him when he said that. And, after a moment's consideration, he did take a breath.

"I'll pick the stuff out for you if you want," David said. "I'm not going to say I know what's cool. But, I know what my sons wear. You don't have to try it on here. If it doesn't fit when you put it on at home, I'll take it back and exchange it. Okay?"

Xavier nodded. He followed David around mutely while he pulled things off the rack. For Xavier, he chose simple. Navy blues, grays, khakis, denims. He would want to blend in at school. Hollister didn't sell invisibility cloaks, so he had to go with the next best thing.

"So, I take it you don't like shopping," David said. "What do you like?"

By the look on Xavier's face, David might have asked the question in German.

"What do you like to do for fun?" David asked.

"I don't know," Xavier said.

"Shawna from the shelter said you liked to watch movies. Maybe you want a television for your room? Or a video game console, maybe. My other sons certainly like video games."

"I don't want you to buy me anything. You have too much stuff. Wizards aren't supposed to care so much about Earthly things."

Three full sentences. Score. The fact he'd said anything at all seemed more important than *what* he had said, but David didn't miss it. With Evangeline safely tucked away in a dressing room, out of earshot, Xavier still called himself a wizard. He believed it, too.

"Okay," David said. "I'm sorry. I don't know much about wizards. You'll have to tell me what I need to know."

Xavier scoffed pointedly and walked away from David.

David would count that as engaging him in conversation. He had to start somewhere.

David holed up in his home office and forced himself to review the budget projections Liza had sent. He found himself developing a case of adult-onset dyslexia. The numbers swam around the page and lost meaning. It couldn't be right. One disaster couldn't bring down his whole business. 347 jobs. 347 people. 347 families. Because of one minor decision he had made one afternoon seven years ago, when twenty million seemed like enough coverage.

And *his* family.

As Xavier said, they had too much stuff. A massive mortgage, three car payments, a boat payment. Private school. Five looming college educations. Why in the hell did they have a boat?

David rubbed his temples and watched the numbers on the screen turn into hieroglyphs until Amanda knocked on the door.

"Are you okay?" she asked.

He stared at her.

"The point of working at home to watch your kids is so you can actually watch them."

He perked up. "What are they doing?"

"Go get your daughter for dinner," Amanda said. "She's being odd. And she won't talk to me."

Whenever *their* kids did something bad, she liked to refer to them as *his* kids. Now she meant it literally.

"Where is she?"

"Backyard."

Evangeline sat on the back lawn with her bare legs folded under her. The ground must be wet and cold. From behind, she looked how David imagined Crystal as a child. She had her thick, brown hair in a messy ponytail and she wore the lacy white sundress David had bought her. He should have made sure she picked out *winter* clothes.

"Are you all right?" David asked.

"I'm fine," she said. She didn't take her eyes off something in the palm of her hand. He thought it might be her magic rock. On closer inspection, he saw a pill bug rolled into a ball.

"What are you doing out here?"

"Practicing."

"What?"

"I'm trying to get the bug to trust me and unroll while it's still in my hand."

"How do you do that?"

She shrugged. "I just focus on making my hand feel safe."

"Does it work?"

"With some of the bugs, it works right away. With others, it never works."

"Dinner is ready, if you'd like to come inside."

"Can I ask you something?"

"Of course."

"Why do you ask me about magic if you don't believe in it? Are you humoring me?" She said the word 'humoring' as if she had recently learned the word and wanted to try it out.

David weighed his possible answers.

"Because it's important to you. I want to know about the things that are important to you."

She carefully placed the still-rolled pill bug on the ground. She gave him one of her mother's inscrutable expressions. His chest swelled with grief. *Because she taught it to you. Your words are her words. I want to hear her echo.*

"Are you thinking about my mother right now?" she asked.

"How did you know that?"

"Your eyes look different. And, I can feel you being sad."

He kneeled down next to her and as he suspected, the knees of his slacks sank into the wet ground.

"We could have a memorial service for her, if you want."

All of her muscles seemed to tighten at once and she shrank slightly. "I don't want to."

She picked up another bug and the back of her dress

shifted, showing more skin around her neck. He saw two tick marks peeking out from behind her dress. His head swam. Good thing he had already knelt.

"We can remember her however you want. Whenever you're ready."

She nodded.

"Is something bothering you?" he asked. It sounded stupid when he said it out loud. Of course, something bothered her. Lots of things. He had meant, *is there anything causing you to be more bothered than usual right now?*

"Amanda said I can't do magic anymore. Not while I live in her house."

A burst of anger made his knees sink farther into the lawn. David couldn't imagine why Amanda would do something as unnecessary and cruel as taking away her fantasy. Not like Amanda at all.

"You must have misunderstood her," David said.

"She said magic hurts people. And, that I should know that better than anyone."

David stood up and knocked the mud off his pants. "No, there is some mistake. I'll talk to her. Come inside for dinner."

He took off his jacket and draped it over her shoulders. It had Crystal in it and he thought about taking it back, but Evangeline wrapped the jacket around herself tightly.

When she stood up, David leaned down to flick the mud and grass off her legs, but stopped himself before he touched her.

Dinner featured no fighting or breaking glass. Emmy graced the table with conversation about student government. She considered running for class President and evaluated her competition. It felt forced, as if Amanda had ordered Emmy to talk about student government at dinner.

Xavier wore some of the shelter clothes. David ignored it, which took some self-control. Samantha sat too close to Jude for David's liking. She ate her macaroni noodles one at a time. *Weren't her parents supposed to pick her up today?*

"I'm going out," Jude announced.

"It's a school night," Amanda said.

"It's Halloween," Jude countered.

"Where do you want to go?" David asked.

"Party at Trevor's house."

"Alcohol?" Amanda asked.

"No. Just milk and cookies," Jude said.

"Don't joke around," Amanda said. "Answer the question."

"His parents are home. I doubt they're buying us a keg. It's not a big thing. Just some people hanging out."

"Be home by eleven," Amanda said.

"It's *Halloween*," Jude argued.

"Then make it nine," Amanda said.

"Eleven is fine," Jude said. He grabbed his plate and left the table in a rush. David guessed he wanted to leave before Amanda changed her mind.

After eating, they all took their plates into the kitchen. While David passed by Amanda, he put his hands on her waist without thinking about it. She pulled away as if he'd burned her.

"Don't touch me," she cried.

All his kids, minus Jude, turned to look at them.

"I'm sorry…it was just habit," he said.

"Break it," she said, and left the kitchen.

Emmy took Amanda's spot by the sink and started loading dishes into the dishwasher. Her cheeks had turned red. Samantha rinsed out Amanda's wine glass. Xavier and

Evangeline stood off to the side, not yet having a spot on the after dinner cleaning assembly line. He handed them rags and asked them to wipe the counters and the table. They did.

David followed Amanda out of the kitchen and hoped she had cooled off. He could feel his own anger simmering and knew approaching her now carried some risk. And even the slightest annoyance in his tone could set off the epic rage she could barely contain.

Amanda folded clothes in their—now her—bedroom. When upset, she liked to get her hands in things. And the house had looked extra clean lately.

"I am sorry for what happened in the kitchen," he said.

"It's okay. I probably overreacted. But, you can't do stuff like that. We're separated. I don't want you to get the wrong idea by me letting you live here. We're not a couple."

"I never noticed how much I touched you, until I wasn't."

She let out a long breath.

"We need to talk," David said, his tone dark.

She raised an eyebrow that looked like a challenge.

Before she could say anything, he continued. "You said this was about the kids, not us. And, what I'm about to say to you is about the kids. Keep that in mind."

"Okay."

"Why does Evangeline think you forbade her to do magic?" David asked.

She unfolded and refolded a pair of David's jeans and didn't look him in the eye.

"Oh," she said. "She told you that."

"What did you say to her?"

"I did tell her she can't do magic. Not while she lives here, anyway."

Anger bubbled up from his stomach and hardened in his shoulders. "What is the matter with you? You said on the first night that they hadn't done anything wrong. That you were mad at me, and not them. She needs her beliefs to cope. Why in the world would you take that away? It makes no fucking sense."

"David," she said. Then she stopped. She smoothed out the pants. "David," she started again.

"What?"

"I understand it's hard to tell someone you love something you know will hurt them. It's not an excuse for not telling me about them sooner. But I understand."

"Okay…"

Her statement didn't cool his anger, but it did confuse him enough to throw him off track. If he yelled at her, she yelled back, even when they were happy.

"Why don't you sit down?" she said.

"I'm not in the mood to sit." He paced at the foot of the bed.

"You should probably sit for this."

"Amanda, if you have some brilliant explanation for why you decided to crush Evangeline's magical narrative, go ahead and spit it out. Or, admit that you had no reason, and just did it to be cruel."

"I have a secret, too, David."

David stopped in his tracks. "A secret? You mean…like my secret?"

"Not exactly. Not an affair. I've never cheated on you. But, I have lied to you."

David's heart raced, and he noticed the rage in his head morphing into something else, something more like fear. His tongue felt too dry.

"To be honest, I never intended to tell you at all," she said. "But, life works in weird ways. Eventually, it will come out, whether I want it to or not. So, I think it's better that I just tell you."

"I know I'm just as guilty, but if there is another man, I

swear, I will...kill...him. I don't care if that makes me a hypocrite."

"I told you, it's not another man."

She finally put down the laundry and stepped toward him. She leaned in and examined his eyes as if trying to solve a riddle printed on his pupils.

"Sometimes I wasn't sure if it really worked," Amanda said. "Or, if we just didn't talk about it. But, I guess it worked."

David thought he wouldn't be able to breathe until she spit it out.

"Amanda." He said her name like a curse. "Tell me. Now."

"I asked Evangeline not to do magic because she *is* a witch. Xavier, too. And magic is extremely dangerous. I don't want them doing it around my family."

David laughed, the same humorless way Amanda laughed when he told her *his* secret. Amanda never had much of a sense of humor, but this had to be some kind of joke. Some kind of cruel game to get back at him.

Amanda didn't smile. "Some people are wizards," she continued. "But, many wizards choose not to practice magic. They believe the benefits are not worth the risks. People like us...we're wizards who don't practice."

"Amanda, I don't get it. Why are you saying this?"

"Wizards have a choice to practice magic or not," she went on, as if he hadn't said anything. "Magic is tempting, but as I said, extremely dangerous. It's not like in books and movies. It's imprecise. Even the best wizards have to conduct spells without understanding their full consequences. Wizards who practice usually end up destroying themselves or the people they care about. Usually accidentally. My mom used to say humans trying to do magic is like an infant trying to defuse a bomb. They might push the right buttons and pull the right wires by accident, but more often than not, they just blow themselves up.

"Wizards also choose whether or not to tell their kids they are wizards. Wizards who don't practice usually don't tell their kids about witchcraft at all. They think that's easiest. Telling kids they're wizards but they aren't allowed to do magic is like telling them there is a secret closet in the house full of toys they can't play with. They'll just want to do magic that much more. And they'll do it without training, making it even more dangerous. That's the choice we made."

"We?"

Amanda went on without clarifying. "My parents told me and Carson we were wizards, but also told us about the dangers of magic, hoping we would make the right choice on our own. I thought that was a risky choice, which is why we chose differently, but in retrospect, they did the right thing. Carson and I did make the choice not to practice. Now I see what can happen if you don't tell your kids. Crystal's parents never told her she was a witch. But, some part of her knew. It nagged at her. I thought about telling her, but it wasn't my place. Obviously, you must have felt the same.

"I guess she found out eventually. When she did, she probably jumped in with both feet because her parents never warned her, and neither did I. I regret that. To answer your question from before, we weren't close, but witches have a way of finding each other. We always seemed to be at the same places at the same times, and so we talked, became friends, even though we didn't have much in common. Well, there aren't too many dark witches walking around, so I suppose we had a lot in common."

She laughed coldly. "Well, I suppose we had even more in common than that." She gestured toward him. "But, you know what I mean. I should have known you'd keep running into her, too. Now that I look back, I should have been suspicious about the fact you *didn't* seem to know her. Of course, you would know her eventually. Any wizards living that close to each other will meet. I should have known you were lying."

"You're saying I am a wizard, but I haven't figured it out for over forty years because my parents never told me?"

"No. Your parents were practicing wizards."

David laughed. That had to be the punch line. But, Amanda's lips didn't even quiver. He had never seen her more serious.

"Practicing wizards?" David asked. "I don't think so."

"They were. You just forgot."

"Oh, I don't think I would forget that."

"I haven't cast many spells in my life. But I cast one on you. A long time ago. There were things from your childhood…memories…that were hurting you. You never talked about it, but I knew you were suffering. I hated seeing you in pain."

Tears pooled in her eyes. Something frozen inside of David melted, something he didn't understand, but something he'd prefer to keep solid.

"I shouldn't have done it. You probably would have healed on your own. In time. But, I decided to remove the memories from your head using magic. It was very complicated magic. I had to do it gradually. While you slept. Over the course of six months. It was terrifying. I was so afraid to make a mistake. Remove something you needed. It was your *brain*, after all. In the end, I did a pretty good job, I think. You didn't talk much about your childhood, so I wasn't even sure it worked until we saw your parents over the holidays. You acted completely different around them. You didn't remember. In time, I realized I removed something else. Since we weren't practicing, it took a while for me to notice you had also forgotten you were a wizard. I guess it was too tied to your childhood memories. It was just gone. And, I felt no reason to enlighten you. Until now."

David's lips had gone numb. He had always had a sixth

sense about whether or not someone tried to deceive him. Amanda believed every word she said. But, he didn't need to read her intentions to know she told the truth. It felt true…like a word that had been on the tip of his tongue for years and someone had finally said it aloud.

"Breathe, David," she said.

He continued to stare at her.

"Are you okay?" she asked. "Let me see your eyes."

She grabbed his face and pulled it toward hers and studied him.

"I don't know if anything bad happens when you tell someone about memories you've removed. I thought it might be like waking a sleepwalker. Please say something. Tell me you're okay."

He pushed her away from him. "You've lost your mind."

"You don't really think that. I can see it in your eyes. You know it's true."

He felt dizzy and sat down on the bed.

She sat next to him and squeezed both of his hands into a tight ball, as if molding clay. "I don't know a lot of magic," she said. "But I can show you some. If you want proof."

He would have welcomed her hands on his a few hours ago, but now they felt confining and threatening.

He had never asked Evangeline or Xavier for proof. He didn't want to embarrass them. But, maybe part of him also feared they would say, *Sure, I'll be happy to provide a practical demonstration. Stand back and I'll burst into flames for you.*

"It's okay," she said. "I have a good one. It's not scary."

What followed may not have been scary, but he had never experienced anything so odd and unsettling. He could tell he hadn't left the room or himself. He could feel himself sitting on the bed, Amanda's hands on his, and his neck hurting from stress and sleeping on an air mattress, but another experience superimposed itself around him, literally at two places at once.

He experienced the feelings first. Happiness. Excitement. Immense hopefulness. His body felt warmer. And, younger. The stiffness and achiness of age he didn't even know he felt, disappeared…such a wonderful feeling, his eyes got wet. The smells came next. He smelled Italian food, and chocolate, wine on his own breath, Amanda's perfume…but not the Amanda sitting next to him. He needed only the smells to know where he had arrived. His wedding reception.

The sounds came next. Music. The loud din of talking. Then everything, just as if he travelled back in time into his own younger body. He danced with Amanda. Not their first dance, but one later in the night, when they had danced off the nervousness and stress from the day and only the delirious happiness remained. He could count her twenty-five-year-old eyelashes. The diamond sparkled on her finger the way it could only when it was brand new. Right behind them, David's mother wore a green dress. She danced with his father.

The image faded back the way it came. The sounds left first, then the tactile sensations. He couldn't feel the smooth satin of her wedding dress on his palm. Then the images, then the smells…then at last, the feeling. Then they returned fully to the present moment. The disappointment felt painful, like waking up from a good dream, but far worse.

"I probably shouldn't let you see me looking like that," Amanda said. "I must look really old to you now."

"You don't look old," he said, almost as reflex. "How did you do that?"

"The only magic I really know has to do with memories. I learned as much as I could so I could manipulate yours. The side effect was, I also learned how to manipulate mine. When I'm feeling happy, I make the memory…sticky. It's almost like turning on an internal video camera. Then I can pull it up whenever I want to. I have lots more, if you ever want to see them. You can see our kids when they were still cute." She chuckled to herself. "Smell their little baby heads, feel their smooth baby skin. I also saved the time we had sex under that big red umbrella in Cabo."

Her cheeks reddened and she dropped his hands. She looked as if she had forgotten they were separated for a moment.

"Do you still have the ones you took from me?"

Fear replaced the wistfulness in her eyes. "Well, I didn't make them sticky, if that's what you mean. I wouldn't…" She shook her head. "They're gone, David. Permanently. Magic is destruction, at least our magic is. Once you destroy something, you can't bring it back. It's gone."

"What did you take out of my head?"

"Just bad memories."

"I have the right to know."

"I took them out for a reason."

"Dammit, Amanda. You had no right. If you can't put them back, at least tell me what you took."

"Abuse."

"What do you mean, *abuse*?"

"I'm not going to describe it to you. I didn't enjoy seeing the memories when I took them out. I didn't hang on to it."

"You mean…by my parents."

"Your father, yes."

"What did he do to me?"

"All sorts of things. He was messed up. He was a practicing wizard, and the magic addled his brain, destroyed his soul. It's not an excuse or anything, but that's what happens."

David shook his head. What she said sounded… right… but he couldn't attach the feelings to any real memories. Distant fear and shame seemed to hang in the air, with nothing tangible to cling to, like a faceless cloud of black.

"But, I remember my childhood, Amanda." A terrifying idea popped into his head. "Are my memories real? Did you give me new ones?"

"No. As far as I know, I can't do that. I can only take away, or enhance, real memories. I can't just add things. I would have no idea how. Your memories are real...just edited."

He thought about the *About Me* storyboard he'd seen online. *Was that who I am? A man filled with blank lines? Could I fill out a storyboard for myself if I tried?*

"So, you have seen all of my most painful memories, and I don't even know what they are? I can't keep them private from you even if I want to. That's such a...violation."

"I was trying to protect you," she said.

David met his saturation point. His brain had doubled in weight. He left. He didn't know if she said anything as he went. Or even if any of his kids said anything to him on his way to the car. He got in the Mercedes and started driving.

He made it halfway to Austin before he stopped to think about his plan. *What was my plan? Drive home?* Someone else owned his childhood house. His father had died five years ago from a sudden brain aneurism, and a year after that, his mother had killed herself. It sounded suspicious now. Did his father's brain explode because he destroyed himself with magic? Did someone kill him with magic? His mother? His brother?

He knew what he had to do, but didn't want to. He knew he couldn't have this phone conversation while driving. He felt lightheaded before he even dialed. So he exited and parked at a gas station.

The sound of the phone ringing rattled around in his brain.

"David? Motherfucker. I have been calling you all week. Why aren't you returning my calls?"

"Hi, James. I'm sorry. It's been a rough week."

"Yeah… I know. That's why I was calling you. I heard about my secret niece and nephew. Holy shit, David. Why didn't you tell me?"

"I didn't even tell Amanda…so…"

"Well, I'm not going to tell you you're an asshole. I'm sure you're being punished enough. If you need someplace to stay, you can come always come here."

"Thanks. I may need to. I don't know yet. She's letting me stay in the house for now. But she wants a divorce."

David heard James's partner Justin in the background asking, "It that him?"

"Yes," James said.

Justin said something else David didn't catch.

"Leave me alone, I'm talking to my disgraced big brother," James said. "Anyway," he said back to David. "Justin isn't as forgiving as I am. Probably doesn't like the idea of Vandergraff men cheating."

"I need to ask you something," David said.

"Sure."

"It's going to sound weird. Can you answer without making fun of me? I'm going through a tough time."

"No promises, but I'll try."

"Are we wizards?"

Silence.

"Are you okay, David?" The timbre of James's voice changed so much it sounded as if a different man spoke now.

"Not really. Just answer the question."

"Yes. Of course, we are. You know we are."

It took a while for the words to settle in his brain. The words kept slipping thorough him without sticking as if the blank lines in his brain had guards knocking words away. Maybe that had been part of the spell. Even when the truth stood right in front of him, his brain rejected it.

"Why did you ask me that?" James asked.

"One more question." He didn't know how to do this one. "Was our childhood….bad?"

More silence.

"You're scaring the shit out of me right now. You were there. Why are you asking me? Do you have amnesia or something?" A heavy pause. "Did you do magic? Did it do something to your brain? Come here right now. Or, I'll come get you. Where are you?"

With every question, his happy-go-lucky brother disappeared more and more. He sounded like someone else. Someone David didn't remember.

"No, I'm fine. It's not like that. I didn't do magic. Amanda did. She manipulated my memories."

"What? She knows better than that. When did she do this?"

"She didn't say exactly, a long time ago."

"Like, years?"

"I think so."

"You've been walking around without memories for years?"

"I guess."

"That's not fucking fair."

To me or to you? he wanted to ask.

"Don't worry about me," David said. "Please don't. I'll get it all worked out."

"Just answer my calls, okay?"

"I will."

CHAPTER TWELVE

Patrick froze mid-stride on his way into the family room. Samantha sat in his spot. Of all the places in the house she could have sat to read her book, she chose the exact spot he sat in to play video games. She would get it all warm and smelling of her. Her blonde hair spilled across the cushions like white neon light. The closer the got to her, the sweatier he got, and probably smelled fully funky when he sat down next to her.

"You're still here," he said.

"Disappointed?" she asked. She tucked a bookmark into her book and placed it aside.

"No."

"My parents were in a skiing accident," she said.

"Oh my God," he said. "Are they okay?"

"They're okay. Just some broken bones. They're in a hospital in Switzerland. So I'm staying here a little longer."

"Okay…"

Just some broken bones. Just in a hospital. No reason not to sit here calmly reading a book. She said it so quickly, and calmly, he thought she might be lying, but couldn't imagine why she would.

"It sucks you have to be stuck with my family. I'm sorry they're so messed up."

"They're not so bad," she said. "I like it here."

He laughed. "Sure," he said, his tone dripping with skepticism.

She laughed, too.

"Saaamaanthaaa," Emmy wailed from downstairs. "Come on."

Samantha dutifully answered the call. Patrick didn't realize he had followed Samantha, as if she had him on a leash, until he had walked halfway down the stairs behind her.

Emmy held out her hand at the bottom of the stairs and grabbed Samantha's as soon as she could reach it. She pulled her toward the downstairs family room.

"I picked out the movie," Emmy said.

Patrick followed them into the family room, where Emmy had some Japanese horror movie pulled up on Netflix.

"I didn't invite you, Patrick," Emmy said.

"You can't watch this," Patrick said. "It's too scary for you."

"Yeah right," Emmy said. "Besides, it's Halloween."

"It has subtitles," Patrick said.

"Uh…. we can read, Patrick," Emmy said. "Unlike the Colters."

"We can read," Xavier said.

Patrick jumped. Perfectly placed to argue this point, the Colter siblings sat on the floor in a blind spot behind the couch, pulling books off the bookshelf and placing them in piles. Flushed patches appeared on Emmy's neck. She had intended her mean comment to be of the behind-their-backs variety.

"I didn't know you were there," she said.

"What are you guys doing?" Mom came into the room as if she had smelled the confrontation brewing. She saw the movie on the screen. "No. It's too late. You all need to start getting ready for bed."

"Jude's not home yet," Emmy said.

"Let me worry about that," Mom said.

"It's only 11:15," Patrick said. His own words surprised him. Since when did he stand up for his brother?

"I'm sure he'll be home any minute," Mom said.

"Where is David?" Evangeline asked.

Patrick hadn't even noticed Dad's absence.

Mom hesitated. "Away," she said.

Evangeline stood up. "You can't send him away." Her voice had a higher pitch than usual. "You can't be apart."

Patrick's eyebrows knitted together. *Who was she to say anything? What did she care?* By the indignation on Emmy's face, she thought something similar.

"If you really cared about their marriage, you should have thrown yourself off a cliff," Emmy said.

Okay, he didn't think *that*.

"Emmy!" Mom shouted.

Everything in the china cabinet along the wall shattered.

"Xavier!" Mom shouted. "No magic."

What?

"Magic isn't a choice," Xavier said. "The only choice is whether or not you control it or let it control you."

The light bulbs in three of the lamps shattered. *What the fuck?*

"Stop it," Mom cried.

Xavier's chest rose and fell rapidly as he breathed. His gray eyes darted back and forth. Looking for something else to break?

Then something even more disturbing happened. Samantha ran at Xavier and thrust her body against his. He stumbled back at the influx of her weight. She wrapped her arms around him, plastering his own arms to his sides and pressed herself…close. Patrick's throat got dry. It looked so…intimate. Xavier sort of grunted, in surprise, but it also sounded kind of private, like the sounds people make during sex.

After what seemed like several years, she released him. An odd way to calm someone down, but it worked. Xavier didn't speak or move. Patrick supposed that would shut any guy up. Distract him, at least.

"That was weird," Emmy said into the silence.

Then a few seconds of calm passed over them. Like the eye of the storm.

Then all hell broke loose.

The whole house shook in a deafening crash of shattering glass and splintering wood. Patrick grabbed Emmy and tried to shield her, but he couldn't tell where the danger came from. He grabbed her by the waist and pulled her back as bits of glass grazed his arms.

When the terrible crunching and shattering sounds had ended, Patrick raised his head. He had somehow guessed right about where to pull Emmy. In the spot where she had stood, he now saw the front bumper of Jude's truck.

Patrick scanned the room for everyone else. Where had they stood? He even wanted to glimpse the dark-haired heads of Xavier and Evangeline. He saw them first. They had backed into the hallway and huddled together, looking as shocked as he felt. Mom? Samantha? Where?

And what about Jude?

He heard his mother's voice. "Emmy!"

Patrick released Emmy from his grip and saw blood on his hands. Emmy stayed standing when he released her, a good sign, but her stomach and chest were red with blood. She clutched at her heart, breathing heavily.

"What happened?" Mom ran over and pulled up Emmy's shirt. "What got you?"

"Glass, I think," Emmy said.

She had a deep cut right under her bra. Patrick could see blood pulsing out of the gash with each heartbeat.

Xavier came from nowhere and pressed a folded throw blanket against the wound firmly.

"Thank you," Mom said.

Samantha made her way to Emmy's side. Bits of glass sparkled in her hair, but she looked okay. What about Jude? Patrick climbed over the pile of wood that used to be the coffee table and scrambled over to the driver's side of the truck. The door was cracked open, but wedged shut against the side of what used to be the couch. Patrick heaved his weight against the couch and moved it out of the way. The door came open and Jude fell out on top of him. He reeked of alcohol and needed to cling to Patrick to keep from falling over. But, still conscious. Lucid. And, by the look on his face, he sobered up fast.

"Emmy," he said.

As soon as he said her name, his blue eyes stilled, as if they had turned to glass. Then they melted. Patrick held his brother up while he cried.

David had made it back to the Expressway when his phone rang. Amanda.

"I'm almost home," he said.

He heard silence on the other line.

"Amanda? Did you pocket dial me?"

"No. I am here."

"I'll be at the house in ten."

"David."

"Yes?"

"Something happened."

His stomach got heavy. Dear God, what now? His stress headache already made him nauseous. Not today. Nothing else today.

"What?"

"First, everyone is okay. Or will be okay."

"What?"

"Jude crashed the truck into the living room. Emmy was hurt, but she'll be okay. She needs stitches and a blood transfusion. We just arrived in the ER at Memorial Hermann. Please come here."

Patrick sat with Xavier, Evangeline, and Samantha in the hospital lobby. They all had blood on them, but Patrick had the most. They could have walked out of the horror film they never got to watch. They sat in four uncomfortable blue chairs facing each other in a tight little square, with Samantha and Patrick on one side and the Colters on the other. They didn't say anything to each other for a long time.

Tears streaked Samantha's cheeks. If his sister's blood and his brother's alcohol-saturated tears weren't soaked through his shirt, he probably wouldn't have done it, but he felt reckless. He took Samantha's hand and held it. She squeezed it back and the squeeze sent a rush of blood through his body like an extra heartbeat.

Uncharacteristically, Xavier finally broke the silence.

"She'll be okay," he said.

He turned to Patrick when he said it. For some reason, the statement made Patrick angry. He wanted to punch Xavier in the face, although he couldn't remember why. Then he remembered what had happened right before Jude drove his truck into the house. Xavier and Mom arguing about magic. Glass breaking for no obvious reason. Samantha subduing Xavier with an aggressive hug. He dropped Samantha's hand.

"What's going on?" Patrick asked.

"What do you mean?" Xavier asked.

"The glass breaking," Patrick said.

"I think we've been pretty open about it," Xavier said. "I'm a wizard."

"You're saying you broke the glass with your mind?"

"I was mad."

Patrick laughed. "You guys really are bat shit crazy."

"How do you explain what you saw, then?" Evangeline asked.

She had him stumped there.

"How do you explain your mom telling him to stop? Not to do *magic*?" Evangeline asked. "She knows. She's a witch, too."

Patrick wanted to cry. He didn't want to act like a kid, but he just wanted everyone to stop acting crazy. He wanted everything to be normal. He didn't even care so much that Xavier and Evangeline lived with them now, he just wanted them to start doing things that made sense.

He got up and went to the water fountain for something to do. He sat back down and everyone looked at him, waiting for him to say something, as if he hadn't left.

Patrick turned to Samantha. "What about you?"

She bit her upper lip. He didn't feel like waiting and pushed harder.

"What was that hug thing?" he asked.

"It was….maybe you should ask your mother," Samantha

said.

"Are you kidding me?" Patrick asked. "Tell me."

"I don't want to get in trouble," Samantha said. "I like it here. I don't want to be kicked out."

Xavier rolled his eyes.

"She won't kick you out," Evangeline said. "I mean….if she didn't kick David out, I can't imagine she would really kick anyone out."

"I think she knows she couldn't kick him out. Not really," Samantha said.

"I don't think she knows," Evangeline said. "Part of her knows. But, she doesn't *know* know. Her parents weren't practicing. She doesn't know much. She let him stay for reasons of her own."

"And if she does know, she wouldn't kick you out either," Xavier said.

Samantha blushed. "No. I'm no one's. I don't think so, anyway."

"Stop it." Patrick shouted it loud enough that a man in a wheelchair who he had previously worried might be dead, looked up. "Just stop it," he said more quietly. "Stop it." Once more for emphasis. "If someone doesn't say something that makes sense right now, I'm going to freak out."

They all stared down at their laps, as if Patrick had asked for the impossible.

"Samantha," Patrick said. His voice sounded tired and pathetic. "I know these two are playing a few cards short of a full deck. I mean, no offense, guys. I'm not trying to judge you. You have every right to be a little…different. But, you, Samantha. Why are you in on this? That's what's freaking me out."

"I'm sorry, Patrick," she said. "You say you don't want to be freaked out and you also want me to explain. I can't do both. And, right now, you're upset and tired. I can't think of anything to say that won't freak you out."

"The truth."

She cocked her head and considered him, then said. "I'm a witch, too. And you're a wizard."

Patrick laughed. It felt good to laugh. But, he didn't laugh because he found it funny. He laughed because he felt…happy to hear it? Her ridiculous claims made him want to smile all the way back to their busted house. But, he couldn't quite let himself believe it yet.

"I don't think so," Patrick said. "I never got my owl from Hogwarts."

They all smiled, even Xavier, the first time Patrick had seen him smile. It made him look like Dad. Patrick didn't like it.

"No owls. No Hogwarts," Samantha said.

"It sounds a little disappointing," Patrick said.

"Sometimes," Samantha said.

The ER resembled an extremely ill-fated Halloween party. A fairy crying in a wheelchair. A zombie covered in real blood. A giant mustard bottle holding up a limping giant ketchup bottle. Halloween. Amanda's most hated holiday. David guessed that made sense now.

He found Amanda and Emmy tucked into a quiet corner with the curtains partly drawn around Emmy's bed. The hospital gown made Emmy look younger, as if every other day she wore an adult disguise, and now the real her lay before him. A little girl. She hardly moved, like she feared if she did, she might split in two.

Amanda and Emmy spoke in whispers.

"I thought you were a Christian," Emmy said to Amanda.

"Have you been pretending all these years? Why even take us to church?"

"What you are is different from what you believe. We can believe whatever we choose to."

"Do you believe in God?"

"Yes."

"Do you believe in the Devil?"

"Yes."

"Can wizards get into heaven?"

"They have the same chance as everyone else."

"But, you don't know for sure."

"Emmy, no one knows *for sure*. Not about any of this."

"We know what's in the Bible. And there are no wizards in it."

"Are you sure?"

Emmy knitted her brows together. "No," she said firmly.

"Hi, Emmy," David said.

Amanda jumped. "Don't sneak up on me."

She let out a deep sigh and ran into his arms and squeezed him tightly enough that Crystal's box dug into his ribs. He had forgotten how great it felt to have her soft, warm body pressed up against his. He never wanted her to let go. When she released him, he approached his daughter.

"Are you in pain?" he asked.

She moved a shoulder, as if she wanted to shrug, but couldn't quite manage it. He took her small hand in both his own.

"I'm so sorry, Emmy," he said.

She pulled her hand free.

"I already have Mom here," she said. "You should go be with Jude."

"Where is he?"

"The police station," Amanda said quietly, as if saying it softly made it less true.

"You had him arrested?" David asked.

"I didn't intend to. We just called 9-1-1. For Emmy." She turned back to her daughter. "Honey, if Dad wants to be with you in the hospital, you have to let him. He loves you very much."

"Does he love Jude?"

"Of course, I do," David said.

"Is Jude going to be okay?" Emmy asked.

"He's just a little banged up," Amanda said.

"I didn't mean physically."

Amanda paused to consider the question. "Yes, he is going to be fine."

"Please don't kick him out," Emmy said.

"He's not going anywhere. Literally. He's grounded until he leaves for college. What do you think, David?" Amanda asked.

Jude nearly killed everyone David loved, including himself. It didn't seem like enough. But, what else could he do?

CHAPTER THIRTEEN

David couldn't think for about three days. *My business is finished. I am a wizard. My father abused me. My memories are gone. My son drove his truck into the family room and almost killed my whole family.* Had all that really happened in only one day?

He had never felt so tired. He pretended to work from home, but really played hours and hours of FreeCell. He emailed Liza and told her about what had happened with Jude and that he needed a few days to sort things out. She didn't complain, but it didn't mean she and the others didn't secretly resent him for abandoning them. As nice as he tried to be, they feared him. This meant he could do what he wanted, but would have to do it knowing that 347 people hated him behind his back and went home and complained about him to their significant others. The tough times defined a good leader, and a good man. He played FreeCell and ignored calls. But, he didn't know how to take things apart. He built things. He built his business, created jobs, and he excelled at it. Disaster recovery. Bankruptcy. Layoffs. Severance. He couldn't do that.

Besides, what did it matter? His business would fail with him or without him. Gracefully or painfully. Either way, it would fall.

Amanda kept grabbing his shoulders and examining his eyes as if she had taken up amateur optometry. She did it again before she went to bed that night. Instead of a goodnight kiss, she leaned in close to see his eyes, and then pulled back.

"Stop that," he said.

"I'm worried about you."

"What are you looking for, exactly?"

"I'm not sure. I just hope I'd know it if I saw it."

"It hasn't been the greatest few days of my life. And, I know it hasn't been for you, either. If I seem upset, it's because I am. Not because my mind is addled by magic."

"I know." She paused and picked up his glass paperweight again, and rolled it from hand to hand. "Did you call that private school like I asked you to?"

"No. I must have *forgotten*."

"Okay, so we're still on that."

"Yeah. We're still on that. Three days later, I'm still upset to know my wife has been treating my life story like a rough draft she can change however she likes."

"I don't just change things as we go. I did this one time. I finished in 1995. Since then, I haven't touched anything."

"What else did I forget?"

"What do you mean?"

"You didn't mean to take out memories of magic. What other mistakes did you make?"

"There may be a few small things."

Another rush of anger settled itself in the middle of David's chest. Honestly, he hadn't expected any more.

"Like, what?" he asked with his teeth bared.

"*Small* things. Little things I've noticed. Like, you forgot you were allergic to strawberries."

"I had to go to the hospital for that. Yeah, in 1995. You could have killed me."

"I didn't know you would forget."

"What else?"

"Well, when the kids asked for pets you told them you didn't get to have a dog when you were a kid. But, you did. You told me about him before the spell. A border collie mix named Max."

"I had a dog? Max? What happened to him?"

"I'm sure he died a long time ago. Before you met me. I just remembered you mentioning him…before."

"Anything else?"

"That's it. Really."

"There could be more. Things I forgot that I had never told you about. Things you wouldn't notice. Do you have any idea how upsetting that is? Who knows what I could be missing?"

"If there was anything big, I would have noticed. I knew you well both before and after the spell. I watched you very carefully. There is nothing else."

A week later, the construction team started to fix the hole in the house. It took great willpower for David to keep from overseeing every detail of the project. His time ticked away. They planned to close Vandergraff Home Builders right before Christmas. He had to tell Amanda…he promised himself he'd tell her before Thanksgiving…or more specifically, before she drained their bank account on Black Friday.

Jude didn't total his truck, but he lost his license, so when the vehicle came back from the shop they put it in the garage and promised to give it to Patrick when he turned sixteen. Jude accepted his punishment of permanent grounding without complaint. David's instinct told him that even if they ungrounded Jude, he still wouldn't go anywhere—not that he planned to test the theory. Jude didn't seem to want to. He became even quieter than Xavier. And, according to Emmy, he broke up with his girlfriend, the beautiful and popular Avery Mathison, who he had wanted go out with for years. When David and Amanda sat him down to tell him he was a wizard, he said, "Yeah, I know," and refused to discuss it further. Apparently, one of the others—most certainly Emmy—had told him, even though David had asked Patrick and Emmy to let him do it.

Emmy's happiness seemed directly related to Jude's and went down in equal measure. Amanda seemed to have given birth to conjoined twins four years apart. Emmy stayed his most talkative child, but she had turned it down considerably, and ran at only about fifty percent Emmy. David might have preferred this, since he'd asked her to dial down her volume on so many occasions, but he missed the other half of her.

Then, David got a call at his office from Coach Ward.

"I assume you know why I'm calling," the coach said.

"No."

"You don't know that Jude quit the team?"

"I don't think he did."

"He told me this morning. He didn't show up for practice. Came to my office right before first period and said he was quitting. He didn't tell you?"

"No."

"Do you know why he might have quit?" the coach asked. "I don't want to pry. I just want to make sure he's okay. He has seemed off for a while. I didn't know if anything was going on at home."

"Well…yeah, he's been having some problems. But, I think he should keep playing football. He loves it. And he's good at it."

"I'm glad to hear you say that. Perhaps you can talk to him.

I hope this is just a lapse. I don't need to tell you I want him back. If he needs some time to deal with personal stuff, I am fine with that, but I need him in the play-offs. When he wants to be, he's an excellent running back. I've hardly ever seen anyone so determined to get the ball across the field. And, he's fierce. I swear I once saw a defensive linesman with a hundred pounds on him just step out of his way and let him pass. It seems like half the defenders fall down when he gets within a foot of them, like he's got a tailwind. I don't know how he does it, but I don't care."

"Huh."

The Coach had a point. Jude did have an uncanny ability to avoid getting hit. Like so many things, before David had known about magic, he hadn't thought twice about it. He didn't question the fact that Jude usually remained unscathed during the game. Had Jude done some kind of football magic? Or did Amanda knock over the poor boys from other teams from her spot on the bleachers?

"I'm sorry, what did you say?" the coach asked.

"Yeah, I'll talk to him."

"Listen, I didn't take his name off the roster. I marked him as injured for now. I don't want him to make a big life decision on a whim. The scouts don't need to know about this."

"Thank you."

That night, when David headed toward his office-slash-bedroom, he felt a pull toward the kids' bedrooms. He didn't know how else to explain it, as if some extra gravity had accumulated there. A cool blue light emanated from under Emmy's door. If he believed in such things, he might have guessed alien abduction.

He opened the door and saw the coolest thing he had ever seen. Samantha lay on the floor making white droplets of light drip upward from her palm like slow upside-down rain. Emmy sat on the bed, watching. The light droplets faded and popped when he opened the door. Darkness bathed the room again. David turned on the light.

Samantha sat up, as if prepared to run. "I'm so sorry," she spluttered. "It wasn't serious magic. Just a little light."

Emmy stood up, ready to come to her defense.

"It was, uh…cool," David said. "You're a witch? I suppose I should have guessed."

She nodded.

This fact made him consider her and everything he knew about her differently. "Where are your parents really?" he asked.

"They were in a skiing accident," she said.

She didn't lie well.

David had last seen Samantha's parents, Penelope and Aaron Carthage, in August. He had never met any two people who could make him feel so uncomfortable so fast. He didn't go over to their house unless he absolutely had to.

He had dropped Emmy off for a sleepover and when the girls ran upstairs, Penelope ushered David inside. She had the body and tan of a beach volleyball player. Large, but very real, breasts. And, a toothpaste model's smile. None of this really tempted David. He couldn't call himself a one-woman man, but he certainly could call himself a two-woman man. He didn't sleep with anything with breasts for the hell of it. But, any woman that beautiful and that friendly had some inherent risks.

She welcomed him to her home as she would welcome Santa Claus bringing presents. Four thick candles burned on the coffee table. From what he could tell, each candle had a different scent and it the combination made his head spin. She picked up the first one.

"What do you think?" She put the candle right under his nose, practically singeing his nose hairs.

"It's uh…nice."

"Does it remind you of anything?"

"Um…vanilla?"

"No, vanilla is wrong," she said dismissively. "Breathe deeply. Relax. What does it remind you of?"

An image of the green moss that grew behind his childhood house popped into his head. But, he didn't say it out loud because it sounded crazy.

"I really don't know."

She put the candle down and held up the next one.

"Try this one. What does it smell like?"

This one made his heart race and his stomach ball up into a fist inside him. He pushed it away.

"I don't know," he said with a nervous chuckle.

"You reacted to that one. What did it smell like?"

"Fear," he said.

She nodded as if he had said something normal such as 'cinnamon' or 'pine trees.'

"Very interesting," she said. "Anything else? Any images?"

"I'm sorry, I don't know what you mean. Listen, I have got to get going…"

"No, wait. Please stay. Have a drink."

"I don't think so."

"Come on, David. Stay," said Aaron Carthage, who had appeared through the patio door. He had dirt all over his jeans and twigs in his hair. His had a deep tan on his bare chest, and a few red patches from sunburn. His brownish red hair had become streaked with blond from too much sun.

"What have you been doing outside?" David asked. "It's 110 degrees."

"The heat doesn't bother me. Good for the soul."

Then Aaron proceeded to kiss Penelope as if he hadn't seen her in a year. He tugged at the little knot on the back of her halter-top as if he planned to take it off right then and there. David backed toward the door.

Penelope giggled and pushed Aaron away. "Stop it. You're making David uncomfortable."

"No, it's fine. I just have to go."

"You have got to try Penelope's Sangria," he said. "It's amazing. She uses Texas peaches and Texas wine. It's worth a taste, I promise you."

"I made it without strawberries just for you," she said with a pout.

Well, if she still wanted him to have a drink with her husband there, at least that must mean she didn't intend anything inappropriate. Unless they were *both* coming on to him, an idea too distressing to consider.

"Okay," he said, cautiously.

They looked way too pleased.

"Have a seat," she said and pointed to their couch, a morbidly obese version of a regular couch. David sank into it so deeply, he knew he couldn't get up quickly he wanted to. Penelope went into the kitchen and Aaron sat in the armchair across from him. *Personal space. That's better.*

"Smells interesting in here, huh?" Aaron asked.

"Interesting is a good way to put it," David said.

"Smell the green candle," he suggested.

"I can smell it from here."

"What does it remind you of?"

"Shush," Penelope said. "I already asked him. He doesn't know." She put down a tray with three glasses of candy apple red wine with bits of fruit floating in it. She handed one to David and one to her husband. To her credit, the Sangria *was* amazing. It took only a couple sips for the drink to spread warmth into all of his extremities. He felt as if he had had a two-hour massage.

"What is in this?" he asked, putting the glass down.

"Just wine, brandy, juice, and ginger ale," Penelope said. "Do you like it?"

"Yes. It's delicious."

"Drink up," she said.

David took another sip.

"Tell me about your childhood," Penelope said.

"Uh…like what?"

"What were your parents like?"

"Normal."

"Normal," she repeated, as if she'd never heard the word.

"Yeah."

She sank back into the couch, looking defeated.

Aaron showed David a blue and green marble in palm of his hand. "Do you know what this is?" Aaron asked.

"A marble," David said.

Aaron dropped it into David's hand.

"Now what is it?" he asked.

Okay. That's enough. World's greatest Sangria or not.

"A marble," David said.

Aaron glanced at Penelope and shook his head. They looked at him as if *he* acted crazy.

"I really don't think he knows," Penelope said.

"Destruction," Aaron said. "Has to be."

After the Carthages' Sangria, David had gone home, took the dishes Amanda washed out of her hands, and pulled her by the arm to the bedroom without so much as a hello. After having animal sex with her, he slept for twelve hours. Yes, very good Sangria.

He'd seen Penelope Carthage one more time after that, about a week later. This time, she had come over to their house, just long enough to collect Samantha and Emmy to drive them to the movies. The girls dragged their feet getting ready and Amanda had gone out shopping. So, he had no choice but to make conversation with Penelope. She sat in the living room and looked around the room as if the cream-colored walls made her want to cry.

"So, it's been pretty hot, huh?" David said. "Is your lawn dead, too?"

"No."

"Wow. That's impressive. You must have a high water bill."

"Samantha really likes it here," she said in baffled tone, as if she couldn't imagine why anyone would.

"She's a nice girl. We're happy to have her around. She's very helpful."

"That's good."

They nodded at each other awkwardly for a moment.

"Is anything new with you?" she asked him.

"No. Same old stuff. Still working in construction, of course."

"So nothing new? Nothing different? Since I saw you last?"

"Uh…no. I guess not."

She nodded grimly.

"I know it's not my place. I just can't help myself. You're like fireworks with no match. It bothers me."

"Yeah, they banned fireworks because of the drought," David said.

"May I show you something?" she asked.

"Okay," he said.

She scooted closer to him and David leaned away.

"Just real quick," she said. "Don't worry."

She clasped her hands on his forearms. He tried to pull away, but she squeezed forcefully. He could only describe the sensation as *invasion*. At the time, he didn't think much of it. A woman he didn't know well had grabbed his arms for no clear reason and dug her fingernails into his skin. Invasion. Boundary violation. Excessively strange. A sense of violation seemed appropriate. Later, he realized the invasion had not been an illusion. Tiny needles poked his brain. It hurt. It troubled him. He remembered feeling defensive. He wanted her off him at any cost and instinctively focused all his energy on counterattack.

And, it worked. At the time, he didn't have the words to define what he had done. Now, he did. He did magic. He would never attack a woman, not with his hands. But, he didn't know he could do it with magic, so he didn't know how to stop himself.

She gasped and shrank back from him as if she expected him to hit her. Her hands trembled as she pulled her keys out of her purse.

"I have to go home," she said.

And, she did. Right there and then, without another word. David tried calling her but she didn't pick up. He told the girls some nonsense about her having to go into work and took them to the movies himself. He never saw Penelope Carthage again.

Reflecting on his memories, he realized how much he had missed. The mind heard only things that made sense to it.

He didn't really want to know more of the story. He had heard enough terrible things. But, that didn't stop him from pounding on his former bedroom door.

Amanda opened the door looking like she might pound him right back. She wore her stretchy gray pants and he could see her belly button. He tried not to get distracted staring at her middle.

"What?" she asked.

"What happened to the Carthages?"

She sighed. "Come in."

He closed the door behind him. She sat on the bed, but he couldn't rest enough to sit, and paced around the foot of the bed.

"I had wondered why you were waiting so long to ask. I wasn't sure if you believed the skiing accident thing, but you didn't ask me."

"I might have, but was distracted by the truck in the living room. They're wizards?"

"Yes."

"Why is she here? What did they do to her?"

"The Carthages are nice people. Do you really think I would let us associate with dark practicing wizards? Never."

"So, they're good wizards. I thought you said wizards can't be good."

"I did not say that. It is true that it's less dangerous for some wizards to practice than for others. Everyone's magic has a different…color…flavor…you might say."

"Like, how they say auras are different colors?"

"I guess so. Since when did you know about auras?" Amanda asked.

"I know about things like that," David said. Or, Crystal knew about things like that.

"It's not just about which spells you choose to use, it's about the type of magic you use to do them. That can't be changed. It's like the color of your eyes. That's why dark wizards can't practice. Even if they want to be good, they can't. It's too dangerous. Dark magic is about destruction. Breaking things. Breaking people. Even my spell was destruction. I *destroyed* your memories. I didn't create anything."

"So, you're saying we're dark wizards."

She bit her lip. "It's all on a spectrum. There are not just good and bad wizards, there are infinite colors of magic, and some are darker than others. You can't classify everyone's magic as good or bad."

"I already know the answer, so you don't need to tiptoe around it for me." He couldn't say why, but he already knew the color of their magic.

"Fine. We're dark wizards. Both of us. And our kids. But, that doesn't make us *bad*. As long as we don't practice."

"If the Carthages are so good, then why do they have their daughter living with dark wizards?"

"They aren't dark wizards, but I don't know if I'd classify them as 'good.' They're…well…they're practicing wizards. That should tell you enough."

"It doesn't. Although it does explain a lot. They definitely have their own way of doing things. Like, when Penelope took her top off at the swimming pool. Was that a wizard thing?"

"I'm glad that's the first quirk you noticed. Is that moment burned into your memory, too?"

Her eyes looked angry, but she smiled. He didn't know if he had gotten himself in trouble or not.

"I am a man. If you want me to forget it when one of our kid's friend's mothers unexpectedly shows me her breasts, you are going to have to remove it on your own. And I'm not offering."

"I'm just messing with you. I'm grateful all you've done is see her breasts...knowing what I know about you now."

David ignored the jab.

"She wanted to get our attention…our magical attention," Amanda continued. "In a lot of ways, they're really tolerant of us being wizards who don't practice. Practicing wizards and non-practicing wizards generally hate each other passionately.

The Carthages know it's different for dark wizards, and let it go for the most part, especially because Samantha and Emmy are so close. But, they just can't seem to help themselves. They're curious about us. They want us to practice, if just to see what we can do. They're like children. All about curiosity and immediate gratification. I think Samantha is the only reason they made any attempt to behave."

"Come on. Give me the worst. Where are they? Do you even know?"

"Of course I know. Sort of. I *did* know."

"Where?"

"Rehab," Amanda said.

"Drugs? Alcohol?"

"Magic."

"They're in magical rehab?"

"No, of course not. It's a regular rehabilitation facility for drugs and alcohol. They didn't know what else to do. They thought the 12-steps might help them. The problem is, rehab works in part because you are separated from your drug. And, when it's a spell, you can't separate. I don't know much about the spell they got addicted to. But, it's some kind of pleasure spell. They did it so much they couldn't stop doing it. Just like a drug. They lost everything. Their jobs. Their home.

"They had been using all their energy trying to keep the spell going and eventually didn't have the mental or physical energy left to do anything but stay home and cast the spell. I noticed Samantha was here a lot, but I didn't think much of it. She worships Emmy. Then it's like she ate dinner here every day. And, I saw her taking food out of our pantry. Pop tarts and stuff. There wasn't any food in her house. She was doing her homework here. Because, they didn't have electricity anymore. Or Internet."

"So, Samantha knows her parents aren't really in Switzerland?"

"Of course."

"How long has this been going on? The addiction?"

"Samantha told me her mom started acting funny right before school started. And then her dad did, too, not long after that."

"August?"

"I guess."

"Do you think...something could have happened to Penelope then…something that messed her up?"

"I don't know, maybe. I suppose it's like pain pills. She might have started doing the spell to feel better about something that had upset her and got addicted. I don't know her well."

David wondered if she could see his heart hammering through his shirt.

"Eventually, I did something," she continued. "Although probably not soon enough. I gave them the money for the rehab. You didn't notice it was gone. I should have told you, but I didn't know what to say."

"How long is the rehab?"

"It doesn't matter. I called the place yesterday. They checked themselves out."

"And…"

"And, I have no idea."

"So, they took our money for rehab, didn't even stay, and abandoned Samantha on our doorstep."

"They are in a bad place. They wanted to get better. Maybe they can't."

"You don't think they're…dead?"

"I really have no idea."

"Does Samantha know they might not come back?"

"No. The last thing they told me was that they planned to be back before Thanksgiving. And, that's the last thing I told her. It could still be true. They're so flighty. They could appear on our doorstep any minute, or never, or anything in between."

"What sort of stuff did they do? The Carthages? What do good wizards do when they practice?"

"Like I said, they aren't exactly 'good,' just not *dark* wizards. But, I guess you could say if dark magic equals pain and good magic equals pleasure, then the Carthages are really good wizards. They are hedonists. They like sexy magic."

"Sexy magic?"

"I know only what I kind of guess. And, Penelope is definitely a too-much-information type, so she is more than happy to tell me about her sex life randomly when I drop off Samantha. I'm always just grateful she's not naked when she comes to the door."

"She has been sometimes?"

"Once. They have this gazebo thing where they have sex in the backyard. Witches prefer to do magic outdoors. And, for them, that includes sex. They know spells to enhance the sexual experience. Like, magical Kama Sutra. I mean, I'm sure sex spells aren't all they do, but it does seem to be their specialty."

"So basically you're telling me I've been having human sex all my life when I could have been having secret wizard sex?"

"I've been having human sex all this time, too, and that's been fine with me. I'm sorry it wasn't enough for you."

She got so angry so fast. In their easy conversation, David had forgotten that fury simmered right under her layer of composure.

"I didn't say that. It has been enough for me. More than that. I love having sex with you. I really, really love it. A lot."

"Stop it. That part of our relationship is over." She sighed pointedly. "You know what, I'm tired and I want to go to bed. We can talk about the Samantha thing later."

CHAPTER FOURTEEN

On the Monday morning before Thanksgiving, before the kids came downstairs, David walked in on Amanda crying in the kitchen, her hair an eagle's nest of pale gold. Her hands covered her face so tightly she looked as if she thought her face might fall off. She didn't even notice him until he placed his hand on her back.

"Don't sneak up on me," she said.

"What's wrong?"

The red in her eyes made the blue brighter.

"Nothing," she said, her voice thick with tears.

"Of course not," he said tenderly. "You cry tears of joy every Monday morning before work."

She laughed weakly. "It's really stupid," she said. "I don't want to say."

"What?"

"I didn't really know how stressed I was," she said. "Until the tiniest thing goes wrong, and I fall to pieces."

Then he saw the tiniest thing that had gone wrong. A pile of broken glass sat on the burner where the coffee pot should be. Someone had broken this pot with magic. The glass fell too evenly. Many of the broken pieces still clung together, to form

119

the shape of the pot. The pot looked as if it had self-destructed. It pricked his senses in the wrong way, too. He got an anger headache that made his brain run hot. He didn't need the caffeine so badly. But, he couldn't stand the wanton disregard for their possessions. The idea that if one coffee pot broke, David could supply infinite future coffee pots with the high-paying job he would have forever. He also fumed at the lack of consideration for Amanda, the first person to the coffee pot every morning—a premeditated destruction of one of her small joys in a day otherwise full of unfaithful husbands, surly sons now with criminal records, and a hole in the house still not repaired.

He bounded upstairs with his eyes pulsing from his headache.

He found Patrick first, sleepwalking to the bathroom.

"I want you and your brothers and sisters downstairs in the kitchen in two minutes," David shouted. He had made a point to use the plural.

"Why?"

"Downstairs. Don't make me come back up here and drag you down."

He pounded on doors as he went back downstairs. Amanda waited at the bottom.

"It's a coffee pot," she said.

"No. It's a symbol of disrespect."

"Why don't you and I just go to Starbucks right now? Maybe…cool off a little."

"I don't want coffee."

David waited while his children filed into the kitchen half-asleep. They all still wore their sleeping clothes and hadn't brushed their hair. Emmy had spots of white acne cream on her face.

"Who did this?" he asked, pointing at the impossibly stacked pile of glass.

They all looked at the coffee pot mutely.

David's glare went straight to Xavier…the amazing glass-breaking boy. He made it over to him in two strides. Xavier's gray eyes widened, then went oddly still. Xavier blinked at him patiently, but didn't seem to look at him quite right. He stared into the air in front of David's face.

"You did this," David said. "Why?" he demanded. "You hate her for not allowing magic? Think it's clever to use magic to break something she likes? If you want to make a case for magic, why don't you do something a little more interesting than breaking glass? Anyone can break glass. You don't need magic. Glass is easy to break. It's one of its defining qualities. Where's the challenge? What's the point? If you're going to break things with magic, you better be prepared to fix them, too. Use magic to fix the coffee pot. Right now."

Xavier said nothing.

"He can't," Evangeline said. "It can't be done."

"Then I suggest you get creative."

David shoved a coffee cup and a bag of coffee beans into Xavier's hands.

"You're going to make her a cup of coffee one way or another. Use magic to make coffee. You're not leaving the kitchen until there is coffee in that cup."

Xavier looked at the things in his hands as if he couldn't remember how they got there.

Jude stepped in front of Xavier, the only one tall enough to look David right in the eye.

"I broke the coffee pot," Jude said.

"No, you didn't," David said.

"Yes, I did."

"Why?"

Jude shrugged. "Just felt like it, I guess."

"How did you break it?"

"Smashed it against the counter."

"It was broken with magic."

"You're mistaken," Jude said. His eyes…Amanda's eyes…locked into his gaze. He knew that look. He had seen it on both Jude and Amanda. Jude had dug his heels into the ground and wouldn't budge, like Little League Jude who had made David pitch to him late into the night until he hit one over the fence.

The sight snapped David back into rationality with painful crunch. Jude protected his brother…the brother he despised. From him. David's skin prickled all over. He had gone too far. He had forgotten whom he yelled at. Even Jude had known better.

CHAPTER FIFTEEN

Evangeline and Xavier had begun class at Blue Oak Academy, a secular private school. And, according to Amanda, not a wizard school, even though the brochure advertised it for students "too creative" for normal learning environments. With them away during the day, and Emmy healed enough to go back to school, David had no reasonable excuse to continue working from home. His ship was sinking, and he had to jump on board to go down with it. Fresh from his obscene overreaction about missing his morning coffee, David went into work. After nodding hello to everyone, he headed into the break room to get the coffee that seemed so important he had yelled at his abused son.

Liza stared at her computer screen as if it made mean faces at her. Not an hour into Monday, and the frizz around her hairline already started to show, as if the stress made her electric.

"Good morning, Liza. You all right?"

She sighed deeply. "Fine. Updating my resume. Why do I sound so crappy on paper?"

"Well, you must be doing something wrong, because you're far from crappy. I'll be happy to be a reference for you."

"Thanks, David."

He started to walk past her when she said, "Oh…there is someone named Colter here to see you."

"Excuse me?" He splashed coffee over the rim of his mug and burned his fingers.

"Rachel Colter. She's in your office." She lowered her voice conspiratorially. "I think she's one of those…what do you call them? Those birds that pick at the carcasses on the highway?"

"What?"

"Scavengers," Liza concluded. "She buys dying companies."

"You mean The Reaper?" Mark asked as he emerged from the office next to David's.

The terror on David's face must have shown through. Mark chuckled. "Calm down, David. She's not really the Angel of Death. We have to joke around a little to stay sane, right? I know a thing or two about Rachel Colter. She's a legend in the investment world. If anything, her being here is a good sign. Hell, maybe it means we should try to stick it out."

"Why?" Liza asked.

"She has the best eye of anyone. She buys businesses for dirt cheap, businesses other investors don't see much value in. But, she must see things the others don't because she gets massive returns. Sometimes, she just sells their assets at a profit, but other times she does some realignment and reopens the business with a new brand, and what seems like the exact same business with a different name and logo becomes profitable. Just like that. Everything she touches turns to gold." He pointed his coffee at David's door. "Be careful with this negotiation, friend. She's going to make you think you don't have anything of value and need to be rescued with her tiny offer. But, that's not the case. If she's here, you must have something of value. Something she wants. Don't just give it away."

"No," David said too firmly. "Never."

Mark and Liza shared a glance that may have meant, *God help us. He's lost it.*

David fingers tingled. He had stopped breathing properly, and nothing Mark had said helped at all.

The only thing he had heard - *Death in is your office. And, her name is Colter.*

If a style existed called 'wizard business professional,' Rachel Colter had mastered it. She wore a black skirt and jacket and patent leather black pumps with straps that looked distinctly 'witchy' while still appropriate to wear to the New York Stock Exchange. She wore her pitch-black hair in a layered bob that went down only to the nape of her neck. The black hair in contrast to her too-perfect pale skin and her candy-apple-red painted lips made her the investment banker version of Snow White.

She waited for David to speak first. He couldn't bring himself to enter the room, and stood in the doorway. He could feel his eyebrows knitted together. He knew he looked threatening. He *wanted* to look threatening.

"Who are you? What do you want?" he asked.

She didn't look the least bit threatened. She smiled.

"Well, that's disappointing," she said. "If there is one thing I like about Southern men, it's the manners. Where is my 'howdy ma'am, what can I do you for?'"

Her smile broadened to show a set of unnaturally white teeth.

"Answer the question," David said.

She snorted in exasperation and met him in the doorway.

"My name is Rachel Colter. I am an investor and am interested in Vandergraff Home Builders."

She held out her hand. Out of habit, David shook it.

"That's a little better," she said. "I feel like I should ask you to come in and sit down, but it is *your* office. Do you always perform your business from the doorway?"

He said nothing.

"I ask you for ten minutes of your time," she said. "That seems only fair considering the fact I flew all the way from New York."

"In a plane?"

Rachel laughed as she would with an old friend. "I knew I would like you, David Vandergraff. Can we sit?"

His neck tightened with tension and he could barely move his head, but entered his office and sat down behind his desk. He nodded toward the chair and she sat.

"I can tell this will be one hell of a negotiation," Rachel said. "It was quite a feat getting you to just enter your office and sit in your chair. That's a first." She pulled some files out of her briefcase. "But, I didn't come here for a tough negotiation. I'll get right to the point. I am prepared to offer you three times what your assets are worth." She smiled at him in an overly familiar way. "And I'll even throw in an extra one hundred thousand just for those wounded puppy eyes of yours." She picked up the family photo he had on his desk and smiled at it warmly. "You're breaking my heart with the whole dark wizard family man thing you've got going on."

She pushed some papers toward him. "I drew up the offer in writing. Of course, I am happy to discuss the finer details and negotiate changes once you have your lawyer look it over. But I'm sure you'll agree the deal is in your favor."

"That is awfully generous," he said in a tone so cold it could reverse global warming. "But you'll have to forgive me for not crying tears of joy. Ms. Colter, I am in no mood to play games. Least of all with you. Tell me what you really want. Why would a businesswoman make an offer that wasn't in her favor?"

Her smile faltered slightly and she leaned back in her chair and looked at her hands. "Well, assuming you aren't this rude and aggressive with all your business associates, you must know who I am...and why I might give you a...family discount."

"We're not family," he said.

"Actually, if you did a little research into your genealogy, you'd see we are sixth cousins. You know how wizards are. So hopelessly connected. But, of course, that's not what I meant. You'll have to forgive me David, I'm not good at...delicacies."

"What is your relationship to Whitman Colter?"

"You really don't know who I am. I get all that hatred from you simply because of my surname? Or was it because you pegged me as a practicing witch? Too good to do business with my kind? You castrated wizards are all the same."

"What did you call me?"

"I apologize. I didn't come all the way here to argue wizard politics or sling insults. To answer your question, I was Whitman Colter's little sister. Well, I *am* his sister. It's a permanent condition, I suppose. But, I hadn't seen my brother for seven years. Not until I was called to Odessa to identify his body. I was the only person close enough to him to even recognize his body. Can you imagine? A sister he hadn't seen in years. How sad is that?"

"The only sad thing about Whitman Colter's death is that it didn't happen sooner and more painfully."

"You don't have to tell me he was an evil man. I knew him much better than you."

She absently twirled a locket she wore around her neck. Talisman.

David exhaled. The lack of oxygen from infrequent

breathing had made him lightheaded.

"I don't accept the offer," David said.

"You didn't even read it."

"I can't accept money acquired using dark magic."

She laughed humorlessly. "I'm not going to say I never use magic in my work, because I am proud to say I do. But, don't imply I snap my fingers and make money appear. Even a wizard who doesn't practice knows magic isn't as simple as that. I am a businesswoman, and a damn good one. I am a successful because I work hard and am good at what I do."

David opened his mouth to say something else, but stopped when Rachel suddenly stood. She picked up the papers and put them in her briefcase.

"As a dark witch and a businesswoman, my bouts of compassion are few and far between. And I don't have the patience for your bigotry or ungratefulness. I wish you the best of luck feeding your family without money and without magic. Goodbye, David Vandergraff."

David left work to pick up Xavier and Evangeline from school. He didn't trust the school bus with them yet. Today, David got good old-fashioned butterflies in his stomach when he saw them leaning against the wall in their school uniforms, wearing backpacks. He didn't look forward to the talk he would have with Xavier. His apology.

David always did a double take when he saw them in their school uniforms. He barely recognized them. Navy blue polo shirts. Evangeline in a knee-length pleated khaki skirt and Xavier in khaki chinos. No embellishments allowed. They didn't complain, but David imagined they hated it. It felt cruel to make them dress that way. How many days would it take wearing khakis and living in a magic-free household before they snapped? Or, just ran away and he never saw them again? They wouldn't give him any heads-up; he'd just wake up and they'd be gone.

They climbed in the backseat together. Neither one of them had ever sat in front with him. But, he had no interest in fighting small battles.

"How was school?"

"Fine," they both said.

No surprise there. A normal response for teenagers of any variety. Except for Emmy, who would have given him a play-by-play of every moment of her day, including trips to the water fountain and what everyone she knew had been wearing.

"Did you learn anything interesting today?" he asked.

"No," Evangeline said.

"Did you learn anything boring, then?" David asked.

Evangeline giggled. "Lots."

"What was the most boring thing you learned?"

Evangeline paused to consider while Xavier stared out the window.

"Hmm…" she said." The most boring was Social Studies. The three branches of the government. I hate the government."

David laughed. It sounded so odd to hear those words in her sweet twelve-year-old girl voice.

"Sometimes I do, too. But, they do some good on occasion, if only accidentally. Xavier, what about you? Anything you find particularly loathsome about school?"

The tiniest of smiles broke free. It reminded him of Crystal's accidental smiles that slipped out despite her permanent vow of seriousness. So beautiful and unexpected. David stopped watching the road for a second and had to hit the brakes hard at the light.

"I don't know. Geometry is okay," he said. "I like that it

makes sense."

"I don't know if I've ever known anyone to like geometry because it makes sense. You must be quite the intellectual, son."

Son. It had slipped out. It had felt so good to say. *Please don't freak out on me.*

Xavier didn't react in any obvious way. But, he never did. He continued his staring vigil.

David saw his opportunity when Evangeline darted to her room to take off her school uniform immediately upon entering the house. Xavier wandered into the kitchen. He at least shared one trait with his brothers, the need to re-fuel frequently. If David wanted a chance to talk to him without Evangeline answering for him, he had to act now.

Xavier stared into the pantry and then turned around with a box of Wheat Thins in hand. He started when he saw David.

"I'm sorry. I thought you knew I was in here," David said.

Xavier shrugged one shoulder.

"If it's okay, I wanted to talk to you for a second."

Xavier said nothing.

"I'm really sorry about what happened this morning with the coffee pot. I shouldn't have lost my temper over something so small. I am very sorry."

Xavier stacked his crackers into a star shape that defied gravity. He might not want to speak, but the bold display of magic seemed to speak for itself.

"That is…very cool," David said.

Xavier removed one of the crackers and popped it into his mouth, causing the structure to fall.

"Even if you did break the coffee pot, it's not a huge deal,"

David continued. "If things upset you about living here or about anything, I just wish you would tell me instead of breaking things. If you tell me, then maybe I can change it, or at least we could talk about it so you could understand why things have to be a certain way. But, you have to tell me. I don't know what you're telling me with a broken coffee pot. It's frustrating…because I want to understand, and all I can do is guess."

Xavier rearranged his crackers into a standing stick figure.

"What do you think about what I said?" David asked. "Can you please say something?"

"I'm good at magic. I don't just destroy things like you said."

"I know. I can see that."

"But you don't care about the magic I can do," Xavier said. "You pretend it's not even real. That we're crazy or something."

A surge of anger bubbled up in his chest, but at Amanda, not Xavier. Choosing not to practice seemed bad enough, but David must have looked like a complete asshole pretending magic didn't even exist.

"I'm sorry about that," David said. "I guess I forgot some things."

Xavier narrowed his eyes, but didn't ask for clarification.

"I care about the magic you can do," David said. "I want to know about the stuff you like and the stuff you're good at. I really do."

Xavier raised one eyebrow skeptically. "Magic is forbidden."

"Just describe it to me. What spell are you best at?"

"Best at?"

"Yeah."

"Well, I can…leave."

"What do you mean?"

"I can leave my body. I mean...I don't actually go anywhere. It's more like closing the curtains in a house. I don't know what's going on outside. I turn my senses off."

Like a turtle in a shell.

"Sounds peaceful."

"I guess."

"Do you do this often?"

"Not that often." He flicked off his cracker man's arms, then his legs, and head. "I got a little too good. I do it on accident sometimes."

"It's cool you can do that," David said. "But I would like it if you stayed here as much as you can. I like it when you're here."

"I try. I have to stay. To protect Eve."

David nodded. He wanted to say she didn't need protection anymore. Not here. Even so, Xavier didn't protect her alone anymore. David had that job now. But, he doubted Xavier felt that way.

"And try to stay present during class, okay? Even if it's something terrible like a grammar lesson."

Another tiny smile. "All right."

CHAPTER SIXTEEN

David spent his first Thanksgiving with Amanda's parents in 1995, the year he gained a wife and lost a childhood. He had spent Thanksgiving and Christmas with them every year since. His in-laws, Erastus and Eloise Oppenheimer, lived in Ezra, Texas, a town tucked so deep in the woods of East Texas that time, civil rights, and wireless Internet couldn't find it. On the drive in 1995, Amanda seemed quieter than usual. She peppered him with random questions about his family. *What does your father do for a living? Where did the Vandergraffs come from? Have you always lived in Austin? What are your parents doing for the holidays? Where does your brother go to school?*

He answered all the questions pretty much the same way. "Amanda, you *know* that. Why are you asking me?"

"I just want to see what your answers are. In case my parents ask."

"Why? Are they really that judgmental? Are you afraid the Vandergraffs are secretly black and your parents are going to run me out of town?"

"That's not nice, David. They wouldn't care if you were black."

"I'm sure. But, they do need to know exactly which town my grandfather lived in before he immigrated? Are they really going to ask me that?"

"Just forget it."

"I'm not trying to fight with you. You're just being weird."

"I'm nervous."

"It's going to be fine, babe. And, it's not like we've never met. I spent lots of quality time with your parents when they came down for the wedding. I remember it vividly."

"That's good," she said. "But you don't remember which town your grandfather was from?"

"No," he said. "Who knows things like that?"

"You do," she said quietly.

It all made more sense now. She had tested her handiwork. She didn't want her parents to find gaps or suspicious answers and guess she had used magic. She did have one thing going in her favor. Her parents *never* discussed magic, so they wouldn't say anything to prick David's bubble and disturb his newly remodeled mind.

Amanda's parents found their magical abilities deeply shameful. They believed only God should have the power to make miracles, and any magic from humans came from the Devil. As David suspected, Amanda's parents didn't approve of his family heritage, but not because of the color of their skin or their nation of origin. They were practicing wizards—the worst type of family she could have possibly married into. Although as long as David himself didn't practice, they could live with it. That had to be okay, since there were hardly any non-wizards in their family tree. Wizards were drawn to other wizards, and most often drawn to wizards with 'like' magic. Pure and simple. Their daughter choosing a dark wizard for a husband didn't surprise them. It would have surprised them if she hadn't.

When David walked into the Oppenheimers' home, he

could tell right away they loved their children, Jesus, and slaughtering animals, hopefully in that order. David could hardly spot a piece of yellowed paisley wallpaper not covered by a family photo, wooden cross, stitched Bible verse, or hunting trophy. Their house smelled of bacon grease, bug spray, and a mild whiff of taxidermy chemicals. In time, this potpourri became a welcoming fragrance. This house would later become Me Maw and Papa's house, a place his kids loved visiting as much as Six Flags.

Eventually, it would also feel like David's own 'coming home' because his own family would become less and less a part of his life, especially after he had kids. He imagined Amanda had faced a serious challenge over the years, keeping David and their kids away from David's parents without having any obvious reason. Fortunately, David never argued this. He wondered if part of him knew, on an instinctive level, to keep his kids away from his father. Or, perhaps from the memories she left him, he could at least piece together the fact that the Oppenheimers easily beat out the Vandergraffs as the better holiday visiting family and the better grandparents. Not a tough decision, since the Vandergraffs ignored Christmas.

After dinner, which had consisted entirely of four whole barbequed chickens, sausage links, dinner rolls, and a pitcher of sweet tea, David didn't think he'd ever get the grease or smoky smell off his hands. David sat next to Amanda and her brother, Carson, on the couch, and Mr. Oppenheimer stared David down with his gray eyes from his armchair. Erastus Oppenheimer was a massive building of a man, with an untamed appearance, as if he lived in the wild…which he pretty much did. His blond hair had turned gray early, or stayed so dirty it looked gray, and he cut it himself at home with a hunting knife. The same blondish-gray fur covered his whole body. He shaved only once every few days at most, and always had a thick gray scruff on his face. Something about the gray beard made David picture Mr. Oppenheimer as a backwoods version of Zeus.

Mr. Oppenheimer said, "Eloise, bring it on out now."

"Bring it on out yourself," she said from the kitchen.

David thought Mrs. Oppenheimer had a wispy, ghost-like quality. Everything about her, from her clothes to her pale eyes and hair, looked faded. Although she was quiet and demure most of the time, no one except her would talk back to Erastus Oppenheimer.

"Jesus, woman," he said. "I just sat down." Mr. Oppenheimer grunted and stood back up. He returned a few minutes later and approached David with the last thing he wanted to see his new father-in-law holding: a rifle.

"There you are," he said, handing the rifle to David.

David held it in his lap and stared at it.

"Oh, sweet," Carson said. He took the rifle out of David's hands and looked through the sight as if prepared to assassinate the porcelain angel on the mantel.

"That's a fine piece," he said and handed it back to David.

David had hoped Carson would hang on to it. He held it awkwardly in both hands, afraid to touch anything and accidentally shoot someone.

Amanda elbowed him in the ribs. "It's a gift."

"Oh. Thank you. Thank you very much. It's really nice."

"You ever shoot a gun like that?" Mr. Oppenheimer asked.

"No. I've never shot any gun."

David remembered Carson had glanced at Amanda and she nodded her head. At the time, he assumed his brother-in-law was appalled to learn his sister had chosen such a pathetic, non-gun-shooting man for a husband and she had nodded to mean, 'yes, he really is that lame.' Now he knew what it had meant. Amanda had told only one person about her memory spell: Carson. Carson wanted to know if David had answered the question correctly.

"Why?" Mr. Oppenheimer asked. "You're not some kind of vegetarian, are you?"

David chuckled. "I wasn't one at dinner, remember?"

Mr. Oppenheimer narrowed his bushy gray eyebrows in confusion. David guessed Mr. Oppenheimer didn't understand the meaning of the word 'vegetarian' and had meant it as a general definition for non-animal killing people with whom he would never see eye-to-eye.

"Go easy on him," Mrs. Oppenheimer said from the kitchen. "He's from Austin," she added kindly, as if he had some sort of disability they should be sensitive about.

Mr. Oppenheimer laughed. He didn't laugh often, but when he did, he had a hearty, joyful laugh, like the Ghost of Christmas Present.

"Well, this sweet little flower made her first kill when she was six." He tousled Amanda's hair as if she was still six. "Maybe I shouldn't teach you a thing," he said to David. "That way, she's always got the upper hand. You know if you do her wrong, she won't hesitate."

He mimed shooting David and laughed again.

"Yeah," Carson agreed. "You don't want to cross her. A six-year-old girl who can kill Bambi's mom without batting an eye?"

"Shut up," Amanda said. "You made your first kill when you were four."

"You." Mr. Oppenheimer pointed at David. "Tomorrow morning. 6:00 a.m."

After Mr. Oppenheimer had disappeared into his shed to do God only knew what someone might do in a shed after dark,

David said, "So, he's going to make me kill something, isn't he?"

"Yes," Amanda said.

"I suppose it's not optional," David said.

"Oh, come on, David," Amanda said. "It's obviously a big deal to him. Just do it. It's not hard."

"Are you coming, too?" David asked Carson.

"Hell, yes," he said. "I have got to see this."

"So, in your Dad's head, I have to perform some kind of ritual of animal sacrifice to be part of the family?"

He had meant it as a joke, but Amanda and Carson's faces grew funeral serious.

"No," Amanda said. "It's not like that. It's *nothing* like that. Plenty of people hunt, David. It's a completely normal thing to do."

"It's not animal sacrifice," Carson added. "Hunting game is a well-known, established sport. It's not weird."

"God, relax," David said. "I know. I was joking. What the matter with you guys?"

Amanda gave a forced laugh. She patted him on the leg. "We know you're joking."

"Message received," David said. "I won't joke about hunting."

David might not spend his holidays with the Oppenheimers ever again. At least, not this year. Instead of an evening discussing football, and only football, with Erastus and Carson Oppenheimer while the girls made the house smell like happiness, David would spend this Thanksgiving avoiding an assassination attempt. David had caught parts of several over-the-phone arguments between Amanda and various family members about Thanksgiving arrangements. Yes, they wanted to see Amanda and the kids—the original kids—but they had not invited David and his other kids to Thanksgiving, or anything else, and they considered simply allowing David to live a gracious act of kindness. In the end, the Vandergraffs and the Oppenheimers decided to have Thanksgiving separately.

However, on the Wednesday before Thanksgiving, Grandma and Grandpa Oppenheimer wanted to spend the evening with their grandchildren. So Amanda took Jude, Emmy, and Patrick to Carson and Jess's house to spend the night with their grandparents and cousins.

Around eleven, David heard the front door open, followed by voices he recognized. Amanda, Jess, and Carson had dressed up for an evening out. So, they must have left the kids with their grandparents. Their slightly raised voices implied some measure of wine or cocktails had been involved in their evening. David stood at the bottom of the stairs wearing flannel pajama pants and waited to get his ass kicked by his brother-in-law and former best friend, Carson Oppenheimer. He had known it would come eventually, and hoped the fact Carson had come escorted by his wife and sister might mean David would at least avoid getting shot.

Aside from also loving Jesus, family, and hunting, Carson and Jess Oppenheimer could hardly be less similar to the elder Oppenheimers. As some of David's favorite people, he had chosen them as the guardians of his children if he and Amanda died. Despite appearances needed for networking, David had never felt as if he fit in with anyone other than his brother and sister-in-law. This had turned out to be far truer than he had ever imagined. According to Amanda, wizards made up a minute fraction of the population. Perhaps .0001%. David didn't know how many non-practicing dark wizard Christian businessmen resided in the Houston area, but he had the feeling he now looked at the only other one.

Carson loved yelling at football players on the television screen, doing anything outdoors, and more than anything else, he loved his wife and kids. He looked like a ruddier and balder version of Jude. Amanda had told David Jess was a witch. David hadn't asked if she was a dark witch, but he didn't need to. She was too warm, the human equivalent of apple cider with cinnamon. Her hair was the color of cherry wood and she usually painted her lips a matching color. She had lightly freckled skin, eyes the color of Saint Arnold Brown Ale, and an over-sized Julia Roberts-type smile. A physical therapist by trade, she had recently returned to the profession after spending ten years as a full-time mom. She also taught yoga classes on the side. David wondered if she truly excelled at yoga, or if she used whatever physics-breaking trick Xavier used to stack crackers to stack her body.

"Hello," David said. "I thought you were going to stay over," he said to Amanda.

"We wanted to talk to you," Jess said. The women had drawn eyes and mouths in straight lines. Carson had his arms crossed and his face turned away from David. They had moved beyond mad and had gone straight to showing the sad faces they had prepared for his funeral.

"Where are they?" Amanda asked, and David knew she meant Xavier and Evangeline.

"They went to bed."

"Maybe the dining room," Amanda said to Jess.

The three removed their jackets, then Amanda grabbed David's arm and pulled him. He could tell by the way she walked Amanda had the most to drink. The other two looked more composed.

"What's going on?" David asked.

"Should I open a bottle of wine?" Jess asked.

"Yes," Amanda said.

"Can I put on pants?" David asked.

They ignored the request. Jess came back with four glasses and a bottle. She poured wine into only two of the glasses.

"None for us yet," she said to David, and handed glasses to Amanda and Carson. "I need you sharp. Have you had anything to drink tonight?"

"What are you talking about?"

Amanda's wine started to disappear as soon as it hit the glass.

"Just do it," Carson said. "Don't give him time to prepare."

David took a few steps back.

"I have to tell him what I'm going to do," Jess said. "It works much better that way. As soon as you tell someone you're trying to find their secrets, their secrets float to the top of their mind and are much easier to find. With wizards, I *have* to tell them, they're too good at keeping secrets."

"If wizards are good at anything, it's keeping secrets, right, David?" Carson said.

"Amanda?" David asked.

"Carson and Jess came to an agreement," Amanda said. "Carson has agreed not to kill you if Jess does a spell to scan your mind and look for secrets. She's really good at it. I've always told her she should have been a cop or something."

"It's a fairly useful trick for a wife and mother, as well," Jess said.

"I don't keep secrets," Carson said. "I am an honest man."

Jess put her hand on Carson's arm. "Calm down, honey. I was making a joke."

"I thought you didn't practice," David said.

"We don't," Jess said. "We don't do this every day. We just thought it would be the best way to decide if we could trust you."

"Amanda, you can't let them. What about your secret? You

want her to know that?"

"What secret?" she asked.

"*Your* spell."

"She knows. Carson told her years ago," Amanda said. "Since we hadn't told our kids about magic, and they don't want to tell theirs, for the most part, it was fairly easy to keep it from you. No one ever discussed it around the kids. But, we spend time with Carson and Jess alone sometimes. Eventually, they would have said something about magic. She had to know."

"So, let me get this straight," David said. "None of you practices magic…until it benefits you. Then, all your beliefs go out the window and you do whatever you feel like."

"It's not like that," Amanda said. "It's complicated. Everything in life is complicated."

"Well, I at least agree with that last part," David said.

"I thought you were a good man," Carson said. "You're as rotten as the rest of them."

"Carson, chill out," Amanda said. "He betrayed me, not you."

"I'm sorry, Carson," David said.

Jess approached David and stood with only a fist's worth of space between them. She looked in his eyes in the same probing way Amanda did. She grabbed his hands. It reminded him of his odd moment with Penelope Carthage.

"Stop." He pulled his hands away and stepped back. "It's not safe. I don't want to hurt you."

"Hurt me?"

"Someone did this to me before," David said. "Penelope Carthage. It was before I knew I was a wizard. I thought she was just completely crazy. She grabbed my forearms and it made me feel weird. I felt myself attack her…with my mind. Some sort of defensive thing, like a skunk's spray. She freaked out. I thought it was all in my head. But now that I know what

I am…I don't know."

"When was this?" Amanda asked.

"August," David said.

"Nice try," Carson said. "I will hold you down for this if you make me."

"I'm trying not to hurt your wife," David said. "I don't know shit about magic. I don't know what I might do by accident."

"I'll be fine," Jess said. "You won't feel anything."

She reached for him again.

"Okay, Amanda, there is one thing I haven't told you," David said.

"Nope," Carson said. "You're not getting out of it that way either. You don't get to share some decoy secret and avoid the spell. You might as well just let Jess tell us."

"The more you fight this, the more scared I get," Amanda said. "You really *are* hiding something."

"Nothing about us."

"Just let her do it," Amanda said.

David took a deep breath and held out his hands. "You just have to hold my hands?"

"Relax. You won't feel anything." Jess took his hands and stood close enough that he could feel her breath on his neck. She inclined her head to look in his eyes. He didn't know why she had to stand so close. Did she need to listen close to hear the thoughts in his head? Read miniscule writing on his eyeballs?

She stayed in that position for a painfully long time. He didn't feel any magical sensations, but that didn't make it any less weird or uncomfortable. He focused on breathing to keep himself from panicking, as he had with Penelope, tried to keep whatever attacked her tied up in back. He wanted to close his eyes, but didn't know if Jess would let him. Amanda and Carson watched as if they waited for a doctor to give them the results of a biopsy.

"He is keeping something," Jess said. "But it doesn't feel romantic or sexual. He feels embarrassed. Maybe in denial. It's big, but not well defined, like he's trying to ignore it. He doesn't want to tell you because he's ashamed. Feels like he's not a man."

"Jesus, David, what is it?" Amanda asked.

"That's it?" David asked. "You can't even tell what the secret is?"

"Magic is vague," Jess said. "I can't read your thoughts like they're a movie screen. I get general impressions of feelings and then from there, try to guess what it is based on what I know about the person. I'm not finished. There was something else."

She took his hands again.

"It's strange. I think there is something about a woman. She did tempt him in some way. But, I don't think it was with sex. She was frightening. A witch."

"Just let me tell her," David said. "You're making it sound worse than it is."

"She likes to guess," Carson said. "She likes the game."

"It's not a game," David said.

"Magic?" Jess asked. "She wanted you to do magic and you were tempted? No, wait. Maybe that's a part of it, but that's not what you're trying to hide. It's more like…you feel like a failure. You didn't want Amanda to know. You were tempted by a chance to keep that private."

Jess dropped his hands.

"I know what it is," Jess said. "It's about money. You don't have any." She said it with inappropriate triumph, as if she had just solved a riddle.

Despite the terrible violation, David had to admit she had impressed him with her skill. "All right, Jess. Stop. That's very terrifying and remarkable. I'm glad I'm not Carson. No wonder he's an honest man. Now are you satisfied I'm not having any other affairs? That I've never been with any woman besides the one you know about twelve years ago?"

Jess squinted at him. "I can't guarantee it. It's possible you have, but don't feel bad about it. If it's not overwhelming your mind, I might not see it."

"Fuck, Jess. What was the point, then?" David asked. Carson moved in on him. "And for the record, if I had had any other affairs, the remorse would be overwhelming my mind. I'm not a sociopath. I may not be perfect, but if I do something wrong, I feel fucking bad about it. So, I passed your test."

"You're right," Jess said to David. "I believe you." She patted Carson's arm again.

"May I speak to my wife privately, please?" David asked. "Or, are our money problems your business now?"

"Of course," Jess said. She poured herself a full glass of wine and towed her husband into the family room, now boarded up to keep out the winter air.

"Money?" Amanda asked as soon as they disappeared.

"I'm sorry I didn't tell you sooner. I really didn't mean for you to find out like that."

"Tell me."

"Vandergraff Home Builders is shutting down. I have my last paycheck scheduled for the Friday after Christmas."

Amanda sank into a chair and stared at David's knees.

"How?" she asked. "That doesn't make sense."

"There was a fire that destroyed our largest project and we lost a lot of our capital. We couldn't recover."

"How long have you known?"

"I found out on Halloween."

"Shit, David."

"I'll find something else. We'll figure it out."

"Why the fuck didn't you tell me?"

"Why don't you ask Jess? She seems to understand the inner workings of my psyche better than I do. Perhaps because I'm a failure. Not a man."

She poured herself another glass of wine. "So everything falls apart," she said. "Who was the woman?"

"An investor. She wanted to buy us out."

"A witch?"

"Yes."

"Please God, don't tell me you signed a contract with a witch."

"I didn't. Jess was right. I was tempted. But, I said no."

"I can't do Jess's spell," Amanda said. "So, I can't be with a man who requires its use."

"I know I should have told you. I was going to, soon; I just wanted to have a plan first."

"You don't have to have a plan before you tell me something important. We're supposed to be partners in life. We're supposed to make the plans together."

"You're right. I'm sorry."

"We could lose our house," Amanda said. "No, we *will* lose our house. Even if you find a new job quickly, which is a long shot in this economy, you won't be taking home a CEO paycheck. When were you going to tell me we were downsizing? The day the movers came?"

"I'm sorry," David said again.

"I don't even really care about the money. We have too much excess as it is. Our kids could use a little grounding. And you know, you're not the only one who brings in good money."

"I know."

"I don't bring in *your* kind of money. But, if we make some changes to our lifestyle, I still can take care of the family. We don't need you as much as you think."

"You won't have to do that. Like you said, we're partners.

You don't have to support the family on your own. I'll find something."

"No, we *were* partners. Now, it will just be up to me. That's what divorce means. Doing it alone."

"No."

Amanda stood up too fast and grabbed a chair to keep from swaying forward.

"You don't deserve me," she said.

"No argument."

"I am not that kind of woman."

"What kind?"

"I won't be abused."

"Did I abuse you?"

"Yes."

Tears pooled in the lashes under her eyes. For a second, he feared he had abused her and forgotten. But, on a deep level, he knew he wouldn't do that. She didn't mean it that way.

"If you hit me, it would be better. Easier. I would know what to do. I could divorce you. I want to be stronger. Like women are supposed to be. Like what I believe. That women have the right to be loved by their husbands. They have the right to be their *only* lover. That I am enough to be your *only*."

"You are."

"Shut up." She moved closer to glare at him from close range. "Why wasn't I enough for you?"

"I don't know. You are. You should have been."

"You loved her. You really loved her. If it was just sex, it would be easier. But, it wasn't. You *loved* her. You were together for years. You had *two* children with her. You loved her. Don't tell me you didn't."

"I wouldn't have risked what we have for anything less than love," he said.

"You see…that doesn't help me, David. That doesn't make me feel better. I can imagine you wanting to fuck someone else. It's not a great feeling, but I can live with it. It's human nature. I mean, I think about other people. Have fantasies."

David wanted to kick some fantasy ass.

"With who?" he asked.

"It doesn't matter. That's what I'm saying. It's just sex. I wouldn't really do it. And, I don't love anyone else. I *never* have."

"What do you want me to say?"

"What did you love about her?"

"You don't want me to answer that question."

"What did she have that I didn't? What was I missing?"

"Nothing."

"Bullshit. Don't fuck with me. It's too late. Tell me the truth."

"I just…loved both of you. I believed I couldn't live without either of you."

"I've been talking with Carson and Jess, getting some magical consult, if you will. There is something binding me to you. A spell. Otherwise, I would have kicked you out. I would have already served you with papers."

David laughed coldly. "Of course, there is something binding you to me. How about twenty-three years together? I didn't give you any love potion, if that's what you're implying."

"Not a potion," she said seriously. "I don't know what it is. But, it's something. I know magic when it's happening. It has this unnatural feeling. Carson and Jess are going to help me figure out the spell and break it, so I can divorce you."

"I haven't cast any motherfucking spells. You know I haven't. You know I can't."

"I didn't say you did. I don't know what it is."

"Are you listening to yourself? Is this a wizard thing? Blaming all problems on magic? Child abuse? Adultery? Drunk driving? You know, those things happen to Mundanes, too."

"I know."

"You don't want to divorce me because you're still in love with me. Because something I did twelve years ago didn't change everything that happened in between now and then. At least part of you knows that."

"Wizards can become twisted up in each other. My mom believes it. She says 'love' is the only magic she practices. The only magic she believes in. And I always want to punch her in the mouth. It's so sappy. But part of me listened. She says if she and my dad were apart, they would die. She warned me; whoever dies first, the other will follow. One way or another, they can't live apart. The other one will die."

"Like my mom?" David asked.

Amanda ran her fingers across the back of his hand. His words seemed to throw a bucket of water on her anger. He imagined steam rising from her.

"Is that why she killed herself?" David asked. "She couldn't live after my dad died?"

"I don't know, honey."

"But…he abused her?"

"Yes."

"What do you remember? Or, what do I remember?"

"I won't tell you about the memories I removed. I don't care how many times you ask."

"They're mine."

"Not anymore. I will never tell you. Your parents are dead. They can't hurt you, or anyone. You've moved on. You have your own family now. I like the man you are. The man who believes in good magic."

"You don't think I would…if I knew?"

"I don't know."

"If you really think it was the right thing to do, then do the same for them."

He didn't have to clarify who he meant by "them."

"Do you really want me to do that?"

"Absolutely."

She paused. "No."

"No?"

"I love you too much to regret what I did to your memories, but that doesn't mean I can't admit I was wrong to do it."

"You are contradicting yourself. Again, you say magic is always bad, unless you really want to do it. Unless it serves *your* purposes."

"Magic is dangerous. And the magic I did was no different. It is the perfect example, really. It was destruction that was well meaning, done out of love. But, someone was still punished for it, in a way I could never have anticipated. I believe if you had still had your memories, things would have been different. Evangeline and Xavier wouldn't have been abused like that. It's my fault."

"That's ridiculous."

"If you had had your own memories, things would have been different. If you had known about magic, you might have realized what was going on with Crystal. If you had known, you might have been able to protect your children."

"It's *really* not your fault. You can help me protect them now." He brushed some of the hair away from her face. She didn't knock his hand away. "Sometimes I think we'll need magic to protect our children. If dark forces are at work, don't we need to learn good magic to stop it?"

She smiled sadly. "We can't. We're not good wizards."

"Good magic has to exist."

"It does. Of course, it does. But, it's hard. Destruction is easy. Dark magic is like stabbing someone in the heart. And good magic is like performing heart surgery to fix it. Almost no one can do it."

"But heart surgery isn't impossible. It's just difficult. If you go to medical school and study for years and practice your craft, you can do it. There is a difference between hard and impossible."

"I love you, David."

"What?"

"I love you," she said again. "I love that you believe in good magic. I'm sorry I took it away from you. I love you…so much."

"I love you too."

He saw his moment. He took her head in his hands and kissed her, knowing it might not happen again. The wine would wear off. She would hate him again. Their horrible present would return. He circled his tongue around hers. Tasted her. Felt the rough of her tongue. Her smooth gums. Her teeth. The hardness of the roof of her mouth. As soon as his tongue touched hers, he knew he wouldn't stop. Something inside her could fix everything. If only he could find it. If he could only go deep enough inside.

She pressed her abdomen against his. It wouldn't take more than that. He would take her right there. In the dining room, with Carson and Jess one room away. He couldn't imagine anything else happening. Only wizards would do something so incredibly inappropriate.

He lifted her up and put her on the table. She wrapped her legs around him and squeezed. He ran his hands through her hair so roughly he probably pulled out chunks of it. She pulled at his pants, bringing him closer and closer. Clothes seemed like a maddening obstacle. He pressed himself into her as if he could enter her right there, clothes or not. Thankfully, she wore a skirt. He reached his hands beneath her skirt and pulled off her panties and threw them on the floor. She didn't stop him.

And, there on the table, he made love to his wife.

He thought the others might catch them, but fortunately or unfortunately, it didn't last long. He might not be eighteen anymore, but he hadn't wanted anything this badly at eighteen. He thrust into her as if his life depended on it. Maybe it did.

He considered it pure luck she tensed against him and cried out in orgasm. In record time. He thought he wouldn't last long enough to make her come and hardly tried. She wanted him, too.

Then she became angry again. She pulled her panties back on and ran her fingers through her hair to smooth it.

"Damn it, David," she said.

CHAPTER SEVENTEEN

The next morning, David made bacon and eggs while Amanda pulled the turkey out of the fridge with a dramatic, "Ugh." She put the turkey on the counter and rubbed her temples. Hung over.

"I'll help with the meal. I'll make the whole thing if you want," David said.

"Don't be ridiculous," Amanda said.

Samantha stood in the entranceway to the kitchen in an unconscious ballet position. By her stance and the concentration in her eyes, she looked as if she prepared to perform a dramatic ballet routine. She crossed her arms over her chest and set her mouth in a firm line.

"It's Thanksgiving," she said.

Amanda wiped her hands on her apron and chewed her mouth.

"You said they would be home by Thanksgiving."

"They needed to extend their stay," Amanda said.

"Stop lying to me." Those four words had more force than all the other words David had heard her say combined. He worried things would start breaking.

"I'm so sorry, honey," Amanda said. "They checked out of

Magnolia Terrace and haven't contacted me."

"Where are they?"

"I don't know." Amanda pulled Samantha in to her arms. "I'm sure they're fine. We'll find them."

"They didn't say anything about me? Did they leave me here for good? What exactly did they say?"

"They love you. They didn't want to leave you here at all. They fully intended to get better and come home. I'm sure they still do intend that. But you can stay here as long as you need to."

After the kids came back from the Oppenheimers, David overheard Emmy and Jude talking to Samantha in Emmy's room.

"If they won't do anything, we will," Jude said.

"We'll find them and we'll fix them," Emmy said.

"You don't know how," Samantha said.

"We'll figure it out," Emmy said. "There is always a way."

"Don't even worry about," Jude said. "We can handle it."

His kids were loyal friends, but so clearly…just kids. They believed they could do anything.

If you want your kids to do magic, forbid it. Patrick wondered if his parents meant it to happen that way. As if that was the game; wizard parents didn't tell their kids anything about magic because they were supposed to figure it out on their own, or something. His parents revolved in their own world a lot of the time, but they couldn't possibly be that stupid. They might as well have given them all new cars and told them they could drive them.

"No, that's wrong," Evangeline said.

Patrick sat with his legs crossed, facing Evangeline, and she had her hands hovering over his as if they prepared to play that slap-hands game. They had found a good spot tucked behind the house, concealed by trees. Xavier leaned up against the air conditioning unit.

"I have no idea what you want me to do," Patrick said.

"It's not that hard," Evangeline said.

"For you, maybe."

"Ready?"

"No."

"Just defend yourself."

She pressed her palms against his. Her hands burned cold and hot at the same time. He pulled his hands away.

"You're not trying," she said.

"I don't even know how to try. This doesn't make any sense."

"You're not really hurting him," Xavier said. "He doesn't feel like he needs to defend himself. It's not going to work unless you are more aggressive."

"I don't want to hurt him," Evangeline said.

"Exactly. That's the problem," Xavier said.

"I think it's a good instinct," Patrick said.

Evangeline picked up one of Patrick's hands and read his palm, as if he came with instructions.

"Are there any kind of spells I can learn that don't involve hurting me?" Patrick asked.

"I guess," Evangeline said. "Those are harder, though. Dark magic is easy. You have to start with that."

"Maybe the problem is, I don't want to attack you," Patrick said. "I should practice on Jude."

"You shouldn't practice on Jude," she said kindly. "He's a

lot better at magic."

And sports. And talking to girls. And, he's taller and better looking. Now, he can also drive with his eyes closed.

"Maybe this isn't his kind of magic," Xavier said. "What kinds of things are you good at?"

"You mean magic things? Uh…none."

"A lot of wizards have one special thing they're good at," Evangeline said. "Have you ever done magic by accident? It may not be as obvious as you think. Is there anything you're just a little too good at?"

"I suppose you're looking for an answer other than *Call of Duty*," Patrick said.

Evangeline wrinkled her nose. Yes, she wanted a better answer.

"Maybe not," Xavier said. "That's like fighting, right? Maybe you'd be good at fighting."

"I don't know…" Patrick didn't like what that might lead to. He had no interest in wizard *Fight Club*.

"Or maybe you're clairvoyant," Evangeline suggested. "Really good fighters are. And I saw you pull your sister out of the way of the truck."

"I think I would know if I could see the future," Patrick said.

"Not the *future* future," Xavier said. "It could be seeing things a millisecond faster than everyone else. Just by knowing how your opponent is flexing his muscles or positioning his body, you know when and where they're going to strike."

"Why do I think this conversation ends with you punching me in the face?" Patrick asked.

Xavier expelled a breath quickly. He never got much closer to laughing than that. "If you want me to."

"I guess that's what Jude is good at," Patrick said. "He could anticipate the cars on the highway, but he didn't even have to see them."

"That's pretty serious magic," Xavier said. "Or, he just got lucky."

"Your magic probably is like his," Evangeline said. "Related people have related magic."

"Maybe I should try to break a wine glass then."

Evangeline shrugged. "That might be good."

"I can do other things," Xavier said.

"What did Samantha do to you?" Patrick asked Xavier. "Right before Jude crashed the truck?"

"I don't know," Xavier said. His cheeks turned red, which would gnaw at Patrick for a while. "I don't know that spell."

"Yeah, but what did she do? How did she get you to stop?"

"She confused me, I guess. I felt sort of happy. I forgot what I was doing. It only lasted a few seconds."

"What are you guys doing?" Emmy came around the corner with Jude and Samantha.

"Hanging out by the air conditioner," Patrick said. "What are *you* guys doing?"

"If we're all out here, we're going to get caught," Emmy said.

"So go inside," Patrick said.

"It's our turn," Emmy said as if they fought over an invisible swing set. "Go inside and distract Mom and Dad."

"They're not paying attention," Patrick said.

Patrick didn't know when they had split into teams, but they had. Since Patrick disowned Jude as a brother when he had almost killed them, and Evangeline and Emmy couldn't talk for thirty seconds without attacking each other, they had to split this way. He didn't mind, except for the obvious problem…Samantha had chosen the wrong team.

"I've been spending the whole day baking while Mom yells at me for doing it wrong," Emmy said. "Time to switch."

"Fine. I suck anyway," Patrick said, and he and his team

went inside.

The meal that required the combined efforts of eight people—although mostly Mom—cooking over the course of about six hours took about ten minutes to eat. This time, they all managed to eat together without yelling or magic.

After eating, Mom, Dad, Jude, and Emmy sat in the living room watching football, although Mom did more sleeping on the couch than actual watching. Xavier and Evangeline went upstairs to do something weird, no doubt. And Samantha did dishes alone in the kitchen.

Patrick suddenly had the desire to do dishes.

Samantha did dishes as she did everything, gracefully. Patrick heard only the occasional splash of water.

"You don't have to do the dishes while everyone else sits around being lazy," Patrick said. "It's very Cinderella."

She smiled. "I don't mind."

"Want help?"

"If you want to."

Patrick took the plate from her hand and dried it. Somehow, he made more noise with a dishtowel than she did stacking plates.

"Are you upset about your parents?" he asked.

"Of course, I am," she said.

"I guess it was a stupid question."

"A little."

"I'm sure they'll come back."

"I suppose so," she said flatly.

"I don't think Evangeline is a very good magic teacher," Patrick said. "Either that, or I just really suck."

"You want me to teach you?"

"Yeah." He hadn't thought about it until she asked…but that worked.

"I probably can't. I can't seem to teach Jude and Emmy anything. It's like I'm practicing ballet and they're practicing rugby. We can't connect."

"Because your magic is different from theirs."

"And yours. Maybe you should ask Jude. He does fine without anyone ever having taught him anything. That's pretty rare, I think. He's a powerful wizard."

Yeah, yeah, I get it. He's a god among men.

"Maybe my magic isn't like his, either," Patrick said. "I can't connect with my other siblings, anyway."

"You just aren't thinking about things in the right way," she said. "You're still thinking Mundane. At some point, you'll just *get* it, and then it'll be easy."

He moved closer to her and her hip touched his. One way or another, he would probably end up breaking some dishes.

"Jude says you have a crush on me," she said.

His stomach lurched. Thoughts came at him like bullets. His first instinct—deny everything. *No, what? That's crazy. I don't even like you. You're gross.* And, why the hell did Jude tell her? Someone had finally noticed how much he stared at her, but Jude? Magic fighting started to sound pretty good.

"Maybe," he said.

She sucked on her cheeks as if she tried to hold back a smile….or, to keep from laughing at him.

"Is that okay?" he asked, feeling like an idiot as soon as he said it.

"Yes."

She handed him a clean dish and wiped her hands on the towel he held. "I think I'm going to go to bed early," she said, and then left.

Patrick woke up, and then heard Emmy's door close. The sequence seemed out of order. The door closing should have woken him up. But, had he heard another noise before that which actually woke him up, or did he anticipate it, as Evangeline had said? Then, he heard Jude's door open and shut. He looked at the clock. 2:00 a.m. exactly. A pre-set meeting time? His insides hardened with a mix of anger, hurt, and disgust. Did he hear Samantha sneaking into Jude's room?

Patrick's room touched walls with Jude's room. He couldn't imagine anything worse than *hearing* them together…except maybe hearing the same thing from his parents' room. Although, not likely anymore. He tried to go back to sleep, but knew that wouldn't happen. As long as she was in there with him, a band might as well practice in that room.

He heard whispered voices. He put the pillow over his head and then took it back off. The voices didn't have a romantic tone. And he didn't hear the sound of the bed creaking, or rustling sheets. *Emmy* had snuck into Jude's room, not Samantha. He should have known. He thought sneaking into her brother's room in the middle of the night was still creepy, but they wanted to break a different rule.

The tone of their voices shifted. They argued in whispers. Patrick crawled out of bed and entered Jude's room without knocking.

"What do you want, Patrick?" Emmy asked.

"What are you guys doing? Magic?"

"So what if we are?" Emmy asked.

"You don't have to be like that. It's not like I'm going to tell Mom and Dad. I do it, too. I try, anyway."

"Let me help you," Jude said. "I am a good teacher."

"Like how you taught me to drive?"

"Absolutely." He answered seriously.

"Did you have your eyes closed when you almost killed us?" Patrick asked.

"I wouldn't drive drunk with my eyes closed."

"So responsible of you."

"I obviously feel like total shit about that," Jude said. "What do you want me to do? I miss you, man. You're my brother. My *real* brother. At least, let me teach you magic."

"How long have you known you were a wizard?" Patrick asked.

"Since Mom and Dad told me a few weeks ago."

"Bullshit. You knew you could do stuff. You did the driving stunt before that. Why didn't you say anything?"

"And what exactly would I say without sounding crazy? I didn't know wizards were real. I didn't know what was going on. I just knew I was different. And, I did tell you. Lots of times. Like, the driving with my eyes closed thing. And, the time I had Emmy push you out of that tree because I said I could catch you. I mean, I did, didn't I? And, when I threw the knife in the air and caught it by the handle with my eyes closed. All the crazy stuff I've done that you hate. I'm trying to show you what I can do."

"Our conversation isn't over," Emmy said to Jude. "Don't try to change the subject."

"What was the subject?" Patrick asked.

Emmy looked at Jude and hesitated.

"I don't care if you tell him," Jude said. "But don't expect him to be on your side."

"Jude is depressed," Emmy said.

"I am not depressed," Jude said.

"Patrick, tell him he's depressed," Emmy said.

Patrick opened his mouth to say who knew what, but Emmy continued.

"You quit football. You don't do your schoolwork. You broke up with Avery. And you've spent most of the

Thanksgiving break in bed."

"You got drunk and drove your truck into the house," Patrick added and Emmy gestured toward him as if to support this point.

"See, he's worried about you, too," she said.

"I didn't hear him say that," Jude said.

"You never do anything or go anywhere," Emmy said.

"I'm grounded."

"That doesn't mean you're not allowed to take showers or shave."

"I shower and shave. Occasionally."

"And it doesn't mean you can't talk to your friends at school. Why are you eating lunch alone around back like some kind of loser?"

"My friends go out for lunch. I can't drive."

"But, you are allowed to be inside cars while other people do."

"You should play football again," Patrick said. "You're going to lose your scholarship."

"See, he is on my side," Emmy said. "Don't you want to feel better?"

"You won't be able to do it," Jude said.

"Don't tell me what I can't do."

"All right," Jude said. "You can try."

Emmy placed her hands on Jude's chest and took a deep breath.

"Hang on…what are you doing?" Patrick asked.

"I'm going to try a spell," Emmy said. "Samantha taught it to me. It's for depression and anxiety."

"Wow, that's so…useful," Patrick said. "I was beginning to agree with Dad, that magic is all breaking stuff."

"Shut up, Patrick. I need to concentrate."

Emmy moved closer to Jude and kept her hands on his chest. She closed her eyes and breathed deeply. Jude closed his eyes, too. After a moment, Patrick noticed Emmy trembling. She scrunched her face and bit her lip,

she didn't pull away. Patrick moved next to her and touched her arm.

"Emmy?" he asked.

At the sound of Patrick's voice, Jude opened his eyes, too. He gathered Emmy's hands in his and threw them off him.

"Are you okay?" Jude asked.

"Yes," she said flatly. She continued to tremble. She wrapped her arms around her chest, leaned over and moaned.

"Emmy?" Patrick asked again.

Jude reached out to her but she stepped back, out of his reach. Without a word, she turned and left the room. Patrick and Jude followed on her heels. She headed for the stairs. Evangeline had been right. Patrick did know what would happen next. But only a second before. Too late for it to be worth a damn thing.

She turned around and looked back at them, then threw herself down the stairs.

CHAPTER EIGHTEEN

David watched Amanda stare at her water glass with an odd urgency. She could have been watching Emmy's surgery on the surface of the water. *Could she actually do that?* No. She would have let him watch, too.

David didn't know what had woken him, at first. He turned over and listened, trying to figure out if the sound had come from a dream or not. Then he heard his oldest son's voice. One word, dripping with more fear and alarm than a bomb warning. "Emmy."

The fear in this son's voice infected David. He stumbled into the dark hallway and found the source.

His sons knelt over something at the bottom of the stairs. Halfway down the stairs, he saw her. Emmy—unconscious, her arm twisted under her at the wrong angle. Wrong. Wrong. Wrong. David made it down the stairs with the urgency reserved for a parent making their way to their hurt child, and toppled his sons like bowling pins as he tried to get between them.

Then it all happened fast. They waited in the ER again. For Emmy, again. Wondering why they had freaked out so much about a little cut. This time she had a broken arm. Broken ribs.

Dislocated knee. Internal bleeding. Head injury. Critical condition.

Jess had gone to the house to keep an eye on the other kids, but Jude and Patrick refused to leave the hospital. They hadn't said much. Except for one conversation. "No, I didn't push her. How can you even ask me that?" … "Then how did she fall?" … "She jumped." … "Why?" … No answer… "*Why?*" … "Magic."

Magic.

David guessed Amanda had no space left in her for anger. Worry filled her to capacity. Once Emmy got better…if she got better…no, she *would* get better…then there would be hell to pay.

The surgeon estimated an hour and a half. He took three hours. This was routine for him. Another night putting someone back together. Did he have any idea what it did to the people in the waiting room, when he took twice as long as expected?

Then, finally, he came out to give the prognosis. "She's stable… She'll be admitted into intensive care for monitoring… Don't worry… She'll be fine… No spinal issues… Should recover… She's a tough little girl, that one."

David took the boys home the next day. Amanda stayed. They decided someone would stay with Emmy all the time. That evening, David returned to relieve Amanda. He would stay the night in Emmy's room. They had moved her out of intensive care, which seemed encouraging, and meant a much more comfortable room and fewer visits from the nurses.

David took one of the deepest breaths of his life when he saw Emmy's blue eyes wide open. He hadn't breathed right since she fell.

"I'm not sure I'm ready to go," Amanda said.

"I want to be with her, too," David said. "And someone has to watch the kids at home."

Amanda hovered by Emmy's bed like a bodyguard, although he couldn't imagine what she guarded her against now. The damage was done.

"It's okay, Mom," Emmy said in a scratchy voice. "Go home. You're a mess."

Amanda kissed Emmy and gushed enough *I love you*s for several weeks' worth of life outside of a hospital room. Amanda nodded to David as she gathered her things, with the intimacy of a shift change. David stood in her way and wrapped her into a hug before she had time to protest. He laid his hand on her head and held her to him.

"Are the boys okay?" she asked.

"It depends on what you mean by 'okay,'" David said. "But…no…I mean, yes, they're fine. Just worried about you," he said to Emmy.

"It's not his fault," Emmy said.

"Do you have everything you need?" Amanda asked.

"I'm fine. Go home," David said.

She kissed Emmy one more time, and then left.

David sat in the chair Amanda had vacated. Casts and bandages held his daughter together and she had an ugly purple bruise on the side of her face. She hated to be still. He couldn't imagine Emmy bedridden. This would be hell for her.

He took her hand and she didn't pull it away this time. Too tired, perhaps.

"Mom told me a little bit about what happened," he said. "Was she angry with you when you told her?"

"She tried not to be. But, I know she is," Emmy said. "Are you mad at me?"

"I've been too scared to be mad," he said. "For what it's

worth, thank you for trying to do good magic."

Emmy smiled stiffly.

"I really thought I could do it. And if I couldn't, I just thought that *nothing* would happen."

"What did happen?"

"It's fuzzy. Mom asked me what was going through my mind and there wasn't really anything. I just felt so sad, I wanted to do anything to stop the feeling. It was intense. I never want to feel like that again."

"I'm sure you won't."

"I don't know how the spell went wrong. It's supposed to work by releasing the bad feelings from the person. Samantha thinks maybe I left myself too vulnerable to Jude's depression, so it came off him and right into me. Does that mean Jude feels like that all the time?" Emmy asked.

"I hope not," David whispered.

"I asked him," Emmy said. "He said no. He said he wasn't suicidal. I don't know if he would tell me the truth, though. But, I guess if he did feel like that all the time, he would already have killed himself. It didn't feel like a choice to me. I didn't have to think about whether or not I wanted to die. It was like a reflex. Samantha said maybe it didn't work because I am a dark witch. What does that mean? Does that mean I can't do good magic?"

"No, of course not."

"Are you just saying that, or do you know? Because that's not what Mom says."

"I hope she's wrong," David said.

"Me, too."

David barely slept that night, and neither could Emmy. How could anyone sleep in a hospital room when a nurse came in every hour to prod and poke and question? In this case, prod and poke his little girl. Amanda came back around seven in the morning, much earlier than she had planned. She said she couldn't relax at home. David ate breakfast with Amanda in the hospital cafeteria, and then he went home.

Amanda had pulled all the Christmas decorations out of the attic, either by her own hands or by the art of delegation. But, David guessed in this case, she had done it herself to busy her hands. Strings of lights lay in single rows on the living room floor where she had detangled them. The stockings sat on top of the mantel, but she hadn't hung them yet. He imagined her standing there with the three stockings. Only three. He could see her starting to hang them, and then realizing…panicking…not knowing whether or not she should buy two more.

They had decided not to tell the kids about their downswing in fortunes until after Christmas, and would try to rein in their Christmas spending in subtle ways, such as putting up the Christmas lights themselves instead of hiring help.

David saw Evangeline sitting on the steps of the back porch. She wore the jacket he had bought her, and huddled over her notepad. When he opened the patio door, she pressed her notepad against her chest so he couldn't see it.

"Is she okay?" Evangeline asked.

"She'll be okay," David said.

"We didn't teach her that," Evangeline said.

"I know."

"I'm glad she's okay," Evangeline said. "She looked so…broken…when I saw her on the floor."

"You don't want me to see what you're drawing?"

She squirmed and leaned over the pad.

"You don't have to show me if you don't want to."

"It's for therapy."

"That was smart of her to ask you to draw. I know you're good at it."

"Okay…here."

She handed him her notepad. David's breath caught in his throat. He saw a sketch of Crystal, as detailed and realistic as if she had handed him a photo. More so. Evangeline had captured a certain glow about her in the shading of her skin. The pride in her eyes. Evangeline drew her in a sleek, black evening gown. Instead of the angel wings tattoo on her back, she had two large, very real, black wings spread out behind her.

"It's my mom," she said unnecessarily.

"I know. I recognized the wings." His voice cracked.

"You're crying."

"I'm just tired."

"You did love her."

"I told you I did."

"Just not enough, I guess."

David bit his lip and tried to keep himself together. He knew he couldn't handle this right now, but as a parent, he had no choice. He sat down next to her and immediately wanted to lie on the porch and fall asleep.

"I tried to find you," he said. "You weren't in any records or in any computers. I tried really hard."

"If you had used magic, you would have found us," she said.

David had no response to that.

"I asked her about you," Evangeline said. "All the time."

"You did?"

"Of course. You're my father."

"Did she say why she hid from me?"

"She said she was destroying you."

"She wasn't."

"Maybe your marriage, then. She told me you needed to be

with your wife because she is your talisman."

"Talisman? I thought those were like your rock and Xavier's cross."

"Those aren't the real ones. Just objects. My mom was really into to object talismans. She created hundreds of them. Rocks. Jewelry. Trinkets. All sorts of things. Different ones for different purposes."

Evangeline pulled her magic rock out of her jacket pocket and laid it on the porch. "This one is you."

"What do you mean?"

"She told me to think about you when I held it. And if I did it enough times, my thoughts would stick to it, and it would really be you and your protection."

David looked at indentation in the rock.

"Did I turn out to be anything like what you pictured?"

"Not really." She smiled. "In some ways, I guess. But, I always thought you would be a wizard. A real one. A really good one."

"I'm sorry I'm not."

She shrugged. "It's okay. I kept my object talisman for my mom. She wouldn't want me to go anywhere without it. But it's just a symbol. My stepfather told me that. He knew more about magic than my mom. He said they weren't real talismans and they wouldn't really do anything. He said only people can be talismans, and those talismans work. They are the most powerful kind of magic. I think he was right. My mom made talismans all the time. But, nothing ever happened. She said it wasn't always obvious, that talismans aren't supposed to stop bad things from happening. They protect you on a deeper level. But, it didn't work for her. She'd been messed up for a long time. At the end, she wasn't really my mom anymore."

"Did your mother have a real talisman?"

"I think you know the answer to that."

"It was me."

She nodded.

"So, I left her unprotected."

"Yeah, but it was her fault. She even set up spells to make it harder for you to find us. Even after she realized you were her talisman. Even after she knew you could fix everything. She kept trying to make her talisman into something else."

Evangeline looked down at her picture. She blinked a few extra times, as if she might cry, but her eyes stayed dry.

"Last March, when we were in town one day, Xavier stole someone's phone. It had Internet on it. He wanted to know everything Mom had ever told me about you so he could look for you. He knew your name, but not much else. But, we didn't know how to use the Internet then and the phone stopped working at our house anyway. Later, Xavier tried to find you with a spell. I don't know what it was exactly, he wouldn't tell me, because he didn't want me to try. I don't know where he learned it or if he made it up. But, it was supposed to bring you to us."

She leaned over her knees and stared at her sandaled feet. She had painted her toenails silver.

"My mom deserved to die."

David thought for a while before he spoke. He put his hand on her shoulder. "She was a good person when I knew her."

David pulled the box of Crystal's ashes out of his jacket. He lay down on the uneven sofa bed mattress in his office. He held Crystal to his chest. If anyone walked in, he would get caught cuddling with a dead woman. Especially abhorrent, since he should be trying to save his marriage with his living one. He closed his eyes and felt her weight on his chest. She moved up and down as he breathed. He felt better.

"You believed in ghosts," he said. "Couldn't you be one for a minute? Come back to me. Tell me what to do."

Like a child, he waited, as if she really might appear there. He watched the ceiling fan spin in a mundane, non-magical way. The clock ticked. The computer whirred.

It did work…sort of. He fell asleep and dreamed about her. For some unknowable reason, his subconscious put her at The Galleria, a place she had never set foot and would never want to. She waited for him in front of the ice rink with the domed glass ceiling. She leaned against the railing and watched him approach her with one of her patented poker faces. But, as she watched him approach, the edges of her lips turned upward ever so slightly and her eyes opened a little wider.

"I'm sorry, Crystal."

She stared at him.

"I know it doesn't help, but I still love you. You saved my marriage by cutting me out. I wouldn't have been able to stay away from you forever."

She still said nothing, but gave a long, slow blink, like an acknowledgement.

"Our children are really amazing. They're beautiful. I'm glad I get to know them now."

Another blink. A longer one.

"Why won't you speak to me?"

Her eyes gazed downward, then back up. She looked like a statue that could move only her eyes. He moved close to her. He feared touching her, as he feared to touch their children, afraid anything he did could hurt her. He touched his forehead to hers. The contact animated her slightly. He heard her breathe.

"Evangeline drew me a picture of your wings. Can I see them?"

He pulled back from her and waited. At first, he thought nothing would happen, but then she pulled her tank top over her head. She pulled her shoulders back and raised her chin, as if she wanted him to know she had no shame in showing her naked breasts. Then it happened. Two massive black wings spread out behind her, twice her height. Her wingspan rivaled a California condor's. He reached his hands out to them.

"May I?"

An infinitesimal nod. He ran his fingers across the smooth feathers. They weren't black. Not really. Each feather had the sheen of a different color. Blue. Red. Orange. Green. Yellow. Violet. The feathers fell around his fingers like water. She was gone.

CHAPTER NINETEEN

Emmy came home on December 10. The doctors said she healed well. Fast. She said she would recover quickly, and she did, as if she could somehow will her bones back together. *Who knew what was possible anymore?* She wore a cast on her arm and a brace on her knee. She couldn't do much, but insisted on walking into the house on her own two feet. David and Jude walked on either side of her, ready to catch her if she stumbled, and she kept swatting their arms away.

"I can walk," she screamed at Jude as he grabbed her elbow to help her over the threshold. "Let me go."

"Whoa," she said when she entered the house. "It's just as bad inside."

Christmas had hit the Vandergraff home with the subtlety of a tidal wave. Amanda had coated the outside of the house with Christmas lights. And not just the house. Every branch of every tree. She even ran strings of lights along the ground. She had placed two Nativity scenes in the lawn, a giant cross formed out of Christmas lights, and a blow-up Santa Claus with all eight reindeer.

The inside of the house looked the same. Green garlands

wrapped around everything. The whole house twinkled. A twelve-foot tree. A creepy dancing Santa on the dining table. Five more small Nativity scenes. David had seen Xavier and Patrick playing a 'count the baby Jesuses' game. According to Patrick, counting both pictures and figurines, they had twelve baby Jesuses on the property, and they hadn't done a full search yet. Apparently, new ones showed up every day.

Amanda had multiple Christmas candles burning, and the smell of chemically contrived pine trees made it hard to breathe. Trans-Siberian Orchestra played throughout the day and Amanda had made about two hundred Christmas cookies that probably would give David diabetes. Apparently, Amanda thought she could attack dark magic with a relentless onslaught of Christmas.

Samantha and Jude plastered themselves onto Emmy like wings all day. David and Amanda could hardly pry Samantha off Emmy long enough to talk to her, but they did manage to catch Samantha doing laundry alone in the afternoon. David didn't know someone could excel at something as ordinary as laundry, but Samantha did. She folded clothes as if she worked at The Gap and everything came out cleaner than new and smelled of springtime. If she used some kind of laundry magic, he wouldn't stop her.

She looked at them serenely, but David didn't miss the hint of fear in her eyes. She put down a towel and folded her hands in front of her in a docile way. He didn't like her looking at him like that. They had had a "talk" with her about teaching Emmy a dangerous spell which had made her melt like a popsicle in August. She cried silently and didn't say anything besides, "I'm sorry."

Apparently, a "talk" with Amanda and David Vandergraff amounted to the worst kind of torture, although David pegged Amanda as the scary one. In the end, David wanted to apologize to *her*, but Amanda appeared unaffected by the display of emotion. She stayed firm but not cruel, and quite clear. No magic.

"Do you want to sit down with us in the dining room for a minute?" Amanda asked.

"You're not in trouble," David added.

She nodded politely and floated, as she always did, into the dining room.

"We have found a good private investigator," David said. At least, not one of the three different PIs who had failed to find Crystal and his kids. So, no strikes against him yet. "Unless…this may be a strange question…but you don't know where we could find a wizard private investigator? Perhaps it would help if they had all the facts."

"No, I don't know about anything like that."

"David, I told you," Amanda said. "You can't Google 'Wizard PI' and expect to find something."

"That's why I'm asking her," he said.

"Do you know how many wizards there are in the world? Even if there are wizard PIs, what are the chances she knows one?"

"Okay," he said. "Anyway, Samantha, it would be helpful to know more about the people your parents know. Do you have other family?"

He treaded carefully here, he didn't want her to read between the lines and realize they wanted to find her real guardians…just in case.

"My Grandma, my dad's mom. She lives in a nursing home in Baytown. You could talk to her, but she's pretty confused. She would probably say she saw my dad yesterday even if she hadn't."

"And your other grandparents?"

"Dead."

David wondered whether or not he should change his retirement plan based on the apparently shorter life expectancy of a wizard.

"Sorry," David said.

"My dad is an only child. But my mom has two sisters. She hasn't spoken to my Aunt Irene for as long as I can remember. But she does get along with my Aunt Charlotte. I see her a couple times a year."

"Can you write down their full names?" Amanda asked, passing her a piece of paper. "And addresses or phone numbers."

"Aunt Charlotte lives in New Orleans, but I don't know where. My mom is from Nevada and she said Aunt Irene stayed there. Las Vegas. But, who knows now."

"Friends?" Amanda asked.

"My mom is in a coven with some other women. I already called all of them. They don't know where she is. But they are casting incantations to help find her and bring her back. They would be happy to help, I'm sure, but they won't talk to a human PI."

"I suppose we could call them," David said. "Would they talk to us?"

"Maybe. But I doubt they would tell you anything they didn't tell me."

"Does her coven know what spell it was…that they couldn't stop?" Amanda asked.

"No. But, they had a few ideas. They said my Mom had been damaged by dark magic and went to them for help. They said they thought they healed her. But maybe whatever it was came back, and she tried to fix it on her own."

A prickle ran up David's neck. Amanda didn't react. They both knew the dark magic had come from him, when he had accidentally deflected her spell.

"Samantha, you're welcome to stay here as long as you need to," David said. "But hopefully we'll find them soon. Who knows, maybe even by Christmas."

"Or December 21," Samantha said.

"Okay…that seems like as good a day as any," David said.

"It's the Winter Solstice, David," Amanda said. "It's an important wizard holiday."

"Oh. Sure."

After their talk with Samantha, David pulled Amanda into his office.

"Help me out a little bit here," he said. "If there are wizard holidays I'm supposed to know about, I'd appreciate it if you let me know. I don't want to ignore the holidays my kids celebrate. By the way, if we are planning on just ignoring wizard Christmas, I think we should have made that decision together. I thought you didn't want to be the evil stepmother, and now you're taking away wizard Christmas?"

"It's not wizard Christmas," she said with a smile. "It's just a wizard holiday that happens to be in December. It's the last day of the wizard year. The darkest day. On that day, dark wizards celebrate the darkness itself. Light wizards celebrate the triumph of light over darkness. There are no gifts you have to buy, so don't freak out about it."

"When do you think we should call Child Protective Services?"

"About what?"

"Samantha. Her parents have abandoned her. We can't keep her indefinitely."

"I didn't even think about that. Old habit from my parents, I guess. Wizards don't usually involve human authority figures in their affairs."

"All right then, I guess we'll have to call Wizard Child Protective Services."

"There is no such thing."

"Clearly," he said with emphasis. "You know, wizard society is a train wreck."

"Exactly. That's why we're a part of regular society."

Christmas break provided many opportunities for forbidden magic. Mom had to work and Dad said he wouldn't work over the holidays, but he did, holed up in his home office all the time or rushing off to the office saying, "Please, please, please be good while I'm gone. And, don't tell your mother I left you alone. Please, please, please, behave," code for "Don't do magic." By some mysterious Mom logic, she had taken it for granted that she had closed the case on the whole magic issue. That what had happened to Emmy provided incontrovertible proof of magic's inherent evil, and no would ever say differently again. But they didn't fool Dad. Patrick could tell by the manic way he asked them to be good and how whenever he came home, he rushed around the house checking on everyone.

Patrick felt bad about doing magic behind his parents' back, and lying about it. Especially Dad, who seemed so freaked out all the time. Patrick didn't consider himself a goody-goody type or anything, but he had never so willfully and knowingly disobeyed his parents. Although, whether or not Patrick actually did any magic was debatable. He still sucked.

Patrick suspected every one of his siblings except for him, including the Colters, was crazy. And not fun crazy, *real* crazy. Insane. He should feel grateful he had dodged the bullet somehow, but he didn't. For one, keeping them from killing each other on accident seemed like a big job. And, two…he felt embarrassed to say it…but he felt left out. Maybe they acted crazy because they had magic, and he didn't. Could wizard parents have a non-wizard child? No one knew for sure. Perhaps he had no magic and a long life of normal ahead of him. Real dark wizards, like mom and dad, worked hard to fake normal and longed for nothing more than not to be crazy. *What was so great about being boring?*

He'd only successfully seen one second into the future. The worst possible superpower he could imagine. And, it could have been a fluke. Maybe it had happened a few times before, such as when he pulled Emmy out of the way of the truck, but he couldn't call on the power at will. Currently, he had no idea what would happen in the next second, which would have come in handy right about now.

Emmy perched on the edge on the roof.

"Xavier, if you don't help, I might die," she said matter-of-factly. "I know you can, you just don't want to. And that's fine, but then you'll have to be okay with me dying and it being your fault."

"That doesn't bother me," Xavier said.

"Yes, it would," Emmy countered. "Even Patrick is helping."

Patrick paced around with his brothers on the driveway. They reminded him of dogs circling a squirrel in a tree. Evangeline also planned on helping, always keen to participate in anything unreasonable. Or, perhaps she wanted a front row seat for Emmy's ultimate demise. Samantha sat on the backyard picnic table. She decided not to help. She didn't want to mess up the spell with her incompatible magic. But, she sat as if prepared to fly into the air and catch Emmy if she had to. She had become quieter and maybe…less shiny. Patrick figured her parents disappearing and abandoning her understandably upset her. But, Evangeline had said the dark magic hurt her. Living with seven dark wizards could poison the pure of heart.

Samantha glowing less brightly didn't make Patrick want to stare at her any less. If anything, he wanted to stare at her more. All the time. To make sure she didn't suddenly blow away.

"Emmy," Patrick called. "I assume it wouldn't help for me to say that this is the worst idea you've ever had and that you really, really, shouldn't do it?"

"Patrick, I don't even hear you talk when you say things like that. You're just moving your lips."

"Don't count on my magic," he said. "My being here might not make a difference."

"I don't want to hear any 'I can'ts'," she said, like a miniature blonde football coach. "Magic is all about 'I can'. Besides, Patrick, you may be more doing more magic than you think. It's not always obvious."

"It will be obvious if you fall to your death," Patrick said.

"Come down, Emmy," Jude said.

"What? You said we could do it," Emmy said.

"No, I didn't. This one's all you. I thought we would try it with the neighbor's dog and be done with it."

"It worked with the dog," she argued.

"It didn't work with the angel statue," Patrick reminded them. He pointed to the pieces of lawn angel scattered across the drive.

"That's how I know it will work," Emmy said. "You don't care about the statue. But, you didn't want the dog to die. And, you care more about me than you did about the dog. I know you can do it. I want you to see what you can do."

"So, this is for our benefit?" Patrick asked.

"This is exactly like those trust exercises at leadership camp. I trust you. Even the girl."

Evangeline glared up at her with arms crossed.

"Don't insult your net before you jump into it, Emmy," Jude said.

"Get ready," she said. "Five seconds."

"Wait, what am I supposed to do again?" Patrick asked.

"Force field," Evangeline said.

"That's not an explanation."

"It's the same thing as with the dog," Jude said. "Just imagine her slowing down and stopping before she hits the ground. Really *want* it. You have to want her to be okay."

"Xavier, are you going to help?" Emmy asked.

Xavier silently positioned himself as the fourth corner of a square made by Patrick, Jude, and Evangeline, and glared up at Emmy. Which, hopefully, meant yes.

"Ready?" she asked, looking blissfully calm about jumping off their second-story roof onto pavement. She didn't wear shoes. A good sign of crazy in forty-degree weather.

Patrick, on the other hand, could hear his heart beating in his face. Adrenaline shot from his brain to his toes. No one else seemed this nervous, although Jude at least concentrated hard. He had his eyes on her like a baseball player watches a pitch. Evangeline and Xavier had their eyes on her, too, but with emotionless faces, as if whether Emmy lived or died didn't interest them much. Although, they pretty much looked that way all the time.

Emmy took a running start and leaped with abandon, as if jumping into a lake on the first day of summer. It happened so fast. In the seconds they had before she would hit ground, Patrick visualized her slowing down and stopping. He panicked even more when he became distracted by the events of the next several seconds in the future and lost grasp of the present. He heard a crash behind him and turned toward the sound, even though he knew the crash hadn't happened yet. But, with or without his help, Jude and Xavier reached up to Emmy and she grasped one of each of their hands. She hovered and then they helped her down to the ground as if they helped a princess out of a carriage.

Samantha clapped, and Evangeline cried, "Awesome!"

Patrick had to admit he had never seen anything cooler in his life. But he alone knew they would bask in their accomplishment for no more than three seconds.

Dad crashed his car into the mailbox. He climbed out of the car and over the scattered bricks and ran down the driveway. The look on his face, simply...indescribable. Trees blocked the house fairly well, so Mundanes driving by wouldn't see Emmy's trick, but Patrick and the others hadn't counted on the fact that Dad would arrive at the head of the driveway at just the right time to see his daughter leap from the roof into the arms of her willing brothers.

Dad's face had gone pale and his eyes had increased in size and doubled in crazy. He pointed at them with a trembling hand but appeared completely speechless. He leaned over and put his hands on his knees as if he had finished a sprint and might throw up.

"Do you think he's having a heart attack?" Emmy whispered.

He stood back up and blew past them into the house without a word. He slammed the front door so hard the Christmas lights on the house shook.

"I suppose adolescence is the worst possible time to find out you're a wizard," Amanda said in a tone several measures quieter than the one David used. A tone of defeat. "You're losing your childhood and you would do anything to hang on that wonder, that magic. Then all of sudden, you can. You can hang on to that magic forever if you just choose to practice magic. You don't need faith. The magic of the world is right in front of your face. It's an intoxicating thing."

Her words sounded earnest, wistful, as if part of her still felt that way.

David paced in their bedroom.

"When I was young, it was harder," she continued. "I had to get it out of my system. And, I hope that's all that's happening with them. When I was their age, I didn't want to listen to my parents either. But, eventually, what they taught me did stick with me. I knew in my gut they were right. I knew the magic inside me was a bad thing. But, if I had never met you, I don't know what would have happened. When I fell in love with you…it was like the gap inside me wasn't as big anymore. I could cope. The whole world looked different."

She turned away from him and rearranged the books on her nightstand. He didn't think she had ever said anything so romantic, even on their wedding day.

"What I'm saying," she said in a more business-like tone, "is that this could easily be a phase. We just have to keep them alive until they grow up a little."

"How do we do that?"

"Keep them from doing magic."

"How? We can't watch them every second of every day. I feel like I've been pretty close to it. It's like they rush to it every moment I turn my head. Even if I don't go back to work, I have to sleep, for fuck's sake."

"It's the best we can do."

"I don't know if I agree with *our* choice to not practice." David put air quotes around "our."

"To be quite frank, I don't think you're in any place to say. You don't have the information you need to make a decision."

"I'm still not happy about you poking holes in my brain. I wouldn't bring it up as an argument against me if I were you."

"Fine, then, tell me. Why in the world do you think we should practice magic?"

"So we know what we're doing. Even if magic is like a

baby defusing a bomb, wouldn't it be better if the baby had a little bit of training? If the bomb is going to go off either way. You said yourself, wizards do magic on accident. I'm sorry, but that seems a lot more dangerous than doing magic on purpose."

"It's not just the actual spells that are dangerous. It's the magical energy that's created when you practice. I can already feel it in the house. It's like the air is heavier. Can't you feel it?"

Yes, he could.

"That's why I forbid it," she said. "Some accidental magic is better than lots of magic on purpose. The more magic in the house, the more likely it will mess with people's minds. And we have *eight* powerful wizards living here. Six of whom are going through hormonal changes that make even normal teens act crazy. That has a lot of potential for disaster. As you may have noticed, it's not going well so far."

"Yeah, it's *not* going well so far. Because we're doing it *your way.*" He shouted the last two words for emphasis. "Your way—which as far as I can tell, is all just hate and lies. Hating who you really are, and trying to hide it. Hating everyone else who is like you. And, the lies—forbidding magic left and right, but then still doing it yourself whenever you feel like it. That's what you've been doing. And that's what's not working."

She stared him down with eyes that seemed to spit sparks. David backed up. He had to admit, his wife's glares looked more threatening now he knew she was a witch, and a wicked one at that. He hadn't won many arguments in their marriage and felt he had poor odds on this one, too. He also usually didn't get the last word…but he did this time. For once, she had no reply, no counter-argument. She turned away from him and left the room.

David retreated to his office. Being a wizard felt lonely. No parenting books or websites existed about how to guide your magical children effectively through their formative years. And,

David had no one to ask. Not counting his kids, he knew only one dark practicing wizard who hadn't died. Perhaps, he had no better option. He opened a blank email and stared at it.

CHAPTER TWENTY

Patrick overheard his mother on the phone cancelling an appointment with a locksmith. From what he caught from her side of the call, she wanted him to put locks on the outside of all the bedroom doors, but she changed her mind. Perhaps she wanted Patrick to overhear it as a warning. One more magical infraction and she would lock them in their rooms until they were old enough to vote. She might do it, too. His mom loved control, and she would get it one way or another.

For now, all the kids were grounded, but Mom and Dad allowed them to move around the inside of the house at their own free will. Patrick enjoyed this freedom by pacing around the upstairs family room, practicing for imprisonment.

Samantha appeared in his path as suddenly as if she had materialized by magic. From his limited understanding of magic, he doubted anything that dramatic could happen. But she could enter a room like an Olympic diver entered a pool. No splash.

Samantha moved close to him. His heart began its predictable hammering.

"May I check something?" she asked. "I am curious."

"Okay."

She placed her hands on his chest, as Emmy had done to Jude before she went crazy. Patrick pushed her away.

"I know what I'm doing," she said.

"Emmy always knows what she's doing, too."

"It's not like that. I know how to be careful. And, it's not a spell. I just want to taste your magic." She licked her lips.

"What does that mean?" he asked, although he barely cared. He wanted her to do it.

"There are flavors of magic for every second, of every hour, of every day of the year. Every wizard has their moment. The moments closest to the winter solstice are the darkest, and the moments closest to the summer solstice are the lightest."

"Where are you?"

"I'm a spring witch. We're about fertility, and youth, and change."

"We're winter?" he asked. He knew it instinctively.

She nodded.

"The opposite of spring," Patrick said.

"No, summer is the opposite of winter. Spring and winter lie next to each other." She lined up her hands, thumb to thumb, to illustrate her point further, as if she needed to. "And, I am a March. Right where winter and spring touch. The gateway."

That almost sounded like a come-on….maybe. He had enough trouble understanding girls without the magical riddles.

She replaced her hands on his chest and then leaned the side of her face between her hands, right over his heart. He knew she could hear it beating out of control. He could live with that as long as she didn't press herself close enough to feel what went on below his belt. Well…he did want her to do that. He wanted her to do lots of things.

She closed her eyes and inhaled deeply. "Hmm…"

Patrick breathed deeply, too, but his breath sounded jerky.

He wrapped his arms around her and pulled her closer.

She looked up at him and licked her lips again.

"Autumn, I think," she said. "Perhaps even, September." She said the word *September* like she might say the word *chocolate*. "You've been misplaced somehow. You don't belong with them."

"September really is the opposite of March."

"Opposite maybe, but not that different. It's the other equinox. Equinox wizards sometimes have trouble learning magic because their magic is too complex, light and dark in equal measure. But once they figure it out, they can be the best ones. The most versatile. They're more moderate, less overwhelmed by extremes, so they can be more precise. At least, this is what my mother told me, to make me feel better when I couldn't do spells."

She stayed in his arms. Her lips glittered.

"Everyone is in your family is winter," she said.

"You've tasted them?" he asked.

She giggled. "Well, not like *this*. The closer a wizard is to the solstice, the more obvious it is. You're complicated. I had to get really close. The others aren't so complex."

Their foreheads touched.

"They're close to the solstice then?" he asked. "The darkest wizards?"

"I think so. I'm not good enough to pinpoint dates. But I would say they are all either December or January. Some of them could be November, or February, perhaps. I've only really checked Emmy and Jude. She's a January. He's a December."

He couldn't help but picture her 'checking' Jude, and wanted to punch him in the stomach for about the millionth time in his life.

"But, you all shouldn't be so concerned about being dark. Darkness doesn't mean *bad*. Winter isn't *bad*. It's just a season.

The Earth needs winter just as much as summer. And Texas could probably use a lot more of it."

She giggled at her joke. He caught her parted lips in a kiss. He had kissed two other girls before and didn't think it had gone well. But, this went differently. She placed his bottom lip between hers and parted his mouth more. She gently dragged the tip of her tongue along the side of his. He had never felt less wintery.

One of David's earliest memories was about Christmas. Lately, he had run the memory through his head over and over, wishing he could make it 'sticky' so he could live it again. With so much missing, this memory of his childhood felt like a nugget of gold in his brain.

The Vandergraffs didn't celebrate Christmas. As a child, he would have at least known why. They would have celebrated the Solstice, instead. Although, of course, he didn't remember any of that. He just remembered the absence of Christmas and how much he hated his parents for not letting him have Christmas like all the other kids. Even as an adult, he never forgave them for this, especially since, as an adult with no understanding of wizardry, he had seen this as an arbitrary cruelty, and child abuse in its own right, one of the many things that had made Amanda's job of gently removing the Vandergraffs from David's life easy. As she had said, she had removed only memories of the actual physical abuse. David still had plenty left in his mind about his parents to piss him off. And, no Christmas topped the list.

In first grade, right before Christmas break, all the kids talked on and on about Santa Claus. David remembered asking his teacher, Miss Atwood, why Santa Claus didn't visit his house and if that meant he was naughty. He remembered this in part, because Miss Atwood cried when he said this, and he hadn't seen many grown-ups cry. She had seemed old to him at the time, but David guessed Miss Atwood had just graduated college, in her early twenties. She had very curly blonde hair and wore glasses.

She told him, "No. It doesn't mean that you're naughty. You're a very good boy. Santa tries very hard to visit every child, but sometimes even Santa makes mistakes. Sometimes he will spill milk on parts of his list or he will accidentally leave pages at home. He has a very hard job, you see, and he's very old."

The next day, she pulled him aside before recess and said, "I called Santa and he wanted you to know he's very sorry for missing your house. He said one of his reindeer ate some pages of his list. The missing pages were from the Nice List, and you were on it."

"Really?"

"Yes. He wants to make sure he doesn't miss you this year. So he wants you to write him a letter telling him what you want for Christmas. He said to give the letter to me, and I'll make sure he gets it."

David rushed home that day and told four-year-old James all about how Santa Claus had missed them by mistake, and would come this year. They just had to write him a letter. James opened his eyes wide and ran to find David a piece of paper and a marker. David carefully wrote two letters, one for him and one for James, starting with Dear Santa and followed by a list of toys. When he couldn't write the words, he drew pictures. He signed their names. James leaned over him and watched carefully to make sure he got it right.

David took the letters to Miss Atwood so she could give them to Santa. On Christmas Eve, he started to get nervous. They didn't have a fireplace for him to come down. They didn't have a tree or stockings where Santa could put presents. He should have warned Santa in the letter. Maybe that's the real reason Santa had never come. He saw their house and thought they didn't believe in him.

But lo and behold, Santa came right before dinner on Christmas Eve. Since they didn't have a chimney, Santa rang the doorbell. David remembered a blast of fear and happiness at once when his father opened the door and saw Santa Claus, complete with the red suit, white beard, and bag of toys. He wished Santa had known to come at night while his parents slept, as he did for the other kids.

This bizarre appearance probably baffled David's father so much, he forgot to be angry right away. He said, "I think you have the wrong house."

"Is this the house of David and James Vandergraff?" Santa asked in a deep, authoritative voice.

"How do you know my sons' names?"

"I'm Santa Claus," Santa said, and then he winked at David's father. Grown-up David couldn't help but laugh at this ridiculous act.

"We didn't ask for this," his father said. "You need to leave."

"Just take the presents," Santa said, in a less Santa-like voice. He took a wrapped package out of his bag, "James, this one's for you."

James approached Santa like a squirrel trying to take a piece of food out of someone's hand. Then Santa gave a gift to David.

"Merry Christmas," he said and then left quickly.

David feared his father would take away his present. He looked at his brother and said, "Run."

They ran out the back door before their parents could react, and into the wooded area behind their house. They ran until they had to stop and catch their breath. He had worn only socks and his feet hurt from running across the rocky ground. But, he didn't care. He and James sat down on the ground and opened their presents. David got a Lego set and James got a toy car. They played with their toys in the middle of the woods until their hands got stiff with cold. He didn't remember what happened after that.

The grown-up David figured that memory had stuck with him for a reason. A far more important memory than his little self would have ever guessed. It would have shown little dark wizard David that good magic existed, too. Because if Santa Claus wasn't an example of a good wizard, he didn't know what was.

David had reeled this memory though his mind so much that week before Christmas, he wondered if he had summoned Santa by accidental magic. Santa Claus, played by his brother James, came to the door unexpectedly that Friday. Of course, this Santa Claus dressed in a black V-neck sweater and jeans and didn't have a bag of toys.

"It looks like Christmas threw up on your house," he said.

"Hey, James. I didn't know you were coming."

"I was in town," he said.

"Are you checking up on me?"

"I can't visit my brother and my nieces and nephews on Christmas? Besides, I believe I have two more to meet. I brought them gifts."

"Where?" James didn't have a thing with him. David guessed that meant he didn't plan to stay.

Emmy and Evangeline came down the stairs to see the visitor.

"Gift cards," James said. With a flourish, five gift cards

appeared in his hand, splayed like playing cards. David wanted to ask him to do it again so he could watch more carefully. A common parlor trick or…not?

"Thanks, Uncle James," Emmy said.

She reached for the cards and he held them out of reach.

"Have you been nice this year?" he asked.

She stood there, with her mouth slightly open, and looked stumped.

"I'm just kidding," James said. "You can have one anyway."

She smiled and took a card.

"You too," he said to Evangeline. "Come on."

"This is my brother, James," David explained. "It's okay."

Evangeline approached him slowly and took a card. She examined it with a puzzled look. David would have to explain the concept of gift cards later.

"Attagirl," James said.

"Can I get you something to drink?" David asked.

"Sure."

His brother followed him into the kitchen, and David handed him a Saint Arnold.

"Emmy's gotten pretty," James said. "You should lock her in a tower until her twenty-first birthday."

"We considered something like that."

"Ha. Sounds like Amanda. She here?"

"Work. Where's Justin?"

"He already left for his parents' house for Christmas."

"You mean you don't spend Christmas together?"

He shrugged. "Nah, it's easier this way. Fewer questions from his relatives."

"I didn't know you were always alone on Christmas. Why didn't you tell me? You could have been coming here."

"It's not a big deal. I have friends."

"But, you visit me *this* Christmas. Is that a coincidence? I mean…it's nice to see you and all."

James peeled the label off his beer. "So, I can't check up on you?"

"I told you, you don't have to worry. I'm fine."

"There's magic in this house," James said matter-of-factly.

"It's the kids. We can't keep them from doing it. We're trying."

"I've just been thinking. If you don't remember magic, then you don't remember why you shouldn't do it." James continued to stare at his bottle while he created a pile of shredded label on the counter.

"Trust me, I have Amanda for that. I'm not planning on practicing magic. At least…not dark magic."

James winced. "It doesn't work like that. Dark wizards can't do good magic."

"As Amanda tells me again and again," David said. "But, I'm not sure if I believe that. Being evil is a choice. No one is born that way."

"I read about the wildfire in the news. That was your development it wiped out, wasn't it?"

"Yeah. I can't believe you noticed that."

"Did you do that?"

David huffed. "Did I set that fire and destroy my company? No, of course not."

"Then maybe Amanda, or one of your kids."

"You're accusing them of arson? That's out of line. Besides, no matter how much they hate me, none of them wants to be poor." As he said it, he couldn't help but think about what Xavier had said when he took him shopping. *Wizards shouldn't care about material things.*

"Wizards don't need a match."

"It's a drought year, James. The wildfire was caused by a jackass with a cigarette butt or something like that."

"Can I tell you something in confidence?" James asked. He

looked up at him for the first time in the conversation.

"Sure."

"Five years ago, I cast a spell. I don't practice…but I thought it was a special case. Justin was really unhappy. He had this horrible job. He worked fourteen hours a day and on weekends and his boss treated him like shit. We never saw each other and when we did, he was so tired and stressed, he was an ass. I thought it was going to break us up. So, I cast a spell. I should have known better than to do one so complicated. Even Mom and Dad didn't do this one. It was a catalyst spell. It's supposed to change your circumstances. I cast it around Justin's job, with the goal of positive change, to either make his current job better or find him a new one. The thing about a catalyst spell is that you can only define the consequences, not how they will be achieved. Humans don't have the depth to understand how magic works and can't change the moving parts. They can only push *go*. But if you do it right, you can get the change you want, one way or another."

"It didn't work."

"It did."

"Oh, God…" David put two and two together without James having to explain. He didn't know much about James and Justin's daily life, but he did know about this. The story had even aired on the news in Houston.

"The next day, when Justin was out of the office running errands for his boss, a motherfucking tornado touched down right on top of his office. It was a stormy day, but a tornado didn't touch down anywhere else in the whole goddamn town. Fifteen people died inside that office, including his asshole boss, but also including… fourteen innocent, random people."

James leaned over on the counter and stared at the granite.

"James, you can't…"

"It fucking worked. It took him six months to find another job, but he did. A better one. He's much happier now." James raised his beer bottle in a highly ironic 'cheers.'

"Does he know?"

"That I murdered fifteen people to cheer him up? No, it's never come up. Thankfully, Justin isn't a wizard, so he wouldn't even begin to suspect I had anything to do with it." He sighed. "I've never told anyone about that spell."

"It's not your fault."

"Those people would be alive if it wasn't for me."

"It could be a coincidence."

James laughed darkly. "No."

"I'm sorry, James."

"Listen, I'm not saying for sure that's what happened to your business. I just want you to know. It doesn't matter what your intentions are. Magic sucks."

CHAPTER TWENTY-ONE

On the afternoon of December 21, Amanda returned from shopping all frizzy and sweaty. She put a loaded paper grocery bag onto the kitchen counter and said, "Fine. Here you go."

"What?" David asked.

"You get your wish. As long as it's just observances, and no significant magic. And if someone calls the fire department, you get to explain why we thought we'd light our backyard on fire. Now help me get the wood from the back of the truck."

"We're going to celebrate the solstice?"

"You said you didn't want to ignore a holiday like your parents did. And the kids want to, so I didn't want to be the bad guy all by myself. I figure it doesn't hurt anything to light some candles and have a fire. As long as there is no real magic."

Samantha and Evangeline's voices uncharacteristically lit up the dinner conversation. Apparently, Emmy didn't have a monopoly on the practice of speech. The family had just been having conversations that didn't interest Samantha and Evangeline, until now.

"You don't have to feel bad," Evangeline said to David. "You're already celebrating the solstice. You have lights all over the house. That's what you do. You lights lamps or candles or use Christmas lights. It's for the triumph of light over darkness."

"And you can see our house from space," Patrick added.

"You have a tree," Samantha said. "We always have a tree. We put white lights on it, and drape herbs and fruits on it. An evergreen tree is about life surviving through the winter. Technically, wizards are supposed to have an evergreen wreath, not a tree. The circle represents the cycle of the seasons. But we have a tree to blend in with the neighbors."

"We didn't have a tree when I was growing up," David said. "Maybe a wreath…I don't know."

"I think a lot of wizards celebrate it differently," Samantha said. "We do a bell ceremony where we honor each of the four seasons with a different bell. They sound nice alone, but beautiful together. It's about harmony, you know. A lot of wizards give gifts to each other to make it more like Christmas, and so do we, but the most important thing is you're supposed to give gifts to nature."

"What do you buy for nature?" Patrick said.

Samantha laughed. "It's stuff like grains and seeds for the animals."

"We didn't have a tree either," Evangeline said to David. "We had a bonfire."

"We always have a party," Samantha said. "With lots and lots of food and wine. You're supposed to celebrate, and be with the people you love. The louder and happier you are, the better you can stave off the darkness. Also, you're supposed to celebrate to welcome the sun. We stay up all night and then do a ritual at sunrise to celebrate the end of the darkness."

"No," Evangeline said. "You're not supposed to be loud and happy. You're supposed to be quiet and contemplative. It's a time of darkness and meditation. We'd have to be quiet for hours before the fire was lit."

"That doesn't sound like fun," Samantha said.

"It's not supposed to be fun," Evangeline said. "It's the darkest day of the year. But, it is kind of fun after the fire is lit. We would throw in herbs and seeds representing the trials of the previous year. The fire would spark and spit with all these crazy colors and smells. Then you use the ashes from the fire in potions and spells. They're good luck."

"We're just going to do a simple light ceremony," Amanda said. "You'll get a chance to be sad *and* happy, okay? Everybody wins. I'm the matriarch of this house. I get to decide."

Samantha and Evangeline nodded.

"Could we do it the real way?" Samantha asked quietly. "Please? It's a simple spell…frivolous," she added.

"One spell," Amanda said. "Just the light one."

David and his family plus Samantha stood in a circle around a small pile of unlit firewood in the backyard. They stood arranged by age: David, Amanda, Jude, Patrick, Xavier, Samantha, Emmy, Evangeline, and then of course, David again, all twice as thick with jackets and scarves. The air felt hard with cold, a determined cold that seeped through all of David's layers. They held candles—but no matches—in their gloved hands. The family had gone through the house turning off lights. *All* of the lights. They even turned off the red lights glowing on electronics. They had unplugged the entire house. However, David could see easily. An orange haze of light peeked up from the trees. Millions of lights lit up the world all around them. Darkness didn't exist in the middle of Houston.

As soon as they had managed to arrange themselves into a circle, the kids got quiet without David or Amanda instructing them to. Wizards standing in a circle felt significant to David. When they got in that position, they snapped into place. The air became denser around him and he was rooted to the spot, as if with extra gravity. But he didn't feel confined. He felt powerful. He plugged into an energy source he didn't even know existed. His fingers had an itchy, tingly feeling. He knew he could do magic.

The paper in Amanda's hand crinkled loudly as she held it close to her face. She had done her research, which David found endearing and impressive. She had talked to Samantha and Evangeline and some of the witches Penelope's mom knew, and had created a ritual designed specifically for them, as the matriarch of the family should. The matriarch of the family always directed group spell casting, because she understood her family's magic, the purpose of each family member, and knew how to keep them in balance—a tall order, since Amanda didn't know much about some of the newest members of her family and knew even less about magic. But, David had never known Amanda to say she couldn't do anything, so why start now?

Amanda owning this task shocked the kids, but not David. He knew her better than anyone did. Thus, he knew her mind and the rest of her often disagreed. Her left brain dug her feet into the ground and wouldn't budge. That part of her would say things such as, "We're not practicing magic," and "We're divorced," until kingdom come. She would say it. She'd believe it. And she'd do the opposite, because occasionally the parts of her not governed by her left brain would break free. David may not be able to sway the left-brain side of her, but he could influence her other side, and he thought that maybe he had actually convinced her of something, for once.

And, part of Amanda had *really wanted* to be convinced, because wizards stayed wizards, no matter how many years they'd been indoctrinated otherwise. They listened to forces that had nothing to do with logic or reason, making them stupid, reckless, destructive, and exciting. And they liked to play with fire. Literally and figuratively.

"How I am supposed to read this in the dark?" Amanda asked. "How do people do this?"

"You're supposed to have it memorized," Evangeline said.

"Your eyesight is terrible," David said. "Let me see it."

She thrust the paper out of his reach. "Back off."

"Why don't you just let Evangeline or Samantha speak?" David said. "I'm sure they have some stuff memorized."

"No," Amanda said. "It's supposed to be me. My words." Amanda let out a shivery sigh. "I'm sorry. I know I'm not supposed to do this." She took her phone out of her pocket and turned it on. She illuminated her paper with the dim blue light.

"First we honor the darkness,

For in darkness, our eyes are not distracted by the flash and flare of Mundane sights

So, only in darkness can we truly see.

In the silence of the deepest night, our ears are not assaulted by Mundane sounds

So, only in darkness can we truly hear.

In darkness, we are unable to see danger and are rendered vulnerable

So, only in darkness can we truly feel.

We do not believe that light exists in spite of darkness. We believe that light exists because of it.

Darkness is the only fertile ground for light. It is the only garden where light can be sown.

So, now we experience the darkness. Use this time in the dark and quiet to use your deeper senses. Experience what you are called to experience. The answers wait for you in the darkness. Do not deny them."

And then, she fell silent.

David couldn't hear the cars on the highway anymore. He couldn't hear the music playing down the street. He could hear only the breathing of the others in the circle. And the sky…the orange haze disappeared and the sky reminded David of the one over Big Bend. Millions of stars set against a perfect pitch black. The moon cast a crisp, blue light on the scene. With her words, or perhaps with some other magic deeper than words, she had called the darkness. David pictured it as a bubble around them.

The quiet didn't feel as awkward as David would have expected. No one giggled or even coughed or sighed. His lungs felt larger. He could breathe. This darkness didn't feel frightening. In fact, David couldn't remember ever feeling so safe. The darkness was the foundation that everything else was built on. The garden where the universe grew. The simplest, most basic thing in existence. And it was spectacular.

He supposed that was the answer that waited for him. That darkness in itself was not evil. Darkness was peace. Potential. Home.

"The solstice marks not only the height of darkness, but also the return of the sun." Amanda read from a second sheet of paper. "The cycle of the seasons represents a promise from God. A promise that in darkness, light never truly falters. Although it appears dark here, the sun burns with all its glory on the other side of the Earth. With the change of the seasons, God reminds us that darkness always ends. Light always exists and will always return when missing. There is no night that doesn't end. No nightmare from which you cannot wake. No hurt that cannot heal.

"Remembering this promise, we will now sow light in the garden of darkness. For tonight, the darkness is at its richest and most fertile. Use your deeper senses to find and sow your light."

David's heart rate picked up. Now he and the others would perform a spell. And, not just any spell: a flashy, awesome spell. The first spell he would do on purpose since he had lost his memories.

Earlier, he had doubted his ability and hadn't succeeded in practice. But he hadn't considered the magic the ritual would invoke. He felt confident now. He knew he could do it as easily as he knew he could clap his hands on command.

Evangeline would go first. The youngest always did. She pulled David's oversized man's gloves off her hands and stuffed them in her pockets. She held out her hand, palm facing up, and blew on her palm as if trying to ignite a fire. A puddle of emerald green light appeared in her hand, as if she opened a portal to another dimension. She dipped the wick of her candle into the light, and the candle burned with a green flame.

He knew Evangeline could do it, but couldn't wait to see what his previously unmagical daughter could do. When he saw the look in Emmy's eyes, he knew she could do it. Her reckless determination and confidence would make her a fantastic witch. So much of spell casting was simply about truly wanting something and believing it could be. Sure enough, a ball of fire came from all the way down her arm and rolled off her fingertips, as if she pitched a softball. She tossed it in the air and then it rested in her hand. Way more fire than necessary to light a candle. She only had to hold the wick within the general proximity of the candle to get it lit.

Samantha did something similar to what he had caught her

doing in Emmy's room. Globs of bright white light oozed from her hand, like one of those lava lamps from the eighties. She touched the wick to one of the globs and instead of a true flame, a little ball of light perched on top of the candle.

Xavier's flame mesmerized David. The flame danced, alight with the full spectrum of colors, moved in unpredictable directions, and gave off iridescent sparks. They would no longer need to purchase fireworks for the Fourth of July.

David could tell they all held their breath for Patrick. In that moment, they all wanted him to succeed. David thought their combined magical good wishes would have a powerful effect. Patrick had the face of an Olympian preparing for a race. Not nervous. Just focused. He narrowed his eyebrows at his palm. He glanced for a second at Samantha, and then turned back to his palm. His hand turned bright gold, as if King Midas had touched him.

There was a collective, "*Ooo.*"

Patrick smiled broadly, and held his hand in front of his face to inspect it. Then he touched one golden fingertip to the wick. It didn't work at first, but then he shook his hand and a flame erupted from under his fingernail.

Jude had something impressive up his sleeve. Without even needing a moment to prepare, he sent a golden rivulet out of his palm. It meandered upward like a quickly growing plant. That was exactly what it turned into. The sprout became thicker, grew higher, and branched off into a tree. When he finished, the tree looked as perfect as if sketched on paper, stood five feet above his hand, and flames flickered on the branches instead of leaves.

"Holy shit," Patrick said.

Holy shit, indeed.

"I can't believe I have to follow that," Amanda said. "Well done, Jude."

Jude smiled with full teeth and dimples. He hadn't smiled

that way in a long time.

Amanda had a deep red flame. It swayed hypnotically and turned David into a moth. He couldn't keep his eyes off it and would have stuck his nose in it if Amanda hadn't said his name.

"Go on," she said.

His heart beat faster. He felt the pressure of everyone's eyes and everyone's expectations. What would they think of him if he couldn't do it? As the father, he should come up with something impressive and awe-inspiring. Something worthy of the head of household.

He thought about Amanda's original command, *find and sow the light.* So, first he had to find. He remembered how his fingers had felt itchy and tingly. He only had to recall the feeling for it to come back and spread up his hand and into his arm. It felt hot and cold at once, and built steadily without him even trying. He knew what to do instinctively. He clenched his fist, which was the trigger. He shot a ball of flame out of his knuckles that climbed into the sky like a flare. Thank God he had aimed his arm upward.

His light shot a good thirty feet into the air and then scattered in a rain of what reminded him of pixie dust. He looked at his unlit candle.

He heard a scattering of giggles.

"Hush…" he said.

"Try again," Evangeline prompted.

David held his fist up again and positioned the candle above it. He tried pumping his fist more gently. The same thing happened, although he spanned only about ten feet this time. He tried to follow the light with his candle as a catcher would follow a fly ball, which resulted in even more giggles.

Then, before he could ready himself, another fireball shot out of his fist unwillingly and went straight for Emmy.

She dove to the ground and dodged it.

"Oh, God. I'm so sorry, honey. That one was an accident.

Are you okay?"

She laughed so hard she couldn't answer.

"Why are you doing it like that?" Amanda asked.

"I have no idea," he said. "How do you make it stay on your hand?"

"No, the real question is, how did you shoot it out of your hand like that?" Xavier asked. "That's awesome. Show me how to do that."

"I would if I knew."

"Okay, try it again," Amanda said.

"Picture the light staying on your hand," Jude instructed. "Visualize in your head what you want it to look like."

David followed his instruction and managed to get the orange orb of light to hover only about a foot over his hand. He carefully dipped the wick of the candle into the orb and an orange flame stayed on the candle, while the rest of the orb sprinkled around him.

"Okay, try to get serious again," Amanda said. "We're not done."

She waited for quiet.

"Now we will combine our lights into a communal fire," she continued. "This symbolizes the importance of the connections wizards have with one another. Our lights are how we find each other in darkness. Wizards can always find each other. It is a sign God does not intend for wizards to be alone."

This seemed dangerous to David. He didn't like them throwing random unknown chemicals together to see what might happen. Starting with Evangeline again, they each used their candle to light a part of the campfire. The result prompted many *ooos* and *aaas*. The fire twisted and spat in a swirl of colors that reminded David of the Tasmanian devil. David kept his hand on the jug of water, but the fire relaxed into a more normal, yet multicolored, fire that swayed unpredictably but stayed in its ring.

"Do you think we can cook marshmallows on it?" Patrick asked.

"Yummy. S'mores," Emmy said.

"Just to be safe, let's not cook food with the magic fire," David said.

David noticed Patrick and Samantha held hands. *Okay...that is new.*

CHAPTER TWENTY-TWO

December 22 was a rainy, nasty, muddy day. Everyone stayed indoors except for Amanda, who had to work. David heard the doorbell ring from inside his office, where he attended to some last-minute business matters. When he came downstairs, he saw Emmy at the door, looking at none other than Rachel Colter wearing a black trench coat. David's heart skipped several beats.

Rachel leaned toward Emmy. "Aren't you a pretty little girl?" she said in her best why-don't-you-come-into-my-gingerbread-house voice. "Is your daddy home?"

Emmy peeked outside, and then at Rachel. "You're not wet."

"I have a very good umbrella," she said with a wink.

David stepped in front of Emmy. "What the hell are you doing here?" He scanned the room for Xavier and Evangeline. *They must be upstairs, thank God.* "The kids."

"Don't worry," she said. "They won't recognize me, I expect."

"Why would you come to my house?"

"Who is she?" Emmy asked.

"A business acquaintance," David said.

"Yes, David built the house that will fall on me one day," Rachel said.

Emmy laughed. "So you're a real witch?"

"Well, so are you, sweetie."

"A business acquaintance? Really?" Emmy asked David. "You're such a liar. Don't think I won't tell mom."

"My dear, your father is being quite honest. I am an investor interested in purchasing your father's business. My being a witch is mere coincidence."

"You're selling the business?" Emmy asked.

David glared at Rachel.

"No, that's not what I meant," Rachel said easily. "I am simply referring to the purchase of certain assets. He has many things of value."

"My office," David said in a cold-as-December-22 tone.

He bounded up the stairs and hoped she would move quickly, too. He wanted to avoid any more encounters between Rachel Colter and his kids.

He herded her into his office and shut the door. She glanced at the sofa bed still in the out position.

"You sleep in here?"

"That's none of your business."

"So, your wife didn't know?"

"Tell me what you want. Be mindful of the fact that walking onto a man's property where his children are is quite different from approaching him at his place of business. If you didn't like my attitude as a businessman, it's risky for you to test my attitude as just a man."

"Are you threatening me? So soon into our chat?" she said playfully.

She sat in the chair and lowered her head slightly, as if in deference to the pack leader of the territory she had walked onto. "I apologize. Both for coming here to your home, and for our disagreement in your office. I am here because in my time of sacred reflection on Mid-Winter's Eve, I was called to act. I was called to come here and pay my penance."

"I don't know what that means."

"Would you please sit?" she asked. She raised her eyes to him only slightly. Her statement sounded more like a request than a command. She gave him control.

David sat.

"You emailed me and wanted a favor," she said.

"I expected you to simply hit 'reply'."

Her inkpot eyes blinked at him impassively.

"I would like to hear your proposal," she said.

"It wasn't about money. It's too late for that. My employees have already been given their severance."

"I know. What was it about?"

"I can't believe I'm talking to you about this," he said. He paused and shook his head. "You're a practicing dark witch?"

"Quite."

"How dark?"

"You mean, where to do I sit on the solar calendar?"

"I suppose."

"December 31. Which is quite dark, as I'm sure you know."

"I've done some research on you," he said. "You're well-respected in the financial community. No criminal record. You're successful, and perhaps even, should I say...sane."

"Well, aren't you the charmer?"

"I don't mean any offense. I just want to know how that's possible."

"So, you marvel at my ability to be a practicing dark witch who is less than criminally insane."

"You could say that."

She laughed. "I thought I told you not to believe everything you hear about practicing wizards. Yes, David, you can be a practicing dark wizard and still function as part of civilized society. Dark wizards have a habit of blaming all their problems on magic. Everything they do that's bad is always due to magic, and not their own dark nature. Evil people do evil things and it has little to do with whether or not they practice magic."

"So dark wizards can practice good magic?"

"It depends on what you mean by 'good'. I assume you are asking whether or not dark wizards can do magic that has a positive impact. And of course, the answer is yes. Dark magic is destructive magic. It refers to the type of tool we carry, but not what we intend to do with it. But, we must understand our tool. It is destruction. Which can often be dangerous, imprecise, and quite evil. But it doesn't have to be. I have heard of dark wizards who are healers. Accomplished dark wizards practiced in the healing arts can destroy maladies while leaving the healthy tissue intact. They have their best luck with tumors, but can sometimes also attack bacteria, I believe. In a general sense, dark wizards can be good by destroying things that ought be destroyed. I would even say that those who know the ways of darkness are the best at destroying it. If they have the willpower for it, dark wizards can be excellent protectors. Policemen. Soldiers. Of course, they can also make the most terrible ones. It depends on whether or not they have the strength of character to limit their destruction to those who deserve it."

"You use dark magic in business?"

"Not really. I do use magic. Wizards often have a special skill. Mine is perception. I can see things other people can't. People say I have a good eye. I can buy businesses with potential that others don't see. That is absolutely correct, I just see it more clearly than they could imagine."

"Are you just as perceptive when it comes to people?" David couldn't help but think it. If she could notice things so keenly, she should have noticed what her brother did to his kids.

She looked down at her hands. "No. Not individual people. I'm good at noticing larger trends and patterns in communities and society. I can understand the behavior of groups. I know what they will want to buy." She chuckled. "A romantic power, isn't it?"

"Thank you for telling me all that. But I don't believe you really came all the way here to answer my questions about magic."

"Not as such. I came here to give you something. Something I need to pass along in person. Although in order for you to understand what it means, I need to explain some other things about magic. May I?"

David leaned forward and examined her. If only he knew a spell to learn her intentions. He'd have to ask Jess how she did that terrible secret digging thing. But he knew now, magic wasn't always about spells. As she said, wizards often had innate abilities available to them, with or without the intentional use of magic. Her explanation of her "business magic" had made him think. He had always excelled at sales. With a handshake, he knew whether or not he would make the sale. He could tell how much his target desired the object in question. He could tell if they trusted him. Sometimes it even came in as a message; "She's lonely and wants to talk to you, but she doesn't have any money." Or "He acts like he makes the decisions, but he doesn't. Talk to the wife." Bam. Just like that.

It worked on the other side of the table, too. When he started his own business, people often tried to sell him things. Everything from office supplies to lumber to construction equipment. He could tell in an instant how badly they needed the sale. He could tell whether or not they deceived him or gave him a bad price. It worked in job interviews, too. Even after he hired Liza, he sat in on most job interviews. He could sense fear, even if they hid it well. He could tell how confident they felt. If they told the truth. If they believed they could do the job. He never thought of it as magic. He didn't know how non-wizards experienced things and thought he just had excellent perception.

"Take my hand," he said and reached it out over the desk.

"I thought you didn't practice magic."

He didn't respond.

"I have nothing to hide, but that doesn't mean I'm going to allow you to thumb through my thoughts and memories like it's your own personal library."

"I don't know how to do that. I'm just good at reading people. The handshake always helps. Just a handshake. One or two seconds."

"You do realize I am much more powerful than you, by both magical and Mundane standards? If you cross me, you'll pay."

Then she smiled pleasantly and grabbed his hand. David hadn't prepared himself. He tried to open his mind to receive something. He heard, *You have all the power. She will give you anything you ask for.* He had never had such a sense of total control over any business interaction. Of course, he had met some people he could hit out of the park like softballs, but nothing like this. He should have known, since she had tried to give him an obscene amount of money just a little more than a month ago. He had the sense she would give him anything. Not just money, either. She would give him things more far valuable than that.

She looked at him warily. He didn't know what look he had. Surprise, probably.

"What?" she asked. "What did you get from me?"

"I believe I can trust you."

She nodded, but shifted in her seat, and looked uneasy for the first time since he'd met her. She clutched the locket around her neck.

"Is this all because of guilt?" David asked. "I worry you are a little too guilty. Of course, you feel badly about what your brother did to my children. Disturbed. Disgusted. I'm sure you feel partly responsible. I know I do. But, why so much guilt?"

"What do you know about talismans?"

"A thing or two. There are object talismans, which are protective charms, and true talismans, which are people."

"That's exactly right." She took off her locket. She opened the hinge and four small teeth fell onto David's desk.

A wave of nausea came over him. "Please tell me those aren't children's teeth. Why…why do you have them?"

"Relax, David. They're not Hansel and Gretel's. They're my daughter's baby teeth. They're my object talisman." She put the teeth in the palm of her hand. "I like having a part of her with me."

"Then your daughter…she died?" His stomach tightened. He felt bad to think it, but he didn't want to hear about it. He had heard about enough terrible things happening to children at the hands of wizards.

"Yes, nine years ago. I had her when I was seventeen. I was rather different back then. My parents were travelers. Whit and I never really lived anywhere."

"Whit?"

"My brother."

David felt sick again. He didn't want to think of this man as a child, as "Whit."

"Anyway. I got pregnant in Oklahoma City, but didn't realize it until we were in San Diego. I couldn't remember the young man's last name. It's neither here nor there. But Verity—that was her name—never had a father. It was around the time she was born that Whit and I decided to leave our parents. We lived in North Carolina for a while. He helped me raise her."

"What?"

"He wasn't like that then. He never hurt her. But, we were on different paths. I wanted to rebel against my parents. I wanted to be the opposite of everything they were. I was barely able to afford community college, even with a hardship grant, but that's what I did. I studied business administration. It was the most unwitchy thing I could think of. But all Whit cared about was magic. He didn't care about anything in the Mundane world, especially money. Although, he did work as a tow truck driver to help support Verity and me. Eventually, we were too different and decided to move apart. I found a job as an aide at an investment firm in New York and so I moved there with Verity. Whit moved around doing God knows what, but we stayed in touch. We talked all the time. Eleven years ago, he told me he was in love."

The last word pricked David's nerves. "I don't want to hear about that." The word "love" stuck like a bad taste in his mouth. "You don't love someone and do that."

"I can skip ahead. That's not important to the story, I suppose. Besides, I knew right away they were a bad match. At the beginning, they were kind to each other and all. It seemed like they were in love, but they were too similar. He told me he told her she was a witch; she hadn't known. Why you didn't tell her, I have no idea. But, that's not my business. When she found out about magic, she stopped caring about the Mundane world, too. Magic was the only thing either of them cared about. There was no balance to the relationship; they both fed off each other and there was no one to inject any sense of reason. Except me, I guess, but I failed.

"While I was trying to fit in, in the epicenter of civilization, they tried to escape it completely. They knew the more they were a part of the Mundane world, the less magic they would be able to do. So, they separated as much as possible. Most practicing wizards do this to some extent, but they took it to the extreme. They took everything to the extreme.

"Like I said before, destructive magic is dangerous. It can be used properly, but you have to be very careful. They were not careful. I could tell the magic they were doing was taking its toll. He was so distracted when I would talk to him. Like he couldn't focus. But, it's so easy to be in denial when it's someone you love. You don't want to accept that something is wrong. Besides, I just thought they were like our parents. Our childhood was less than ideal…but it wasn't like *that*. Our parents were inattentive and mercurial. When I read parenting books, for Verity, it become obvious to me that my parents had done almost everything wrong. But they were not abusive. Honestly, I never even considered I should be worried about Crystal's children. Living with parents who were practicing wizards didn't seem like a big deal to me. I survived it just fine. But, I'm digressing again. Do you know why dark wizards need talismans?"

"For protection. Although I'm not convinced they work."

"Talismans don't protect the body, they protect the soul. Bad things can still happen to you if you are protected by a talisman, but your soul will stay intact. That is why dark wizards need talismans, far more than any other kind of wizard. It is very hard to do destructive magic without destroying yourself…destroying your soul. But if you have a talisman, and you are careful, you can do dark magic and keep your soul intact."

"Evangeline told me I was Crystal's talisman. Is that why you're telling me this?"

"I figured as much, at least in retrospect. I didn't know who you were at all until recently. Breaking up with her may have been enough to sever the talisman protection, but if you still cared for her, some of the protection may have remained. I think it was her breaking off contact with you that really did it. She vowed to break her tie with you—a dangerous move. The more distant you are from your talisman, the more vulnerable you are. And I mean distant emotionally, not physically."

"If you're telling me this is all my fault, you can save it. I already figured that out."

"I'm not saying that at all. I'm saying Crystal broke the bond in a much more decisive way than you did. And although talismans are important, it's only one important thing. Crystal made her choices on her own and you had nothing to do with it. Besides, it wasn't just you. Crystal and Whit lost their talismans at around the same time."

"You?"

"Yes, I am my brother's talisman. The difference is, though, he is also mine."

"Whitman Colter was your protector? How could someone like that protect anyone?"

She smiled slightly. "About nine years ago, I decided my brother and I were just too different. I didn't approve of the way he had chosen to live his life and I wanted my daughter to have a more favorable impression of dark wizards. I wanted her to have pride in what she was. So, I told him I was done with him."

She stopped and took a few breaths, as if just the memory of the act hurt her.

"I had no idea how dangerous it was to sever yourself from your talisman," she continued. "Things started to go badly for me. I felt awful. Raw, like the tiniest pinprick could bring me down. I was depressed and irritable. Then, Verity became depressed. She and I were so close. It was almost like my depression was sticking to her. Then, I realized that it really was. She was trying to cast spells on me in my sleep to help me feel better. It left her too vulnerable and my depression seeped into her. I tried to get her to stop. I even locked her in her room so she wouldn't come in while I was sleeping. But, it was too late. She stayed depressed. I tried to get her help. I had her see a therapist. But on January 14, 2004 she jumped out of the window of our fourteenth floor apartment. She was only eleven."

David's heart pummeled his ribs. The story sounded far too familiar. "I'm so sorry."

"She was my everything." She gathered the teeth and put them back into the locket. "If I hadn't severed my tie with my talisman, she wouldn't have died."

"It's not your fault she died."

"Thank you for your sympathy. I know I wasn't directly responsible, but if I hadn't severed my tie with my talisman, it wouldn't have happened. Simple as that."

"But you survived the loss of your daughter even without a talisman. I don't know if I could do that, even with one. So, Colter has no excuse for doing what he did when he lost you."

"He was already vulnerable. Already losing his senses. Already doing too much magic. So yes, losing me was surely enough to push him over the edge and make him what he was. And, I didn't *want* to survive without my talisman. When my daughter died, I didn't care about anything but finding a way to feel better. I looked for him, but I couldn't find him. They had moved to Monahans then. I believe they used a spell to make themselves untraceable. So, neither of us could find them. It was so foolish.

"Perhaps I survived the loss of my daughter, but that's all I've done the past nine years. Survive. I've distracted myself with work. Filled my life with empty things. But I haven't been happy. Not for nine years. The only thing I could think of that might help was reuniting with my talisman, bringing back the bond. I wanted to feel protected again. Connected to someone."

A tear skidded down her cheek. "So, that's what I did. As soon as I had the opportunity. I do feel better. But I can't..."

She trailed off.

"I don't understand. When did you re-connect with your brother? You told me you hadn't spoken to him. That you didn't even know where he was."

"As you know, Whit wasn't connected to society. Almost no one knew him. He had no formal identification. Like I told you before, they called me to identify his body. A sister from New York he hadn't seen in years. I don't know who the police gunned down and put into that bag with my brother's name on it. But, it wasn't my brother. I lied and said it was. Whit is still alive."

David stood up quickly. His chair clattered and almost fell over. He felt as if he needed to do something. Immediately. Check the kids. Check the locks. Call the police. Something.

Rachel scooted her own chair back and flinched, as though she thought he would hit her. He wanted to.

"Please," she said. "Let me finish. I've come here to help you. To protect you, and your family. I swear to you. If you felt anything when you touched me, you know I mean you no harm."

David couldn't speak. He glared at her and waited.

"Severing your tie with your talisman is a dangerous and destructive act. However, there is something else far worse. If you are someone's talisman and you knowingly put him or her in harm's way, or choose not to protect him or her, it is more dangerous still, for both of you. That is what I want to give you. I wish to knowingly put my brother in danger."

She pulled an envelope out of her briefcase with shaking hands. "This is the address where you can find him."

She raised the envelope in the air at her eye level. "I, Rachel Colter, the talisman for Whitman Colter, choose to betray him by aiding his known enemy, David Vandergraff. I give Vandergraff this address so that he may have the opportunity to kill my brother. Thus, I contradict all my protective influence and become instead a contributor to his demise."

She pushed the envelope toward David. "Take it. You must take it from my hand."

David grabbed the envelope and she grunted, as if it had hurt her. He stared at the white business-size envelope.

"Is it important to say the words aloud?" he asked

"It's not critical. But it's so hard to predict the exact effects of a spell. I like to be as precise as possible. I can tell you that one way or another, my brother is now in danger. If not by you, someone or something will be after him shortly."

"Do you think he will come for the kids?"

"I don't know. He's not the man I knew at all, and I can't guess what he might be thinking or be planning to do. He hasn't told me much. However, I do know he is angry. Wants revenge for Crystal's death."

"What do you mean? The motherfucker killed her himself."

She seemed to shrink. She put her head down. "Not according to him."

David laughed mirthlessly. "If not him, then who?"

"Her son, Xavier."

"That's ridiculous. He's a liar."

"I have no idea if it's true or not. I'm just telling you what he thinks. It might be useful to know. And…I'm not saying it's true…but it's helpful to keep in mind. You should be careful about spells you do against Whit. If you say or even think you're casting a spell against Crystal's killer or as revenge for her death…you could misfire and hit Xavier."

"I won't even entertain the thought. It's the ravings of a madman."

"I'm only trying to help."

"You said betraying your talisman hurts both parties. What happens to you?"

"Like I said, destruction isn't always a bad thing."

"I can't let you destroy yourself."

"That's kind of you to say, but I don't plan to walk across the freeway, if that's what you're worried about. If death comes, it comes. And when it does, I'll die with a clean conscience. I'm not sure that will keep me out of Hell, but there's no harm in giving it the old college try." She winked at him. "I'll leave you now."

"Where are you going?"

"Home, of course." She hugged David and kissed him on the check. "Happy New Year. May this one be better than the last."

As soon as Rachel left, David went to check on Xavier and Evangeline. They played *Call of Duty* on the Wii with Patrick and none of them turned around when he came in. His kids pretended to blast people to death, but they were safe and acting more normal every day. David flashed back to a conversation he had once had with Amanda when their kids first starting asking for violent video games. She had argued *for* violent video games, which seemed odd at the time, but David didn't care enough either way to come up with an impassioned *against* argument. She sounded so convincing.

"Kids need to blow off steam," she had said. "It's better than them doing it in real life."

This conversation, as many of his memories, had new meaning now. Had she really meant that fantasy killing would make them less likely to kill people? Did she think this was a real risk? Was that why her parents encouraged her to start murdering adorable animals when she was six?

David's stomach filled with acid. As much as he had denied it aloud…what Rachel had said made him wonder about Crystal's death. The most logical answer would be that the murderous child rapist might have lied or was simply too crazy to have any grasp on reality. So, why did it feel plausible? Evangeline acted so cold about her mother. Said she deserved to die. Didn't want to have a memorial. And Xavier hadn't mentioned her at all. Perhaps they had felt so trapped, they could only escape by killing their parents. Maybe they had planned to kill both of them and Whitman got away. And, if they had? Did that even matter? Whitman certainly deserved to die. And Crystal hadn't been the same person he had loved. Maybe she deserved it, too. But still…he wished he knew. Spells did misfire. James had simply wished his partner happiness and killed fifteen people. What if David's anger toward Crystal's killer accidently became a spell he didn't know he had cast? What if it hit his son?

He watched them for a moment, and then went back into his office. He had expected to find Emmy waiting to assault him with questions about the mysterious woman. Maybe she would wait for a more dramatic moment, such as at the dinner table in front of everyone. He looked at the envelope sitting squarely in the middle of his desk. He could call the police. But, what if they messed it up again? In the spell, she had intended David to kill him. What would happen if he didn't? And if he called the police, he would never get the opportunity to kill him himself. To make sure he really died this time. It scared him that this played into his decision-making. He wasn't a killer. He couldn't even kill a deer without feeling sick. But, the deer had been innocent.

CHAPTER TWENTY-THREE

Talking to Xavier about what he wanted for dinner intimidated David, and now he had to ask him something much more important. He had to know, before he did whatever he would do to Colter. In case he used any magic against Colter, he wanted his mind to be in harmony with the facts.

Later that afternoon, Xavier washed the Expedition in the driveway. The keys dangled from his jeans pocket and David guessed Amanda had let him pull the Expedition out of the garage himself. Seeing him do something as common and domestic as washing a car made Xavier seem different from the boy he had met only nine weeks ago. He looked older, and the same silence that had made him seem timid and afraid now made him seem focused and calm.

"What did you do?" David asked.

Xavier paused his sponging. "What do you mean?"

"You're washing the car. Is it a punishment from Amanda?"

He smirked. "No. I like it. And, I want to be useful."

"Good work ethic on top of everything else. And, you don't want to wash the car with magic?"

"I can't do that. Or if I could, it would take much more effort than just doing it by hand."

"Good to know. I had been wondering if there was a spell for household chores. Tell me, is there a spell for sorting recyclables? I hate that."

Xavier gave David one of his mom's half smiles and shook his head.

"Can you take a break so I can talk to you about something real quick? We can sit on the porch…it's kind of important."

Xavier squeezed out his sponge and looked younger again. "What is it?"

"Just sit down. You haven't done anything wrong or anything like that." That statement could be easily contested and he wished he had phrased it differently. After all, he wanted to ask him if he had murdered his mother.

Xavier sat down next to him on the porch swing. He still had the sponge in his hands and squeezed it absently.

"Um…" David said. He had practiced this, but still, this would be rough. He had thought talking to Jude about condoms had been uncomfortable. "I can't even imagine what it would have been like to live with…that man. I'm sure if it had been me, I would have wanted to do just about anything to get away."

As always, David had trouble reading Xavier's expression. "Okay," he said.

"I think you were brave to be able to escape and save your sister, too." Xavier seemed too still, and David wondered if he was still *there*. But unlike before, Xavier looked him in the eye. David could tell Xavier didn't breathe much. David didn't either, for that matter. He took a deep breath to remind Xavier to do the same. Perhaps subconsciously, Xavier did mimic David with a shallower, but still audible breath.

"Was there anything else you did I don't know about?

Anything you did to save yourself and your sister?"

Xavier sat back in the swing and turned slightly away from him. He blinked his eyes a few times and rubbed them, as if he struggled to stay awake. Maybe he had to focus to stay present, which seemed brave on its own.

"Did she tell you something?" he asked quietly.

For a second, David thought he meant Rachel, but that made little sense. He must have meant Evangeline, the only *she* who would have known what had happened. Xavier put down his sponge, and rubbed his arms as if he wanted start a fire. David didn't know how much longer he'd stay present. He wanted to reach into his mind and take the memory as Amanda had done to him. That way, he would have the answers and Xavier would never have to remember. Then it all popped into place. It came to him so clearly David knew his desire for the answer had manifested itself into a spell. He already had all the pieces, and with a little magic, all the pieces came into place.

David had assumed when Rachel said Xavier killed his mother, she had meant he had killed her in the traditional sense. He hadn't taken magic into account. Evangeline had told David that Xavier had cast a spell to find him. David guessed it had been something similar to the catalyst spell his brother had cast. A spell to find their real father with the ultimate intent of changing their circumstances for the better. But as James learned the hard way, the wizard couldn't choose the means, only the ends. And, if the wizard was dark, the means would be destruction.

"I think I know what happened," David said. "It's not your fault."

Xavier became even more still. David wanted grab his wrist and check for a pulse.

"Xavier," he continued. "It's really not your fault. I'm not angry. You had good intentions. Was it a catalyst spell?"

Xavier still didn't move. David should just shut up, give him some space, but he couldn't resist the urge to unfreeze him. He wanted him to say something…anything…so he knew he hadn't faded into oblivion.

"How did it happen?" David asked. "Did he kill her like they said, or did it happen in some other way? Perhaps even, peacefully?"

"I didn't mean to hurt her." David could barely hear him. "I didn't want to. But, I must not have…said it right. After I cast the spell, she never came back into the house. I found her outside. She had tripped and hit her head on a rock. She was bleeding. I killed my mom."

Xavier stood up as if fire covered him and he needed water.

"Son, calm down. You didn't mean to. You can't even prove it was you. It could have been an accident. A coincidence."

Xavier ran down the steps. David didn't anticipate his plan. He still had the keys. He jumped into the driver's seat of the still soapy Expedition and turned the ignition. As he pulled out, he busted an ornamental flowerpot. The kid didn't know how to drive on a good day, and he could barely stay present while sitting on the porch.

David sprinted into the house to grab his own set of keys and then dived into the Mercedes, but as soon as he made it down the driveway, he couldn't see the Expedition anymore. He drove to the main road, and still didn't see him.

David tried to calm himself. Xavier would cool off and come back. Colter didn't know Xavier was now alone and unguarded. But as soon as he thought it, the panic flooded back in. Colter was a powerful wizard. Who knew what he knew or what he could do? Phrases he'd heard in the past few months swam in his head. *Wizards are hopelessly connected. Wizards can always find each other.*

David drove around looking for the Expedition, but Amanda called him thirty minutes later and said Xavier had returned. He should have known better than to panic. Xavier wouldn't stay away from Evangeline for long.

CHAPTER TWENTY-FOUR

Samantha was officially Patrick's girlfriend, so it took effort not to smile like an idiot all the time. He had to play it cool. If he didn't pretend their coupling made sense, Samantha might notice her choice in boyfriends had violated the rules of time and space.

When Dad talked to him about his newfound good fortunes, he didn't accuse him of using love potions or mind control spells. He only said she couldn't be in his room with the door closed. He said, "The Carthages dropped off one girl with us and I plan to return one *girl*."

Other than that, he got the sense Dad wanted to high-five him.

Patrick and Emmy might end up ripping off Samantha's arms in a tug-of-war match. But aside from that, Emmy tolerated them. When he asked her if she minded, she said, "It's gross. But whatever, I'm just glad she didn't get with Jude."

When he asked why, she just shrugged.

So, three days before Christmas, Samantha leaned into him on the couch like he was her own personal armchair, and he ran his fingers along her smooth thighs while he watched her paint her toenails lavender. It might be all in his head because he knew she was a spring witch, but she smelled of cut grass and honeysuckle. Which made him wonder if he smelled of dead leaves and rotting pumpkins.

"Do you feel different being around dark wizards all the time?" he asked.

"What do you mean?"

"Evangeline said it could be dangerous for you. Sap your energy or something like that."

She huffed. "No. I'm not worried about being around them. They should be worried about me."

"Why is that?"

"What's the only thing that can break the winter?"

"What?"

"The spring, of course."

Patrick laughed. "That's awesome."

"We're the toughest wizards. No matter how cold or long the winter, we break through the ice. Every single year, since the dawn of time."

"And you look pretty when you do it, too. All covered in flowers."

"That's sweet." She wiggled closer to him. He put his arms around her and pulled her even closer, his hands grazing the bottom of her breasts.

"Now I can't reach my toes," she said with another playful wiggle.

"So?"

"I can reach your fingernails," she said, reaching toward him with her brush.

"All right fine. I'll let you go."

"I only need my arms."

"So, what is it like having spring wizards for parents?"

"Mostly…embarrassing. The truth is, I wished they would disappear all the time. But, I do miss them now. Despite being annoying, they have a good attitude about life. They don't get stressed out much and just go with the flow. I've never been quite like that, but I'm more easygoing than a winter witch. Talk about taking yourself too seriously. Your family needs to lighten up sometimes. Have a party. Dance or sing or something. They must get tired of being themselves all the time."

"Yeah. I think they do."

"What about you? What's it like being an autumn wizard?"

"I don't know. I'm the only one I know."

"I think autumn wizards are supposed to be practical and smart. They're the most levelheaded. Like the ducks that fly south, and the squirrels that store their nuts before the cold. They're prepared for what's coming and know how to survive it."

"I don't feel prepared."

"Maybe that's why you know when something bad is about to happen."

"One second isn't a lot of time to store nuts."

"It may get longer once you get better at it."

He didn't like that idea. Patrick had the sense his life would be full of things he'd rather not know about any sooner than he had to. Humans could call it paranoia or anxiety, but Patrick couldn't count on that. His fear could be prophecy.

Patrick woke up at 12:57 a.m. He saw the big red numbers hovering in the dark room. He waited for the sound he predicted. The one that woke him up before it happened. But, nothing came. It reminded him of the feeling he had when he woke up the night Emmy jumped down the stairs. Something was about to happen. He lay awake waiting, but after a few minutes passed with nothing but silence, he fell back asleep.

When Patrick got out of bed the next morning, he found Emmy standing outside Jude's room. She stared at his closed door. She wrapped her arms around herself as if she was cold, but the house felt plenty warm. The look on her face made her look more like Dad than Mom. The slanted eyebrows screamed Dad.

"What are you doing?" Patrick asked. He didn't even know why he asked anymore.

"He's in there," Emmy said.

Patrick looked at the door. "Who? Jude? Yeah, I'm sure he is. I saw him swipe some vodka from the liquor cabinet last night. He'll probably be out for a while. Is Samantha still asleep?" he asked.

"Shower," Emmy said.

Patrick continued past her toward the stairs. "You do know that standing outside your brother's door waiting for him to wake up is really weird?"

"Mmm, hmm," Emmy said absently.

CHAPTER TWENTY-FIVE

On the morning of December 24, David wrapped the earrings he had bought Amanda. He had hoped he would come up with something better, but he hadn't. If he bought something too expensive, she would be mad at him for spending the last of their money on a gift. But, this year, she deserved a truckload of diamonds. He couldn't win. A month had passed since she had given in to him in the dining room and he hoped another holiday would weaken her resolve. But love or lust would have to do it, because the eighty-dollar earrings he had bought her wouldn't have her ripping her clothes off.

He placed the small box under their colossal tree. On his way to the kitchen, he said good morning to Evangeline, who used the bear-shaped honey bottle to design an elaborate pattern on her plate, which looked like a flower or a spider web. While David rummaged through the pantry, Jude came in and poured himself a generous helping of Cheerios. He took the honey from Evangeline and squirted it on his cereal, an act that caused Xavier to appear from nowhere and stand between Jude and his sister.

"What?" Jude asked. "I can't use the fucking honey?"

"Jude, calm down," David said.

Jude slammed the little bear back on the table and took his cereal into the living room. David followed him, although he knew any attempt at a father-son chat would be met with shouting and being doused with Cheerios and milk. But, David wouldn't get the chance to try.

Patrick came from the bottom of the stairs looking like a different person. His hazel eyes had an extra gleam of gold and were locked on Jude. The ferocity in his movements made him look a foot taller. As mad as Patrick looked, David couldn't have anticipated what happened next. Jude turned around in enough time to see Patrick shove him so hard he went careening backward through the glass coffee table.

Without hesitation, Patrick approached his fallen brother and stepped on his neck. After a moment of stunned shock, David moved in to tackle Patrick before he killed his brother. But, he didn't need to. Jude grabbed Patrick's leg and used a spell to make Patrick fall back. Patrick tumbled to the ground and tried to get back up, but stumbled again as if he had suddenly become dizzy or drunk.

Jude coughed and wheezed, clutching his neck. He had spots of blood on his shirt and arms where the glass had cut him, but none of them looked large. David kneeled down beside him, glass digging into his own knee, but Jude knocked his hand away. He wheezed something that sounded like, "okay," scrambled to his feet, and went out the front door.

"What the fuck?" David shouted at Patrick.

Patrick clung to the couch, trying to pull himself back up and didn't respond. David followed Jude, but didn't make it in time. Jude had taken the keys off the ring by the door and had driven away in his truck.

David and Amanda sat across from Emmy at the kitchen table. Emmy looked as if she had dimmed the lights under her skin, in an attempt to become invisible. It wouldn't surprise David if she popped out of existence right there in the kitchen. David put his hand right above his stomach where acid climbed toward his throat. He had already thrown up twice. He wanted to crawl into bed and not come out. But, he had to be a father. He needed to be here, experiencing the worst conversation of his entire life.

"Am I in trouble?" Emmy asked.

"Uh…" Amanda said. Her incoherent spluttering was still better than he could do. "I just don't understand why you didn't tell us sooner," she whispered.

Emmy stared at the table.

"Emmy, answer me." Amanda said. "Why didn't you say anything?"

"I don't know."

They both spoke so quietly, David had to lean in.

"Am I in trouble?" she asked again.

"Well…no," Amanda said. "I'm just trying to understand. I mean, you were there?"

She nodded.

"Tell me exactly what happened," Amanda said.

Please don't, David thought.

"I woke up and saw Jude in Samantha's bed."

"And you're sure it wasn't…consensual?"

Emmy shrugged.

"Because according to what Patrick heard from Samantha, it wasn't," Amanda said. "But perhaps he just heard what he wanted to hear. Or maybe she lied to him. What do you think?"

Emmy stared at the table again.

"Emmy," Amanda prodded. "This is important."

"I know that." She picked at her cuticles. "No. She didn't want him to."

"How do you know?"

"Because she said 'Emmy, make him stop.'"

"Oh…but you didn't?"

Emmy's eyes reddened. "She didn't say anything else. She tried to push him away, but then got really quiet and still. I didn't know what to do."

"You didn't know what to do?" Amanda asked, her volume rising. "The house is big, but not that big. You could scream. You could bang on the wall to wake up Patrick. You could run over to wake up me, or your father. How long would that journey take? Ten seconds? Five?"

David put his hand on Amanda's. "Don't yell at her," he said softly.

Amanda lowered her tone back to the barely-there whisper. "And the next day? It's been over thirty hours. You were all together yesterday like nothing happened. Eating meals at the same table. Watching TV in the same room."

"Samantha didn't say anything either. She only did because Patrick guessed something was up and wouldn't leave her alone about it."

"I don't understand," Amanda said.

"I thought maybe it wouldn't be a big deal," Emmy said.

"What is wrong with you?" Amanda asked. "It is a really big deal. How did we screw you up so badly that you don't see that?"

"Amanda," David said firmly. "You shouldn't be yelling at her. She's….just look at her."

Amanda stood up suddenly. "I'm going to go find him."

"And do what?" David asked.

"I don't know. I just need to find him."

David didn't try to stop her. He knew she had to act. Staying still at a time like this would kill her.

"We're not mad at you," David said to Emmy.

CHAPTER TWENTY-SIX

David felt a fever coming on. He sweat in the creases of his knees and an achy heat settled in his joints. He turned off the heater. The temperature outside had risen to more than 60 degrees, anyway. He guessed the discomfort and achiness came from the *wrongness*, a reminder he would never feel okay again. The heat continued to nag at him, and David wondered if it signaled the start of a nervous breakdown. He felt held together by Scotch tape and chewed gum.

David opened the front door and walked out onto the porch, expecting a refreshing gust of cool, damp air. Instead, he found blinding sun and stifling heat. The sudden blast of bright sunshine turned the rain into steam. He must have imagined it, but the air felt like it had heated to at least 90 degrees. Unless global warming had taken an aggressive turn, something unnatural had happened.

"Excuse me, sir," said a male voice.

It took David a moment before he could place who had spoken. He didn't know why he hadn't seen them right away. Three people stood in his driveway, their little silver car parked next to his still decimated mailbox. They had barely moved down the driveway and didn't move any closer to introduce themselves. They had an odd brightness about them and David could hardly bear to look at them. After a few seconds, he adjusted to the sensation and could focus on them, but it made his eyes hurt.

Two men and a woman. The woman had her hand raised over her eyes as if she was blocking glare. Did she not want to look at him, either? David saw nothing obviously objectionable about them. However, they didn't seem to feel the heat. They wore gloves, scarves, and heavy coats over their business casual attire. The woman had a pale green umbrella open, even though it had stopped raining.

He must be caught in some kind of temperature anomaly, because it took willpower for him not to take off his shirt and mop his forehead with it.

The woman clutched a large white binder and he would have pegged them as salespeople or evangelicals, except he was one hundred percent sure they were wizards. They had the weight about them wizards had, that extra bit of gravity he had never thought twice about. He supposed wizards could also sell security systems or pass out The Book of Mormon.

"Stand down," said one of the men. "We mean you no harm."

Stand down? The man made it sound as if David had weapons. Wait, did *they* have weapons? For some reason, he felt like they did, although he couldn't see any.

"We're here to collect Samantha Carthage," he said.

"Who are you?" David asked.

"Come to us, dear," the woman said. "You're going to be safe now."

David turned around and saw Samantha standing behind him. She had never greeted unknown visitors before. They must have summoned her somehow.

The woman appeared as kind and unthreatening as anyone

could. She was in her late twenties or early thirties, with honey-colored hair, a honey-laden voice, and milky skin. But, his gut felt something wrong about her, something opposing.

David held out his hand to signal Samantha to wait. "Hang on, Samantha. Do you know these people?"

She shook her head.

"We're from the Council of Child Welfare and Protection," said one of the men.

That rang false to David.

"I believe the organization you're referring to is called the Texas Department of Family and Protective Services." He had visited the website several days ago, trying to figure out what to do about Samantha. "It seems like you would know that if you worked there."

The three exchanged bewildered expressions.

"We're not from the Mundane government agency," said the woman.

"You mean you're *Wizard* Child Protective Services?" he asked.

"You could say that," the woman said.

"Where have you been?" he added softly.

"I'm sorry?" the woman asked. She looked at him with the mix of fear and pity one might give to a psychotic blubbering on the street.

"We don't wish to harm you," said the man who hadn't spoken yet. "Stand aside and hand over the child and we'll leave you be."

His had the voice of a cartoon superhero. It struck David that the two men served as bodyguards for the woman.

"You don't have to talk to him like that," Samantha said. "He never hurt me. He's a good man."

They shared looks again. If she had said, *he's an elephant, feed him peanuts*, they would have looked less confused.

"This girl is in my charge," David said. "I'm not letting

strangers take her away. Show me some identification."

"Please, you do it," the woman said to the first man. "I don't think I can."

She pulled a laminated badge on a lanyard out from under her coat and handed it to the man. He approached David slowly and handed him the badge. He was a tall African-American with unusual green eyes that seemed to sparkle as if lit with fireworks from behind. The man swallowed hard, but held his chin up and forced himself to look David in the eye.

David didn't want to stand next to this man any more than the man wanted to be near David. He glanced at the badge. Sure enough, the badge read Laura Hannigan, *Case Manager, Council of Magical Child Welfare and Protection, Southwest Division.* She sparkled even in her mug shot. The badge also had a symbol that reminded David of the sun on the New Mexico flag. He tried to project his salesman magic onto to them to get an idea of their intentions. He could ask to shake the man's hand, but David didn't think he could stand to touch him. He had trouble reading them, both from the distance and through the veil of brightness. They confused his senses. They felt threatening and welcoming, simultaneously.

"To begin, we simply wish to speak with her," the woman said. "Would it be possible for you to wait on the porch while we do?" She smiled at him apologetically.

"No. I think I can be here for whatever you have to say."

"I'm sorry, sir. It's not personal," the woman said. "I need to perform an incantation. I don't think I can if you're close. That's all."

Samantha touched David's elbow. "It's okay. I can tell they aren't going to hurt me."

David backed onto the porch. Patrick and Emmy also stood there watching. "Who are they?" Patrick asked.

"Patrick, go get me my keys. I want to be able to follow if they lead her into the car without warning."

"What?"

"Just do it. Go."

Emmy hovered close to David. He put his hand on her shoulder. "It's going to be okay."

"There is something wrong with them," Emmy said. "I have a bad feeling."

"I do, too. But, I think they're just…different from us."

Next to the three strangers, the normally glowing Samantha looked as gray as the sky. The woman spoke to Samantha, but David couldn't hear her. She placed her hands on Samantha's head and closed her eyes. It reminded David of a baptism. She did this for what seemed like several minutes. Then she took Samantha's face in her hands and looked into her eyes. Then she placed her hands on Samantha's shoulders, with her face very close to hers. David could see Samantha's forehead knitted with nerves. He didn't blame her. Like all wizard readings, it appeared weirdly intimate.

Finally, the woman released her. She spoke to Samantha again, with her hand on her shoulder. Then the three people got back in the car without Samantha and drove away.

Patrick appeared at David's side with the keys. "What did they do to her?"

Samantha didn't turn around. She looked at something in her hands. Patrick and Emmy both started to move toward her.

"Don't swarm her," David said. "Just stay here for a second."

David walked down the driveway toward her. The air already felt cooler and it started to rain again. Samantha's blonde hair lay in wet clumps, and her drenched, mint-green top clung to her back. David realized rain soaked his shirt, too. It must have never stopped raining. He had stood in a full rain shower the whole time he had talked to the strangers. The weather had not really changed at all.

"Samantha?"

She turned around to face him. She held her shirt out in front of her as a shield to protect an envelope from the rain.

"Why did they leave?" he asked.

"March 4," she said.

"What?"

"They said I was a March 4. They take only wizards who fall between the spring and fall equinox. I'm too dark for them, I guess."

It took David a moment to grasp the meaning of this sentence, but when he did, a swell of fury went from his stomach to his heart. Deep disappointment quickly replaced his fury. He had pegged them immediately. Summer wizards. Good wizards. Despite the fact they were his natural enemies, he had felt hopeful. He had wanted to believe three angels had come to save Samantha, to take her to a better place where she would be safe and happy. He had wanted to believe something that good could happen. He supposed that was what he got for being a grown man who believed in Santa Claus.

Samantha handed him a business card. This one had a more familiar Texas DFPS logo.

"They said to give that to you," she said.

"Are you okay?"

She shrugged weakly.

"Everything will be okay," he said. "We'll find your parents. We'll figure something out. I promise."

She shook her head. Her chest moved up and down. If she cried, the rain disguised her tears.

"Let's go inside," David said.

Samantha followed him back onto the covered porch. Patrick and Emmy hovered close to her, but stayed at arm's length. Jude's assault had caused her to grow a force field they couldn't penetrate.

"David," Samantha whispered.

"Yes?"

She pulled the envelope out from under her shirt.

"They said their job is to find homes for *orphaned* children. Does that mean my parents are dead?"

Emmy let out a tiny gasp.

"They didn't say?" David asked.

"No. They just said it all matter-of-fact and didn't explain."

"Assholes," Patrick whispered.

Samantha hadn't taken her eyes off the damp envelope. It had her name written on it in purple ink.

"This is my mom's handwriting," she said. "I'm afraid to look inside."

She handed it to David.

"Do you want me to open it?" he asked.

She nodded.

David didn't want to look inside, either. The envelope came apart easily, since the glue had come undone in the rain. The purple handwriting was messy and smudged, but readable.

Dance then, wherever you may be.

Mom

"What does it say?" Samantha asked.

"'Dance then, wherever you may be'," David said.

"That's it?" Patrick asked.

"That's the chorus to the Lord of the Dance," Emmy said. "The hymn we sing at Easter."

David handed the paper to Samantha. "Does it mean anything to you?"

"I think it's a suicide note," she said.

"No," David said. "I mean, that's quite a leap just from that."

"She didn't make a lot of sense in the end," Samantha said.

She buried her face in her hands. Patrick touched Samantha's shoulder lightly. When her skin didn't burn under his fingertips, he put his arms around her and she buried her face in his chest. Emmy moved in and joined the hug, resting her cheek on Samantha's shoulder.

"Not today. How could this happen today?" Amanda shouted it, as if she expected an answer. As if, she thought she could call God's secretary and complain about the scheduling mix-up. She threw her purse onto the kitchen counter. "I thought this would happen eventually. I hoped it wouldn't, but I feared it would. I…but how could it have happened today? If they had only come to collect her two days ago."

"It wouldn't have mattered because they didn't collect her at all," David said.

Amanda put her face in her hands.

"I'm not convinced they're dead," David said. "'Dance then, wherever you may be'? How is that a suicide note?"

"Why else would they have come for her?"

"Maybe because of what happened. Perhaps, they just know when something bad happens. Can summer wizards do that?"

"I know less about summer wizards than I do about those neon fish that live at the bottom of the ocean. I've never even talked to a summer wizard. Although, I've seen them, of course. They're hard to miss."

David ran his fingers over her hair to smooth down the frizz, but he only made it worse.

"Has he called you?" She whispered it, as if their oldest son's existence had already become a secret.

"No."

"We screwed this up. If we call the police now, it will look like we tried to cover it up. There would be no evidence. It's just the last thing I was thinking of."

"I know."

"What do we do?"

Kill Whitman Colter, David thought to himself. He couldn't say why that answer came to him. He felt furious and sad and likely turning funny in the head, but he just wanted to do *something*. If he had been a man and had killed Colter right away, none of this would have ever happened. He believed it, even though it made no sense at all.

"I think I'm going to go look for him," David said. "For Jude."

He didn't want to lie anymore, but he had to make an exception. If he told her what he planned to do, she would chain him down and not let him do it, or chain him down so she could do it herself.

David turned to go up the stairs.

"You mean right now?" Amanda asked.

"Right now."

"I'll go with you."

"You know you can't. Someone has to stay with the kids. And um…lock the doors and keep the gun handy."

"I always do. But, why are you reminding me?"

"Paranoid, I guess. The bad things seem to come all at once."

"Are you okay?" she asked.

"No. Of course not."

"I know. I just…there is something about you right now. Like, something changed."

"You're imagining things."

CHAPTER TWENTY-SEVEN

David stared at his office. Something was wrong with the image in front of him, but he couldn't put his finger on it. Then it hit him. He had left the envelope with Colter's address right on top of his desk, but he didn't see it now. Maybe, he did move it. He certainly should have moved it. But, so much had happened so fast. His pulse quickened.

He scattered the papers on his desk and looked under his keyboard. He got on his hands and knees and scoured the floor. By the time he started looking through his drawers, he had become frantic. He looked in ridiculous places, such as in the folder with his 2008 tax return documents and under the sheets of his bed. He ripped through the closet and looked in pockets of jackets he hadn't even worn this season. Close to ripping apart his desk with an axe, he noticed something that didn't belong.

A pink Post-it note peeked out from under some of the papers he had tossed around. He didn't use pink Post-it notes. He recognized Emmy's giant, loopy handwriting.

I have left to kill Whitman Colter. Emmy

The words blurred and he blinked a few times to bring them back into focus. It made no sense.

"Emmy!" he shouted.

He ran to her room and threw open the door. "Emmy!" he yelled again, even though he knew he wouldn't find her.

He turned around and saw Xavier and Evangeline watching him.

"She went to a friend's house," Evangeline said. "Remember? I heard her telling you."

David's hands shook so much, he had to grip the phone tightly to keep from dropping it as he dialed Emmy's number. It went straight to voice mail.

Amanda came in the room. "What's going on?"

"Emmy!" David shouted again. His vocabulary had been reduced to a single word.

"Emmy what?" Amanda asked. Amanda glanced at Evangeline. "What do you have there?"

David's heart lurched into his ribs. Evangeline held a pink Post-it note. He must not have noticed her take it out of his hands. Xavier leaned in and read it over her shoulder. They didn't say anything. They didn't even move.

Amanda snatched the note. At first, she had the same frozen expression. Then she said, "I don't understand what this means. David?"

"I can only assume it means what it says," David replied.

"You told me he was dead." She whispered it as if she didn't want the kids to hear, even though they stood right next to her and had read the note themselves. Evangeline and Xavier animated enough to look at him, waiting for an explanation.

Patrick and Samantha entered the family room, too. Samantha didn't look as if she had been crying, but she had a manic vibration about her, as if it all simmered under her skin.

"What happened?" Patrick asked. The tiredness in his voice belonged to a much older man.

David took the note from Amanda's hands and gave it to

Samantha. "Did she say anything to you?"

Samantha stared at the note with a numb expression. She nodded.

"What?" The girl had been raped and orphaned in the course of twenty-four hours and he still wanted to shake the answer out of her.

"She listened to your conversation with that woman. She had her ear against the door. She was worried the woman was your lover or something and wanted to find out for sure. She told me what the woman said, that their stepfather is still alive, and that you were supposed to kill him."

"What?" Amanda interjected.

Samantha paused for a moment then continued. "But she never said she was going to do it herself. She didn't tell me that. I…I had no idea."

"Damn you, David," Amanda said. "You're still keeping secrets from me. Why didn't you tell me the man was alive?"

"I'm not going to waste time fighting with you. I have to find her. Now."

"You're right," Amanda said.

She retreated into the bedroom without a word, but David knew what she had in mind. She would get the one thing that made her feel safe.

She returned with an empty lock box. "She already took it." Her hands trembled and she dropped the box on the floor with a loud clang. "Where is he? Where is she going?"

David opened his mouth as if he expected the answer to come out. Then the truth hit him. "I never even opened the envelope," he said. "I can call the woman who gave it to me."

He ran down the stairs while he dialed. He moved so quickly he missed a step and had to catch himself from tumbling down the stairs. There would be no more discussion. He would go find her right now.

Rachel's cell went straight to a monotone male recording:

"The person you are trying to reach is unavailable now. Please try again later."

He didn't even have the option to leave a message.

"Shit," he said. He would keep calling every thirty seconds if he had to.

He grabbed his jacket and his keys.

"Wait," Amanda said. "Take one of the hunting rifles. I'll get one from the garage."

"I can't walk around with a hunting rifle."

"How else are you supposed to kill him?"

David had no response to this. She asked it so matter-of-factly, as if she wanted him to take an umbrella for the rain, not a gun to kill a man.

When Amanda disappeared to her garage locker, an odd moment of silence passed. His three remaining children and Samantha had followed them down the stairs and stared at him. He had Emmy's face in his tunnel vision and had forgotten this impacted all of them. They all heard him and Amanda talk about killing a man. And, not just any man. He couldn't think of a thing to say.

"Please stay here," he said. "Don't do anything. I just want you to be safe."

"How will you find her?" Evangeline asked.

"I…I'm going to keep calling the woman who gave me his address. She'll answer eventually. She isn't the type to be away from her phone for too long." David's stomach lurched when he said this. Rachel didn't seem like the type to have her phone off at all, or ever roam far from a cell tower. She had said that betraying her brother hurt both of them. Who knew what could have happened to her?

"You can find her with magic," Evangeline said. "Wizards can find each other."

"No, they can't," he shouted with unexpected force. "I couldn't find you. We couldn't find her parents." He pointed at

Samantha.

"I found you," Xavier said.

The words floated around David's ears for a while before he grasped his meaning.

"No," David said. "Don't do any spells. There is too much at stake."

Amanda arrived with the hunting rifle her father had given him so many years ago. She had better, newer guns, but he had actually used this one before and he might remember how to use it again.

"I should be the one to go," she said. "I'm a much better shot."

"Absolutely not. Besides, you would only have the upper hand if you sniped him from 200 feet. He's not a deer. He won't run from you. If he got close, if he somehow disarmed you, you wouldn't have a chance."

"I can't do nothing."

"You won't be. You'll be protecting them." He gestured toward the other children.

He wanted to remind her again to lock the doors and bring her own rifle up from the basement on the off chance Colter decided to come back here for Xavier. But, he didn't want to frighten them. He hoped she would read that between the lines. He realized he had never stopped lying to her. Or at least, he had never got in the habit of telling her everything. He thought about all the things she should know about Colter, about Xavier's spell, about talismans, that he hadn't told her, simply because had grown so used to keeping secrets. And now, he didn't have time.

"You can protect me," David said. "And you don't have to do anything. You just have to want it."

She nodded vaguely, but didn't ask for clarification. She wrapped him in her arms and kissed him once on the neck. The gesture made her seem more like his wife again than she had since he had brought his newest kids home. Even having sex with her hadn't seemed so intimate.

"Bring our baby home," she said.

"I will," David said.

Emmy had taken the Expedition and Jude had taken his truck, so he had only one car to choose from. Emmy didn't know how to drive, but at least she took the tank.

A cold, damp wind hit him that seemed appropriate for Christmas Eve. He flipped up the collar of his jacket and could feel Crystal's box, cold against his ribs. He wanted to tell her he would kill her killer. Not the magic-addled woman who had allowed her husband to abuse their children, but the twenty-something filled with fire and hope. He pushed her out of his head. Even thinking about her might cause a spell to misfire.

"Wait." The small voice seemed to blow away in the wind. He didn't want to stop. "Wait," it came again.

He didn't fully stop his mad trek to his Mercedes until she grabbed his arm and said, "Dad."

Evangeline had followed in his heels with sock feet and no jacket.

"Wait," she said again, this time forcefully.

"What is it?"

"You have to bring her talisman." Her eyes blazed even greener than usual, and they reminded him of the puddle of magic she had pooled in her palm. Perhaps the redness around the rims made them greener. He had never seen her cry.

"Okay," he said. "Hurry. Go get it."

She didn't move from her spot.

"What does she use?" he prodded. "Do you know where it is?"

"Jude," she said.

Just the sound of his name made David's head swim.

"I can't. No," he spluttered.

"Please." She sounded close to tears. "You have to. It's so

important."

"I don't even know where he is, and I don't have time to look."

"He'll come to you. I know he will. Just leave a message on his voice mail and tell him what happened. If he knows Emmy is in danger, he'll come. He wouldn't be able to resist even if he wanted to. But he wouldn't resist. He loves her."

David got on 1-10 and headed west. Eighty miles per hour to nowhere in particular. He felt as if he should head west, but he didn't get any more magical insight than that. And, "West" covered a rather large area. He called Rachel for the twenty-seventh time. No answer. He had also called Liza at home to see if she could find any other numbers for her, an unreasonable request considering she had left town for the holidays and didn't officially work for him anymore, but perhaps the desperation in his voice led her to act. She called him back quickly with the number for Rachel's office. The main line and the direct line to her desk. When no one answered the main line, David wanted to chuck his phone out of the window in frustration. Why the hell wouldn't they pick up the damn main line on a Thursday afternoon? Didn't they have a receptionist? As soon as he thought it, he realized he had forgotten something important, the date. Late afternoon on Christmas Eve, and getting later every minute. He would count himself lucky to find an open gas station, let alone contact a business office.

The dull white sun hung low in the sky. He had several hours until sunset, but the dead winter angle of the sun made it look as if it would sink behind the hills any minute. Amanda had called the police, but had said they didn't seem to understand the seriousness of the situation. Emmy had not been abducted, she had run away, and only a few hours ago. Apparently, the situation didn't call for an AMBER Alert. They took note of Amanda's claim that the dangerous Whitman Colter was still alive, but didn't sound convinced.

David's options ran thin. But, he had to try everything. Even the ideas that made him want to throw up. When Jude's phone started ringing, David wanted to hang up. His temples pulsed with rage and his throat tightened with grief simultaneously. He had no word to describe the feeling. He needed something that meant "disappointment," only exponentially worse.

Not too surprisingly, Jude didn't pick up. He heard his son's voice on the answering machine. His real son. He had recorded those words before he changed into something else. After the beep, David forgot to talk right away. The first part of the message Jude would hear would be nothing but highway noise and his father breathing.

"Emmy's missing. She could be in serious danger. I need you to help me find her." His tone sounded as dull as the day.

Jude called back.

David wanted to let it go to voice mail. Possibly, he could manage to communicate with him by voice mail tag and not have to speak to him directly. But, he didn't have time for games.

"Yes," David said.

"Dad?" Jude's voice sounded far away. "Something happened to Emmy?"

He described the situation as quickly and plainly as he could.

"Why would she do that?" Jude asked. Fear increased the pitch of his voice.

"Because of you," David said.

The vague statement didn't make sense by itself, but Jude

didn't ask for more clarification.

"I'm sorry," Jude said.

"Just tell me where you are."

Jude was in Austin. A friend of his had gone to UT last year and said he could crash on his couch, without asking too many questions. Fortunately, this meant David could keep driving in the general "West" direction. He didn't think he could get his car to go any other way. When he pulled into the dilapidated apartment complex, the sun skirted the horizon. Jude met him in the parking lot. He wore the same blood-spotted clothes he had left in and had no bag with him. He didn't wear shoes. He had a glassy, vacant look in his eyes.

Jude got in the car without comment and avoided David's eyes. From his smell, David guessed that Jude hadn't brought deodorant with him either, and had been drinking. David had expected to want to bash his head into the dashboard, but a different emotion rose to the surface—the deep ache of seeing someone he loved suffering. It made his bones hurt. He wanted to take him home and get him cleaned up, give him a good meal, and put him back in his own bed.

When David didn't start the car, Jude finally looked at him.

"Well, where is she?" he asked.

"I don't know. I need you to find her."

"I don't know what you mean."

"Find her," David shouted. "That's why you're here."

Jude stared at him with his mouth slightly agape. He looked as if he might pass out.

"You're her talisman. And she's yours. You're connected by magic. I know you're a powerful wizard. You could pull her out of the air when she jumped out the roof. Find her."

Jude stared at the glove compartment. Even though the request sounded insane to David, Jude seemed to take it seriously. He took a deep breath and closed his eyes. After a minute or two, he opened them again.

"I don't know," he said. "I've never done any spell like that."

"You know where things are. You know where the other players are on the football field. You can sense them. Can't you?"

"Yes. But they're close. If you put me in a dark room with Emmy, I could find her. But…there's too much noise, or interference, in the world. I can't find her across miles."

"If you don't, she'll face Whitman Colter alone."

Jude lowered his head and closed his eyes again. David could sense his magic vibrating from his skin. He had turned himself on high.

"Leave the city," Jude said. "Go west."

Patrick watched his mother bounce around the house like a pinball. A pinball with a gun. Patrick felt more like an anthill, filled with nasty biting things, but unable to move himself. He should do something for Samantha. Comfort her. Help her. Go back in time and kill his brother. But he didn't know how to help her any more than he knew how to travel through time.

He sat at the kitchen table with Xavier, who created an elaborate house of cards. It had three floors, plus a chimney, and an attached garage. Patrick wondered if anything went on behind Xavier's cloudy no-color eyes. Did he care about any of it?

The pinball bounced into the table, but only a few cards came down.

"Perhaps you could see her future," Mom suggested. "And, tell us where she is in your vision."

"Yeah, I'll be happy to tell you one second before something terrible happens."

"Xavier, there has to be some kind of spell to find a person," Mom said. "Please."

"You asked us not to do spells," Xavier said. He had already said it twice before.

"I know I've forbidden magic over and over again," she said. "But even wizards who don't practice sometimes do magic in an emergency. There comes a time when what's at stake is worth more than the risks of doing magic." She put her hands up as if she wanted to throttle him. "Why are you picking now of all times to start listening to me about magic?"

"I haven't done any serious spells since I've lived here. Not since my mom died."

Mom huffed and ran up the stairs.

"Why did you stop doing magic when your mom died?" Patrick asked.

Xavier looked at him for the flash of a nanosecond, and then shrugged. "Didn't feel like it, I guess."

The house of cards tumbled as if a blast of wind Patrick didn't feel came through the kitchen.

"Why'd it fall?" Patrick asked.

"It happens sometimes," Xavier said.

Mom thundered back down the stairs with Evangeline and Samantha at her heels. She should leave Samantha alone. Of course, Samantha would agree to whatever Mom wanted her to do, but that didn't mean Mom should ask. Mom and the girls sat down at the table with them, making Patrick and Xavier unwillingly parts of a circle of wizards. Patrick could feel the subtle increase of magic, but the magic didn't feel as clear and cold as it had on the Solstice. The magic still felt cold, but had unexplained warm spots, like in a lake. Their magic felt as they did. Distressed. Erratic. Desperate.

Samantha had sat on Patrick's left. Whatever he said would be wrong, so he didn't say anything at all. She placed her hand on his.

"It's going to be okay," she said.

He should comfort *her*.

"How are you?" he asked tentatively.

"I want to do magic," she said.

"She should," Evangeline said. "She'll feel better."

Patrick didn't know much about magic, but he knew enough to know magic didn't make people feel better.

"We're casting a spell," Mom said. She said it with the no-nonsense Mom tone she might use to say, *We will be cleaning out the garage.*

"Whatever," Patrick said.

"No whatevers," Mom said. "This is very serious. And dangerous. You need to give it your full attention."

"Why do I have to do it?" Patrick asked.

"Because you love your sister."

"I used to."

"Is that really the choice you're making?" Mom asked. "That's not the kind of person you are."

Was.

Patrick didn't respond. He didn't fully understand his choices or why they mattered at this point anyway. He glanced at Samantha. She had the stringy hair, red eyes, and sunburned skin of someone who had spent the day at the beach. It would have been lovely if they *had* just come from a romp on the beach, but on someone who had stayed inside all day in winter, it just looked wrong.

"You want to help her?" he asked Samantha. "After what she did…or what she *didn't* do."

"I think you're more angry than I am. Bad things happen. It's done."

"I don't know if you're really tough, really crazy, or just in denial."

"Maybe she's all three," Evangeline said. "What are you picking on her for?"

"I'm *not*," Patrick argued, but the accusation shut him up. Not only had he failed to comfort her, now apparently, he had picked on her.

"I understand there is a lot to be upset about right now," Mom said. Her attempt at "calm" came out as strained and stilted. "But, there is only one thing that can currently be changed. Three of you have been practicing magic for your entire lives. There has to be something helpful you can come up with."

"Why don't you just use the spell you used to find Dad," Evangeline said to Xavier. Everyone's head whipped over to him, Mom's the fastest. Xavier gave his sister a *look*.

"What?" Mom asked. "I thought he just got a phone call. Or, was he lying about that, too?"

"No," Evangeline said. "But, how do you think spells like that work? They work through people and events and things. They change what happens."

"Okay. Perfect," Mom said. "Xavier?"

"It's not a good idea," he said.

"I try to be patient with you, Xavier. But sometimes you make me want to pull my hair out," Mom said. "I can't even begin to fathom why you don't want to help. Tell me, in plain English…in full sentences…why you can't or won't perform this spell."

"I won't do it," Xavier said. A streak of rather Vandergraff-ish stubbornness broke through his barely-there demeanor.

"It was a complete sentence spoken in English," Patrick said.

Mom turned her sights on Patrick, but Samantha

intervened.

"I think I know the spell. I'll do it," Samantha said. Even now, she wanted to neutralize the situation.

"It's simple, really," she continued. "At least…I think it is. I don't know if it's different for winter wizards, but it's so simple, I don't see how different it could be. My parents never taught it to me. They didn't allow me to do serious magic. They said should you shouldn't alter the world to get things you want because people are too stupid to know what they want. And, they don't believe in doing magic to earn things you don't deserve, like to get money or promotions and stuff. If you did, it would be jinxed anyway. But…I think the same concepts would apply here and it's not about getting something you shouldn't have. It's for a good purpose. So, I don't think it would be jinxed."

"Tell us," Mom prompted. She tapped her foot against the table.

"Like I said, it's really simple. All you have to do is think about what you want to happen and it will." Samantha glanced over at Xavier as if she wanted his confirmation, but his non-expression provided so little information, he might as well have been invisible.

"That's it? That can't be right," Mom said.

"It's not as easy as it sounds. I mean, it's really like all other spells. You do them with your mind. You visualize what you want, and find the correct current of energy to make it happen."

Mom nodded now, drinking in her every word.

"But it's easier when you want something simple to happen, like fire to appear in your hand. It's easy to picture in your head. If you're trying to manipulate complicated things, it's hard to find the right thing to focus on. You can't be too specific. There are a limited number of possible things that can happen. And if you don't pick something that's in the range of possibility, it won't work. You have to let the magic figure out the details. But if you're too vague, you might not get what you want, at least not in the way you expect."

"That's the thing," Patrick said. "We can't picture what's going to happen. We don't even know what state she's in. Like, when she jumped off the roof, we knew exactly how it would look for her to slow down before hitting the ground, so we could picture it."

"That's why this spell is more dangerous than jumping off the roof," Xavier said unexpectedly.

Mom cocked her head to the side to consider what he had said. She stopped tapping her foot.

"It really is simple," Mom said. "I don't know why I didn't think of it that way. And if all seven of us…or six…five…all focus on the same outcome while in a circle, it would be extremely powerful."

Samantha nodded.

"What if we simply focus on protecting Emmy? Is that too vague?" Mom asked. "I know it is vague. But, perhaps we could make it into a visual. Imagine a bubble of protection around her, or something like that. What do you think?"

"It seems okay to me," Samantha said. "I've never done this before." She looked at Xavier again.

Xavier got up from the table and left the room.

"Xavier," Evangeline called as he walked away. He didn't turn around. Patrick expected Evangeline to follow him, but she didn't.

"He's not going to come back," Evangeline said. "We should do it with four."

"Why won't he do it?" Mom asked.

"I think he's worried about Dad," Evangeline said.

Mom furrowed her eyebrows. "I don't understand. I mean, I'm worried, too, but I don't even think he'll even get within fifty miles of that man. He has absolutely no idea where to go and he's driving around Texas randomly. If he's in any danger, it would be a car accident, but that's just as much a danger when he commutes to work, probably more since he's driving in Houston."

Evangeline shrugged one shoulder. "Well, Xavier won't do the spell. I can tell."

"Four is the most powerful wizard circle anyway. Am I right?" Mom asked.

"Yeah, but it's supposed to be one from each season," Evangeline said.

Mom swatted the thought away. "This is as close as it gets. We have three out of four. A summer wizard would never sit at a table with a winter wizard." She looked at Patrick. "Are you in?"

"Yeah, okay," he said. "It seems simple enough. Just like prayer."

Chapter Twenty-Eight

Night had fallen. And, in between towns in West Texas, night fell hard. If David cared to look at the sky, he knew he would see all the stars he missed in Houston. No streetlights lit his path. Nothing but his headlights illuminated the patch of black road ahead of them.

In Ozona, Jude had said they shouldn't take the exit toward Odessa. He wanted them to keep driving West on I-10 at ninety-five miles per hour. David didn't think it would make sense for Colter to stay in Odessa. He had successfully faked his own death there and going to the local grocery store would risk exposure. A logical man would flee to Mexico, but David didn't think Colter did that. Frankly, he had no idea what Colter would have done. He assumed logic played no factor in his decision. He could be anywhere.

However, David couldn't fairly criticize anyone's logic now. They currently searched for a person in the place where, statistically speaking, a person was the least likely to be. The country they drove through had an average of one person per square mile and not far from Loving County, the least populous county in the United States, with eighty-two official residents. But, David thought Colter would like that. The man had gone well out of his way to avoid people and society. He would want to be that one person per square mile.

The total darkness made it easier not to talk to Jude. Without seeing him clearly, he could almost believe he didn't sit there next to him.

At least, until he talked.

"Dad?"

"What?"

"I didn't hurt her or anything. It wasn't like that."

David made a disgusted sound.

"I mean, I didn't hit her."

"I don't want to talk about it."

"You're really mad at me, aren't you?"

"No, Jude, I'm *mad* at you when you break curfew."

"So, what are you then?"

"What was going through your head? What makes a person think that's an okay thing to do?"

"I don't know."

"But you know it was wrong, right? You must know. Otherwise, you wouldn't have left. You wouldn't have said you were sorry."

"Yes."

The blue light from the digital display illuminated Jude's face, but David couldn't read his emotions. In the darkness, he couldn't tell his eyes were blue, let alone see any hints as to the emotion behind them.

"Then why did you do it?" David asked.

"What do you want me to say?"

"I really don't know."

"I don't remember most of it. I was wasted. I don't remember starting, I only remember stopping."

"What made you stop?"

David hung on to the silence, waiting. In the end, it made no difference. It didn't matter to Samantha anyway. Or Emmy.

But, maybe it meant something good had remained. Jude still had a conscience somewhere in his drunken, magic-ravaged brain.

"Emmy said my name." Jude turned to the window and covered his face with his hand, as if only that part of the story shamed him. "And I saw her there, watching me." He paused. "Do you think she's going to be okay?"

"And of course, you mean Emmy, not the girl you raped," David said.

"I…"

"Obviously, Emmy is not fine. But you know what, if she doesn't end up getting herself killed tonight because of you, she will be fine. Eventually. So will Samantha. They can heal. You can't."

He heard a pitter-patter on the windshield and David thought they'd hit a large swarm of bugs, but saw the rain streaking up the glass. The drops increased in size quickly and the tiny spot of road he could see in the headlights became distorted from the sheet of water moving across the windowpane.

"When does it rain in the fucking desert?" David asked.

He had meant it rhetorically, but Jude answered.

"Occasionally," he said casually.

CHAPTER TWENTY-NINE

Lightning illuminated the land around the road, and startled Emmy so much, the truck swerved dangerously. The light had come from nowhere. She hadn't even noticed the mountains until they turned into massive blue ghosts in the brief flash.

"Since when does it rain in the fucking desert?" she asked the empty car.

She felt dead tired, but at the same time felt like she could stay up for the rest of her life. The adrenaline worked better than caffeine, but she'd had plenty of that, too. Although, she didn't know if the fiery feeling she had came from adrenaline or caffeine. Maybe magic. She didn't really know where reality ended and magic began. Did everyone feel this way all the time? Like, if they didn't stop moving they would explode? The nice thing about being a witch was now she knew it *could* be magic. She didn't have to be weird or crazy. Anything that went bump in her head, she could call magic.

Maybe because she had gotten closer now, or because lighting had broken the sky into pieces, the fiery feeling had increased. It didn't just come from inside her anymore. The magic swirled around her like a smell in the air. Wet dust from the storm, electricity, and magic.

She worried the address on Dad's desk had been a fake. Some kind of stupid joke. This asshole didn't live in a city, or a town, or village, or places where people can buy food and gasoline. He lived south of Marfa on Route 67, which, according to the conspiracy nut bumper stickers and T-shirts at the last gas station, was the area famous for the "Marfa Lights," these unexplained light balls that shot around the sky. She saw no lights anywhere on the horizon, unexplained or not. She didn't see *anything* out here. That woman had probably just played a mean joke on Dad.

The rain started and didn't kid around. Someone could have poured a waterfall on the car. She had to slow down to a crawl. But, at least no one would hit her from behind like they would on I-10. She hadn't seen any headlights or brake lights for half an hour or more. At least, maybe she'd get to skip driving lessons after this. Well…she'd probably still be grounded when she turned sixteen. Driving came naturally when she did it Jude's way. She had her eyes open, but she kept her other senses open, too.

She found the road from the address. It hardly looked like a road, but she turned down it anyway. Things got really wet really fast. In her headlights, she could see water running down the dirt road so heavily, she seemed to drive through a stream. But, it couldn't be more than a few inches of water. That's why she took the Expedition. Then something weird happened. The wheels stopped scraping the road. The car seemed to float. The steering wheel locked, and the lights on the console went out. The car moved on its own. Backward. With a crunch, the back bumper hit a boulder, and then the water spun the car around so the driver's side of the car smashed into the same boulder.

David parked on the shoulder of Route 67. The rain had become too thick to drive through. To avoid risking gas and battery power, he had taken the keys out of the ignition. He had thought it was dark before. *This* was dark. He couldn't see a damn thing out his window. Not even the road, which he could only assume still lay along the earth, directly to his left. Now that clouds had covered the stars, they could be floating in deep space.

The cold, white light of David's phone flooded the car.

"I don't have service anymore," David said.

"I know. It's like we're *nowhere*," Jude said. He spoke the word 'nowhere' like it named the Promised Land he searched for. David had considered the possibility that Jude didn't plan to take him to Emmy at all, but simply followed a mad impulse to drive away from lights.

"Emmy could be calling me right now. Or, your mother. She's probably freaking out I'm not answering. When the rain lets up, we're going home."

"You're giving up?"

"I would never give up on finding Emmy. But I don't think that's what I'm doing anymore. You can't find a person by randomly driving, making gut decisions about where to turn."

"Why not?"

"Because it makes no sense."

"But, that's because it's magic. Right?"

"I don't know. I don't know when something is magic and when it's not."

"I do."

"You really think you can find her?"

"Do you really want to give up and go home?"

"No." He hadn't meant what he had said about going back. He would never have done it. He would have kept driving circles around the globe until he found her.

"You said I was her talisman," Jude said. "If being around me keeps her safe, why does she keep getting hurt?"

"Probably because you're a terrible talisman."

Jude nodded. "Maybe I should let her go, then. Can I decide not to be her talisman?"

"No…that's not a good idea. You can't be around her anymore. But, you can't cut her out emotionally. It's dangerous to renounce your talisman. The truth is, I don't know if you can be a bad or good talisman. I think you just are one. She still gets hurt because talismans protect the soul, not the body."

"What good does that do? That sucks."

"It does plenty good. But, I'm not surprised you think that. You clearly don't care about your own soul; why should you care about anyone else's?"

"You don't know what you're talking about. You don't know what it's like."

"I don't know what *what* is like?"

Jude ignored the question. "The whole time we've been driving, I've been casting a protection spell for her. If it's working…have I been protecting her body or her soul? And if I am just protecting her soul…then what does that mean? That doesn't do anything. She could still be hurt. She could still be *killed*. And, what? The upside is, her soul floats up to heaven, safe and sound?"

"That's the thing. You have no idea how a spell is going to work. Even if they seem harmless. Stop casting spells and focus on finding her. If we do that, we can protect her soul *and* her body the old-fashioned way."

David glanced at his phone, now nothing more than a light and a clock. 12:00 a.m.

"Merry Christmas," David said.

The door wouldn't open, so Emmy crawled out the window. The water reached past her knees. Her muscles tensed painfully. It seemed to get colder with each passing minute. She had never felt so cold, in fact. The slopes of Winter Park, Colorado must have been colder, but she hadn't been soaked to the waist. And, since she'd had the heater on in the car, she had left her jacket on the floor of the passenger seat, now underwater.

She waded out of the road onto higher land. At least, the rain started to pass. She didn't bring much with her when she scrambled out of the car, but she did bring the gun. In the dark, she couldn't even tell which way to head back to the road, and her cell phone was both out of area and underwater. The night would get only colder. She didn't know how long it took to get hypothermia…but she already couldn't feel her toes. She rubbed her bare arms furiously and then remembered she could do better. She tried to call up the flame as she had on the Solstice, but it wouldn't come. Maybe her hands shook too much.

A glow of light appeared several hundred feet away, as if the fire she had meant to create had gotten lost. It bounced up and down, illuminating short, black trees that looked like charred skeleton hands. She thought about the Marfa lights. Then she heard a light cough. Emmy clutched her gun tightly. It had to be him. She should have realized that in the pitch dark, he would have seen her headlights coming from several miles away. The flood stopping her may have worked out for the best.

The fiery feeling under her skin increased and made her feel warmer. She felt as if she glowed. She looked at her hands to make sure she didn't actually glow. That wouldn't be helpful right now. As long as he had the light, she had the upper hand. The darkness worked as well as an invisibility cloak. She should be scared, but she almost never felt scared. Or, not exactly. The things that scared other people, such as horror movies and monsters in her closet, didn't scare her. Some things scared her. But, right now, she felt better than she had in a while. A pleasant heat bubbled under her skin, the same heat she felt when talking to a cute boy or when on stage for debate or theater.

The light got closer. Now she could hear the crunch of his footsteps on the gravel. She crawled behind a rock to shield herself from a flashlight sweep and tried to breathe as little as possible, a hard task in the situation. He would find the car and that would distract him. Then she could make her move. If only she could snipe him from behind the rock. But, she didn't have a sight and couldn't find a good target in the darkness anyway. She hated waiting. She wanted it done now. It would fix everything and bring the world back into balance. Evil would be punished and good would prevail and it would all make sense. *Justice.* She had to stop herself from saying the word aloud.

His light illuminated the busted Expedition. She could hear splashes and squishes as he moved through the water and mud. Even though he moved close enough that she could hear him breathing and muttering, his light pointed away from him, and she couldn't see his face or any part of him at all. But, he had to be the right man. Not only because no one else would live in a place such as this, but also because she could feel his magic. He had a heavier presence than anyone in her family. She imagined him as a black cloud gliding over the rocks.

The thought gave her the briefest flash of fear. If she could feel him without needing to see him or hear him, he could do the same for her. She guessed her magic couldn't be as black or saturated. She had practiced magic for only a little over a month and he had practiced magic for years. She would look like a wispy breath of steam compared to him. But still, she was the only living thing for miles, and she was a witch. They say wizards can always sense other wizards in their presence.

He aimed his flashlight precisely in her direction. He had to feel something. Otherwise, he would have pointed his flashlight into the car first. The rock did its job keeping her hidden…at least, the self visible to the eye. He pointed his flashlight inside the car. He reached his hand through the passenger side window where Emmy had climbed out and she heard a click and a rustle. He took a white slip of paper out of the glove compartment and examined it under the flashlight beam. Their car insurance slip. Emmy had no idea whether or not the name David Vandergraff had any meaning to him and she couldn't see his face for a reaction. Either way, Colter had her father's name now, and his home address. He folded the slip of paper and put it in his pocket. No going back now. He had to die.

Then he did something unexpected. He turned off his flashlight. He might as well have disappeared.

"Did you see that?" Jude asked.

The rain had lightened, and they headed farther into nowhere on Route 67.

"What?"

"It was like…a light. Way off the road over there."

David pulled over again. A flimsy lead, but the only thing even close to useful they had run into for a while. Jude fiddled with the map on the GPS.

"It looks like there is a road just a few hundred yards up. Go there," Jude said urgently.

"Okay." David's heart rate quickened. It could be wishful

thinking, but he thought he could feel whatever Jude had tracked here. He had the vague sense the two of them weren't alone anymore. Someone or something was out there.

Sure enough, they came upon a dirt road. It had the same barely-there appearance as the one Colter had lived on outside of Monahans. Someone had unscrewed the street sign from its pole. Maybe, against all things rational and logical, they had actually found him. But, if Jude tracked Emmy, then she had found him, too. She had beaten them here.

"Turn off the headlights," Jude said. "We're putting ourselves at a disadvantage. He can see us coming."

"It's too dark to drive without them."

"Let me drive then."

"What difference does that make?"

"I can drive without them.

"You'll drive us off a cliff."

"I can do it. I've done it before. I can drive on I-10 during rush hour blindfolded. Trust me."

David wanted to argue, but hesitated, remembering whom he talked to. "Dear God, you really did that, didn't you?"

"Yes."

"Oh fuck," David said.

He pulled the car over and switched places with Jude. Jude turned off the headlights. David wouldn't say it aloud, but Jude's blind driving impressed David. Jude drove slowly but steadily. Then the sound of the tires against rock changed, more of a splash.

"Stop," David said.

"What?"

"Are we driving through water?"

"There's some water on the road, not much."

"No. Stop."

Jude stopped the car.

"Flash floods in the desert are dangerous," David said.

"The soil can't absorb the water and it rises more quickly than back at home."

"Fine, then we'll walk," Jude said. The determined Little Leaguer remained somewhere. He wouldn't give up, even if it meant walking through the desert blindly.

"Okay."

David had never been a Boy Scout. He had no flashlights, no water, and no compass. As soon as he opened the car door, he stepped into water up to his ankles. Of course, he had no spare shoes or socks. He hadn't brought anything with him but his keys, wallet, and a hunting rifle. And, of course, Jude. He opened the truck and pulled out his rifle, as much use as it would serve in the dark.

David turned on the car's emergency lights. It would drain the battery, but if he didn't do it, they would lose the car as soon as the lights went off. They didn't have cell phone service, so if they lost the car they'd have nothing to help them stave off hyperthermia and mountain lions until the sun rose.

"What are you doing?" Jude asked.

"We can't lose track of the car."

"But…the light."

"We won't be with the car, so it won't matter."

Jude grumbled something, but didn't argue more. He darted along the unflooded part of the road and immediately disappeared into the now total dark. If David hadn't been able to hear Jude's feet against the gravel, he would have already lost him. He scrambled along in his wake, his feet squishing with water with each step. Then, a ball of light shot away from where Jude walked.

"Whoa," he said.

"What was that?"

"I was just feeling the air and it was like it caught on fire."

Jude raked his hand through the air and tiny sparks followed in its wake.

"There's so much magic here," Jude said. "Can you feel it?"

"Yes. Do you think it's coming from him?" David asked.

"No. It doesn't feel like that. It's like it's coming from the air. Or it's in the rocks. The place has extra magic. It would be an awesome place for a wizard to live though, wouldn't it? It would make all your spells stronger. And if anyone saw anything, they'd think it was those ghost lights."

Jude started walking again, slower, perhaps afraid to set off more accidental fireballs. David breathed heavily, searching the horizon for more signs of life.

"I was thinking something," Jude said. "Do you think that killing a person would hurt your soul?"

"Yes," David said without having to think about it. "Why?"

"I'm worried about what you said, about Emmy's soul. If I'm keeping her soul safe, and not her body, then she won't be able to kill him, will she? Because killing him would hurt her soul. I might not be protecting her at all. I could be putting her in more danger. It doesn't seem like both her soul and her body can be safe at the same time. What do you think?"

David's head hurt, from the cold, from exhaustion, from stress, and he couldn't wrap his head around the question.

"I don't know. All I know is that if we get to him first, she can't kill him and he can't kill her."

"Do you want me to kill him?"

"No. Why?"

"Because your soul is still good."

David didn't miss Jude's implication about his own soul. "It's my job to do. If I had done it sooner, Emmy wouldn't have felt like she had to. I'm done asking my kids to take on my burdens."

"It's too late for that, I think," he said matter-of-factly. "Let me know if you change your mind."

Emmy crouched behind her rock. She had her gun clutched in her hand and mentally reviewed her mother's instructions on how to use it. *You can't screw around with guns, but if you're ever in danger, I don't want you to hesitate*, she had said. She took shallow breaths through her nose and felt the air to find his magic. She remembered more of her mother's words. *Only in darkness can you truly see. Only in silence can you truly hear.* She closed her eyes so she would stop trying to see like a Mundane.

She couldn't hear his footsteps. That scared her because it didn't make sense. She shivered so much she feared he might hear the subtle vibration. *Only in fear can you truly feel.*

She stuck her fingers in her ears so she would stop trying to hear footsteps. She had to feel with her deeper senses. It worked. The left side of her neck prickled. She felt him there, on her left. And, he felt close. She sensed that he stood only a few feet away, looking at her. She still couldn't hear him. No breathing, no shifting gravel under his feet. She heard nothing but the wind skating across the earth. He must know some kind of spell to cloak himself. If he saw her there, why didn't he do anything? The fear surged in her again. He wasn't a rational being. She couldn't predict his next move.

Then, he lunged at her.

She couldn't hear him, but she could feel the dark cloud race toward her as if it had been caught in a wind. She scrambled to her feet and ran. The scattering of gravel and her own fast breathing distracted her other senses. She couldn't tell how close he got. She could run fast, but didn't know if it would be enough. For all she knew, he could fly.

Her leg exploded in pain. She had hit a large rock at full speed. Her face hit the hard ground and she could feel the dirt embedding itself in her cheek and hands. She couldn't help but cry out. The anguished bleat didn't sound like her. But, it didn't matter whether she screamed or not. He could find her now. She reached out to feel her shin, half-expecting to feel bone sticking out. Her bones remained inside her, but an egg-sized bump had already surfaced.

The gun. *Where is it?* She patted the earth around her on her hands and knees. The pain distracted her from the use of her other senses, but she guessed he stood right over her. Watching her. Biding his time. Why wouldn't he be? She made as much noise as a rockslide. Then her hand hit something hard and smooth. The gun. She clutched it to her chest again like a teddy bear, but something about it scared her. He had let her find it. Maybe his wizard vision worked only on living things and he simply didn't see the gun in the dark.

She stood up and had to stifle another scream when she put weight on her leg. The end of the line had arrived. She couldn't run anymore, at least, not far or fast. Even as she raised the gun, he didn't move. The clouds parted and the new moon sky gave off enough starlight to show her the outline of a man standing four feet away from her, staring at her, and saying nothing. She didn't understand how a man could be so silent. She didn't even hear breathing. She visualized his heart beating in his chest and tried to feel it, tried to make it her target.

She pulled the trigger. Click. She pulled the trigger again. Click. Something was wrong with the gun. He moved toward her slowly. Click. Click. She dropped the gun and tried to run.

He grabbed her by the hair.

With no options left, she filled her lungs with air and let out a scream that bounced off the mountains, and with it, she unwittingly released a fireball that rose from her chest and shot across the blackness. She wanted someone to find her, although she could tell by the blackness for miles around that no one would hear her scream. He threw her on the ground and she clenched her fists. Part of her had prepared for this moment ever since he turned off his flashlight. If he got her, she would fight to the death. She would bite, punch, kick, claw, and elbow until he killed her. That was the only way Emmy Vandergraff would go down.

But, he took that last choice from her. He put his hand at the base of her spine and she went limp. And, when all the power had left her, she remembered to pray.

"Jude!" David shouted. "Jude!"

He had run too far ahead and had disappeared.

"Dammit, Jude!"

He feared Jude would slip away. Disappear. And, he'd never see him again.

"You're too slow," Jude said. He had stopped to wait.

"Are we still on the road?"

"Sure, it's right there."

"It's still so dark…and quiet," David said.

"So?"

"If she was here, wouldn't we have seen or heard something by now? We've been going down this road for a while."

Jude pointed excitedly as if he had spotted Santa's sleigh. "Look!"

David whipped around. A little trail of light faded into the horizon. Then, in the opposite direction, he saw another one. A basketball-sized globe of light hovered a few feet above the ground, then shot sideways before it diverged into two balls and then disappeared.

"Is that what you saw that made you want to stop here?"

David asked.

"Yeah. I saw a light like that."

David shivered. Now he had stopped walking, it had grown colder. His jacket and the box of ashes within provided little warmth.

"What?" Jude asked.

"It's just…what do you think that was?"

"I don't know."

"I know what it's not. It's not flashlights, headlights, or lights in a house. If I'm not mistaken…they're the Marfa lights. Ghost lights. A mirage caused by temperature gradients or UFOs, depending on who you ask."

"What are you saying?"

That they're completely lost. But, he couldn't bring himself to say it aloud. "We'll keep going. This road has to lead to something; that is, assuming it's really a road and not a dry river bed."

"It's a road," Jude growled back. "We're close."

David followed Jude at a jog. The faint light given by the stars illuminated his outline, and he kept him in sight even though his lungs seared from panting in the cold air and a stitch in his side made him want to double over.

Then Jude stopped. He stared at something in front of him.

"What is it?" Jude asked.

David gave his eyes a moment to make the most of the tiny amount of light. They had come to a massive hole in the earth. Limestone had been cut out in giant blocks, giving the slopes of the hole a stair-step appearance. David scanned the area inside and around the quarry and didn't see any signs of an active dig. No construction equipment, no Porta-Johns, no foreman's trailer. He saw no vehicles or any other sign of man.

"It's an old quarry," David said.

"I don't understand. Does he live here?"

David paused before answering. Even though the man was a snake, David didn't think he lived under a rock. And, he would need a vehicle of some kind to make it out here.

"No," David said finally.

Jude kicked the ground, causing gravel and sparks from his magic to spray out in front of him. "No. This isn't right. I know we're close. I can feel her."

"I'm sorry. I know you did your best." Enchanted Rock had called to David and Crystal. Perhaps that had happened again. The magic of the place drew Jude here, not Emmy. "It could be the magic from the Marfa Lights, whatever they are. That's what you feel."

Jude sat down at the edge of the quarry and wrapped his arms around his knees. David didn't remember him looking so much like a child, even when he was one.

"We failed?" Jude asked as if he had just learned the word. "No. Magic is about believing the impossible is possible. If we believe we can find her, we will."

"We'll keep looking. But, we have to go back to the car. We need to drive back to Marfa where there are cell phone towers. That way I can call your mom. Who knows, Emmy could even be back home right now."

"She's not."

Jude's breaths became jerky. He cried and tried to do it quietly. The sound make David hurt from his head to his gut. He hadn't heard his son cry in more than ten years.

David sat down next to him, not quite sure what to do. "Jude…"

"Leave me alone, please."

CHAPTER THIRTY

Patrick had never stayed awake past four in the morning until tonight. He once stayed up until after three one summer night when he snuck out of bed to play a video game he had been addicted to at the time. But, he didn't feel tired tonight. Or, perhaps, he'd never felt more tired. But, he didn't feel *curl up in bed and rest* tired, he felt *I'll never sleep again* tired.

Samantha had fallen asleep an hour ago, curled up on the couch next to him. Her painted toes pressed up against his leg. He didn't know if she didn't want to sleep in Emmy's room anymore or if she had simply gotten so tired, she passed out where she sat. But, it didn't matter. He liked it this way. He had put a blanket over her and sat at her feet. She didn't need twenty-four hour guard duty, at least now Jude had left, but it made him feel better. If he could work it out so he could stay awake for the rest of his life to watch her sleep, he would.

For hours, he sat there, occasionally visited by Mom to check if he was okay. She got a sarcastic, "Yes, I'm awesome. How is your day going?"

Perhaps she thought his staring into space for hours was a weird way to cope. Mom had been flitting around the house

280

doing ridiculous tasks such as addressing Christmas cards for next year. "I have all the stuff out now," she had said. "I can't believe I never thought to do this before. This is so smart."

Then she baked a pecan pie at midnight, followed by three enchilada casseroles she put in the freezer. All of this punctuated by calling Dad, Emmy, and Jude over and over and over as if she wanted to be the one-hundredth caller in a radio giveaway. None of them answered. Their phones didn't even ring, just went to voicemail. Patrick couldn't imagine any reason why Dad would turn off his phone tonight, and simply the fact that it didn't make sense terrified him.

Patrick didn't stare into space because he had gone crazy. He was paying attention. As stupid as his gift of one-second-prophecy was, he still wanted to know. However, waiting for prophecies didn't work like it did in the movies. He couldn't tell what thoughts and images came from his own brain and what might be a message. After all, he couldn't watch his thoughts like a movie. He *thought* his thoughts. He wrote the movie. He tried to think about Emmy and picture her surroundings. He had a vague sense of fear, but he couldn't picture anything. In fact, thinking of Emmy made his mind go completely black and silent. He had an idea of what that might mean, but didn't even want to think it. He had gotten several other images throughout the night—a rushing stream, a ball of fire, and most recently, a pair of giant black wings.

He heard his mother's voice in her bedroom and shot up from where he sat. Evangeline and Xavier had gone to bed a couple hours ago, and she didn't usually talk to herself, at least not in full sentences. He went into her room without knocking. Sure enough, she spoke into her phone. She put her hand over the receiver and whispered, "I'm sorry, honey, I didn't mean to…it's not them."

She waved for him to come in.

"Thank you so much. Okay. You, too. I will," she said and

hung up.

"Who were you talking to? Grandma?"

"Actually, it was Lydia Armstrong, you know, from church. She's the one who always wears those gaudy pins on her blouse."

"Why were you talking to her in the middle of the night?"

"She's in my prayer circle."

"You mean, they're praying…for us? For this situation?"

Mom smiled a little. "They don't know all the details. Just that Emmy is missing. As nice as it is to think I can cast a spell and protect my family on my own… I feel safer knowing I've consulted an expert."

"You mean God?"

"Yes, I mean God."

"Yeah. I prayed for her, too."

"Thank you, Patrick. You know, I should say it more often. You're a good person. I'm proud of you."

That made him mad. Basically, she meant, *I'm glad you're not pure evil like your brother.* He didn't do anything more special than *not* rape anybody. Yeah, he should get a medal for that.

"Thanks," he said.

"Have you picked up on anything?" Apparently, she knew what he had been trying to do.

"No."

She squinted at him. "Are you lying?"

"No," he said again.

"All right. Come here and give me a hug."

He did as he was asked. She looked calm, but she shook slightly.

"I should tell you to go to sleep," she said. "But I know it wouldn't do any good."

"I'll be right outside if you need me."

She smiled at him warmly, but her eyes stayed sad.

When Patrick went back into the family room, Samantha

sat up with her arms wrapped around her knees.

"I'm sorry, did our talking wake you up?"

"No. I woke up when you left the couch. I liked being able to feel you with my feet. It helped me sleep."

"Oh." He sat back down and picked up her feet and put them back on his leg. "There you go."

"Can I ask you something?" she asked.

"Sure."

"Are you mad at me?"

"Why would I be mad at you?"

She shrugged and didn't look him in the eye. "I want things to go back the way they were."

"Me, too. But, I don't know if that's possible."

She stared at her knees. Her shoulders slumped as if her arms suddenly became too heavy.

"But…I suppose there is no impossible for a spring witch," he said. "You can break through ice with flowers."

She flashed him her green eyes.

"Do you want to go dancing?" he asked.

"Dancing?"

"Maybe not right now…but you know, sometime soon. Would it make you feel better?"

"Yes."

"Just so you know, I don't know how to dance at all."

She smiled, but the smile faded quickly and she looked back at her toes. "Patrick, with everything that happened with Emmy, I haven't had a chance to tell you."

Patrick felt his stomach tighten. He didn't have much experience with dating, but still knew that tone. The "we need to talk" tone.

"What?" he asked, his throat dry.

"Would you still want to be with me, if I left?"

"Left?"

"After the summer wizards came, your mom called my

Aunt Charlotte. She's going to come get me."

"Well, that's good, right?" He didn't really think it was good. He wanted her to live here with him. He didn't care that fifteen-year-olds generally didn't get to live with their girlfriend. He felt like his throat had filled with cement that rapidly hardened. He waited for the axe to fall.

"She lives in New Orleans. I'm going to live there." Her throat sounded like it had hardened too, or she suddenly got a cold. "I don't want to. I know I can't stay here. But, I don't want to leave Houston. Or, you."

"When is she coming to get you?"

"New Year's Day."

"That's soon."

"But, I'm not leaving if Emmy's not safe by then. I won't leave if she's not home. I won't leave my friend. I'll lock myself in the bathroom when Aunt Charlotte comes, I don't care what I have to do."

"I'm sure she'll be back before then." Patrick didn't know if she would be, but that was just what he had to say. "You asked if I still wanted to be with you if you left. Do you mean that?"

She nodded again. "I don't want to break up. Besides, I need someone to text about my crazy aunt. Her house always smells like barbecue, but she's a vegetarian. It's very unsettling."

Patrick didn't know if she meant it as a joke, but he couldn't help but laugh.

"I don't want to break up either. So, I don't think we should."

She leaned in and kissed him, but for once, Patrick couldn't concentrate on it. He just felt like he had started the countdown of last kisses.

CHAPTER THIRTY-ONE

The dawn sky turned a dusty purple, and then the clouds caught the first rays of the sun and erupted into blankets of fire. It looked like a painting. It looked like Heaven might look. Some people might call it "breathtaking," but David didn't give a damn what the sky looked like. His delirious mind couldn't help but think about how Amanda's war between dark magic and Christmas had ended badly for jolly St. Nick. It had been a slaughter. On Christmas morning, he walked down Route 67 looking for cell coverage…because his car's battery had gone dead and they were stranded.

He couldn't remember ever feeling so uncomfortable in his life. No sleep. No food. No water. The cold, dry wind chapped his face. He probably looked twenty years older and he felt about fifty years older. Jude probably felt the same but didn't complain. Jude didn't whine much, but he did complain about much less. He didn't act like himself anymore.

To punctuate this thought, Jude turned and ran straight out into the flats, hurdling a thicket of bush. He acted as if he had an urgent appointment out there he had forgotten to mention. Part of David wanted to shrug his shoulders and continue his walk down the road as if nothing had happened.

But then, he saw what Jude had seen. Among the interminable expanse of brown grass and stout yellow bushes, something reflected the fiery sky. David thought he might pass out. He saw the Expedition.

Unlike Jude, he didn't want to run to it. There was always room for some hope when a child was missing…but when they're found, the truth must be faced one way or another. David ran anyway. Distances were misleading in the desert, and the car didn't seem to get much closer as he went. But when Jude arrived, David could tell what he found by his body language.

Jude ran a few circles around the car, opening the doors, and then he continued to move circles away from the car, darting his head from side to side. He must not see her. When David finally arrived, Jude had climbed on a rock to get a better view of the surrounding area. David examined the car. She had hit the rock, but the collision had been mild, just a scrape. She left the keys in the ignition. That fact made dread creep down his neck. If she had walked back to the road looking for help, she would have taken the keys…and her purse and cell phone…which sat on the floor on the passenger side. He picked up her jacket, desperate to feel some part of her, wanting it to still have her warmth. The jacket dripped all over his shoes. Everything had been soaked. Then, it made sense. She had gotten caught in a flash flood. Most of the water had receded, but the thick mud around the tired remained.

He turned to his son. The longer Jude stayed silent, the more terrified David became. Jude had proven he did have the power to find Emmy. Emmy had a light inside her that Jude had followed across six hundred miles. And now, they had to be closer than ever. So, if he couldn't feel it now…maybe the light had gone out.

"Jude, where is she? Jude?"

He pointed. "I think I see something over there."

His tone sounded flat. The *something* was bad news.

At first, David's eyes refused to let him look. But, he managed to get them to focus. He saw it several hundred yards away, hard to distinguish among the brush, but it looked like clothes on the ground. Maybe, a person.

David ran this time. He could hear Jude at his heels over the sound of his heartbeat pummeling in his ears. As they got closer, David slowed and approached the prone figure. He grabbed Jude's arm to hold him back.

"Is that him?" Jude asked.

"Be careful," David said.

"Why? He looks dead to me."

David prodded the man with his foot. He was face down in the dirt with his mouth and nose pressed against the earth. If he hadn't already died, he would suffocate soon. David used his foot to flip him over.

"Is that him?" Jude asked again.

"I don't know what he looks like."

His unkempt hair was pitch black, like his sister's, although his had strands of gray. He wore jeans that had the thin and grimy look of jeans worn every day. His skin was tanned and aged a decade or so past his years. He looked as Whitman Colter should, but it still didn't seem quite right. David had hunted a monster and found only a man.

"I definitely think he's dead," Jude said. "He's hasn't been dead long though, he's not all rotten or anything. Holy shit…he's dead. He's fucking dead. She did it."

"How?"

He didn't have any blood on him, or any evidence of injury.

"I don't know. Let's ask her," Jude said.

"What?"

"She's over there." He pointed.

David didn't see her, but he did see a tiny travel trailer, so coated with dirt it blended into the scenery. Colter's home.

David ran again. Then he saw her, so dirty she blended in with the scenery, too. She sat in the open doorway of the trailer. She had rolled up one jean leg and pressed a dirty cloth to her shin.

She smiled. "You found me."

David kneeled at her feet and gingerly touched each of her arms and legs like as if one might be missing. He wanted to count all her toes like he did when she was first born. She had bloody scrapes on her face and arms. A deep bruise covered her leg.

She must have read his mind, or he might have literally glowed with rage.

"Dad, you're freaking out. Calm down. It's not like that. I tripped and fell real bad."

He gathered her in his arms and wept into her hair. She felt warm, and soft, and alive. He hadn't appreciated the miracle of a beating heart so much since he had seen Jude's for the first time on an ultrasound inside Amanda.

"Dad…really, I'm fine." She put her arms around him and squeezed him back. "I want to go home."

"I love you so much."

"I love you, too, Dad. And…while you're still happy to see me…you should know I wrecked the car."

"I don't care."

"Can I get that in writing?"

"How did you do it?" Jude asked her.

She had acted as if she couldn't see him there, and David didn't know if she would respond.

After a moment, she did, but kept her eyes on David. "I didn't kill him. But, I was able to fight him. I thought he had won and it was over. So, I prayed. And then I heard God tell me, *keep fighting.* It made me angry at first. I couldn't fight. He had done something to me and I couldn't even move. But, I didn't want to give up and I think God was telling me I didn't have to. So, I listened. I decided I was going to be okay. He wasn't going to hurt me. I kept thinking it over and over, trying as hard as I could to really, really believe it. That was the hardest part. But God said I could, so I believed. I kind of hoped I could get myself to shoot fire at him or something, but that's not how it worked. He just kept getting confused. He would walk away like he forgot I was there, and I'd creep away and it would take him a while to find me again. And it was like his depth perception was off. He would be way off when he tried to grab me. Somehow, I messed with his head. But, all it did was slow everything down. I don't think it would have held him off forever. That's when the black angel came."

"What did you say?" David asked.

"Well, that's what she seemed like. Her magic made air ripple and it looked like wings. It was really cool. She was the one who killed him. She wouldn't tell me how she did it. They shouted nonsense at each other and then he died."

"I don't understand...do you know who she was? Is she still here?"

"Yes. The woman who gave you the envelope. And yes, she's here. She gave me food and water from his trailer and has been sitting by herself for hours."

David's heart sank. For a moment he had thought...well, that would have been impossible.

"Is it okay if I leave you with him while I go talk to her?"

Emmy looked at her brother for the first time. "Yes."

"See if there is more food and water," David told Jude. "You need to drink some water."

David headed in the direction Emmy had pointed. Rachel perched on a rock, watching him approach.

"I thought I felt your presence. David, honey, you look awful."

It's not something you say to a lady, but she looked worse. He hardly recognized her as the fashionable New York businesswoman who had rung his doorbell less than a week ago. She looked as unwashed and unkempt as her brother. A layer of dirt lightened her black hair and it looked as if she had left her hairbrush in Manhattan.

"So you got my message?" she asked.

"Uh…no."

"Oh…well, then, color me impressed."

"Why didn't you pick up the phone? Where were you?"

She cocked her head to the side, as if she tried to remember. "On Sabbatical. But, when I went into town, I got all the texts you had sent me. I replied back, but you didn't respond. I was worried. So, I came here myself."

"Did you drive?"

"Of course, David. How were you imagining it? By broomstick, with my flying monkeys? I parked up the road."

"Do you happen to have jumper cables?"

"I think so. Ask the monkeys to help you."

"Rachel…I don't know how to thank you. I owe you everything."

"No. Maybe, I just owe *you* a little less now."

"I'm sorry…you know…for your loss."

She chuckled darkly. "That's cruel, David. You don't mean it in the least. Why did you say it?"

"I meant it. I'm not sorry he's dead. But, I'm sorry for you. I can't imagine having to kill someone you love, even if they really deserve it."

"Thank you," she whispered. She wrapped her arms around her knees and stared at her toes while she wiggled them. It made her look like a little girl. "Can I see your hands?"

David hesitated at the odd request, but walked closer to her and held out his hands. She took his right one and moved her finger along the lines of his palm, then drew a line from nail to knuckle of each of his fingers and then down each of his finger bones. Then she followed the vein that went from his wrist up his forearm. Her eyes looked glazed and unfocused.

"You have nice hands."

"Are you all right?" He gently extricated himself from her grasp.

"Do you think Verity will have a scar?"

He paused. "Do you mean Emmy?"

"Who?"

"Uh…if she does, I'm sure we can get it fixed. The scrape on her face doesn't look very deep, if that's what you mean."

"That's good."

"How about I help you get home safely. You can ride with us."

"You should be careful. You have two of them," she mumbled.

"Okay…it's going to be fine. Just come with me."

"I don't want to go."

"I can't just leave you here…like this."

"I'm a grown woman."

"I know you're a very capable person. But right now…I think you need someone to help you."

"No, thank you. We two have paddled in the stream, from morning sun till dine. But seas between us broad have roared since auld lang syne." She took his hand back and kissed his palm.

When they got back to Marfa, David called Amanda and she demanded they get a hotel and sleep before driving back. David said he didn't want to spend another moment away from home and away from her. She said it would be stupid for them to go through all that to die in a fiery car crash because he fell asleep at the wheel.

She won the argument, of course.

So, the next morning, David dropped Jude off at James's house in Austin on the way back to Houston. He needed to buy some time before he figured out what to do with him. He doubted he had much time before his brother called and demanded that David take his son back. Even on Jude's best days, David didn't think they would get along very well.

After Amanda had finished her own inspection of Emmy and gotten her own, "Mom, stop freaking out," speech, she fell into David's arms.

"Spend the night with me tonight," she whispered.

"Absolutely."

"But maybe shower first."

David chuckled.

"Seriously…why didn't you shower at the hotel?"

"I didn't think about it. I just wanted to come home."

"You are ridiculous." She whispered it into his ear like her own brand of sweet nothing. "And stinky."

EPILOGUE

Evangeline insisted on wearing a dress and sandals to scatter her mother's ashes, even though it was January and they climbed to the top of Enchanted Rock. However, since Evangeline originally hadn't wanted to come at all, it pleased David that she chose to dress up. She looked lovely. A white party dress with black ivy stitched around the hem. David liked it because, for once, she didn't remind him of anyone. Not Crystal, not David's mother, only Evangeline. Showing a glimpse of the grown-up self she would become. To complete her outfit, she had drawn intricate, colorful butterflies up and down her left arm. They looked so real he worried the people would think he had let his twelve-year-old get tattoos.

They had the rock mostly to themselves, as he had expected for wintertime. The bald face of pink granite had no trees to block the wind. Xavier draped his jacket over Evangeline's goose bump-covered arms before David had a chance to. He didn't have much planned. He had done his research, but hadn't found any wizard rites that seemed fitting. They all mentioned the wizard afterlife, known as the Summerland. Summerland was just another word for Heaven, but he didn't like it. The word alone implied they didn't belong there. So, it would be simple. Just the three of them, and not much would be said. David hadn't really known the woman in the box for a long time, but he thought she would like it.

He pulled the cedar box out of his jacket. He didn't mention he had carried it with him for months. He also handed the opal ring to Evangeline. She accepted it without comment and put it in her dress pocket.

"Is there anything you want to say to her?" David asked.

As expected, they didn't respond right away. He waited.

"Okay," Xavier said. "Um…"

Xavier looked at the box in David's hands and rubbed his arms. "I'm sorry."

His face contorted as if he tried to hold in a sneeze. David realized he tried not to cry. He put his arm around Xavier's shoulder and hugged him. The first time he had ever touched his son. Xavier pressed his face into David's shoulder to dab away his tears covertly.

"She's not mad. She's proud of you," David said. Of course, he had no idea what she thought, but the words had a ring of truth to them. He hoped Xavier heard it, too.

"I'm sorry, too," Evangeline said quietly. "I shouldn't have said you deserved to die. I was just mad. I didn't mean it. I didn't want you to die, I wanted you to get better."

"It's okay. She knows that, too."

David ran his fingers across the smooth cedar. He had lots of things to say. *I'm sorry. I'm mad at you. I still love you. I love our kids. I forgot how it feels to have the tips of your hair brush across my chest when you lean down to kiss me. I wish I could feel it again.*

"I hope you found what you were looking for," he said.

He scattered her ashes in the four cardinal directions. The wind quickly swept her away into the great "more." When the sun caught the ash, it briefly shimmered iridescent, as if she had never been made of anything more than fairy dust.

ACKNOWLEDGEMENTS

I have a wonderful life and for that, I owe many thanks to many people. First, I'd like to thank my husband, for loving me just as I am and for supporting me unconditionally on every step of my writing journey. I'd like to thank my mother being a wonderful mother and grandma, and for the magical inspiration and education. I'd like to thank my brother for being an early reader of *Destruction* and for his words of encouragement. I also wish to thank everyone in my extended family. I'm lucky to have supportive and loving relatives all around me.

I had some incredible beta readers for *Destruction*. Their input helped to make the story and characters what they are today. Thank you to Ben Chiles, Charity Bradford, Dana Edwards, Gwen Gardner, Deana Barnhart, and Leah Deane. Your feedback and support meant so much to me.

And, none of this would happen without the support of Curiosity Quills Press. Thank you Eugene Teplitsky, Lisa Gus, Katie Hamstead, Andrew Buckley, Courtney Worth Young, Nikki Tetreault, Holly Erwin, Clare Dugmore, and all the other goats and minions. Of course, I have to thank my brilliant editor Mary Harris. She really helped me make the story stronger. And, the talented cover artist Michelle Johnson. The cover is everything I hoped for and more.

There are volumes worth of people who deserve my thanks for helping to spread the word about *Destruction*—including everyone who participated in my blog tour, cover reveal, and release day blitz. I also want to thank every single person who purchases this book and writes a review. Your support means so much to me.

I also want to thank J.K. Rowling for inspiring my love for magic and wizards…despite her biased portrayal of Slytherins.

Every night I say a prayer of thanks for everything I have. And, I'll do that again here. Thank you God for all of my many blessings. My family. My safety. My health. I truly love all that you have given me I'll do my best to appreciate every bit of it.

ABOUT THE AUTHOR

Sharon Bayliss lives in Austin, Texas with her husband and children. She hates wearing shoes and loves jogging in the rain. She only practices magic in emergencies.

She is also the author of the young adult science fiction novel, *The Charge.*

You can connect with her at www.sharonbayliss.com, www.facebook.com/authorsharonbayliss, and @SharonBayliss on Twitter.

www.ingramcontent.com/pod-product-compliance
Lightning Source LLC
Chambersburg PA
CBHW051645180726
48284CB00006B/1877